Y0-BQI-073

HOLLYWOOD HOMICIDE

This Large Print Book carries the
Seal of Approval of N.A.V.H.

A DETECTIVE BY DAY MYSTERY

HOLLYWOOD HOMICIDE

KELLYE GARRETT

THORNDIKE PRESS
A part of Gale, a Cengage Company

GALE
A Cengage Company

Farmington Hills, Mich • San Francisco • New York • Waterville, Maine
Meriden, Conn • Mason, Ohio • Chicago

Copyright © 2017 by Kellye Garrett.
Thorndike Press, a part of Gale, a Cengage Company.

LIBRARY OF CONGRESS CIP DATA ON FILE.
CATALOGUING IN PUBLICATION FOR THIS BOOK
IS AVAILABLE FROM THE LIBRARY OF CONGRESS

ISBN-13: 978-1-4328-4164-5 (hardcover)
ISBN-10: 1-4328-4164-5 (hardcover)

Published in 2017 by arrangement with Midnight Ink, an imprint of Llewellyn Publications, Woodbury, MN 55125-2989

Printed in the United States of America
1 2 3 4 5 6 7 21 20 19 18 17

For Kim McCoy, who was the Dayna to my Sienna.

ONE

He stared at my résumé like it was an SAT question. One of the hard ones where you just bubbled in C and kept it moving. After a minute — I counted, since there was nothing else to do — he finally looked up and smiled. "So, Dayna Anderson . . ."

He got my name right. The interview was off to a pretty good start. "So what in your previous experience would make you a good fit for this position?"

He smiled again, this time readjusting the *Joey, Manager. Ask me about our large jugs!* name tag that was prominently placed on his uniform. Since I was sitting in the Twin Peaks coffee shop interviewing to be a bikini barista, said uniform happened to be a Speedo. I pegged him for twenty-two, tops. And it wasn't just because he didn't have a centimeter of hair anywhere on his body. I made a mental note to get the name of his waxer.

"I make a mean cup of coffee," I said. "Not to brag or anything but it's been compared to liquid crack."

I smiled and he frowned. He was actually serious. Maybe a drug joke wasn't the best opening line. I quickly attempted to rectify my mistake. "This position just seems tailored to my competencies. I've always been a people person."

He nodded and glanced back at my résumé. It felt like it took him years to ask the next question. "So why do you want to work at Twin Peaks?"

Because I needed money and this was my first interview since the head Starbucks barista turned me down for being overqualified. "Because it just seems like a great place to work. I've known Richie since I moved to LA five years ago from Georgia."

The Richie thing was the first true thing to come out my mouth. He'd opened the first Twin Peaks down the street from my first apartment. The coffee was good enough that I could overlook the whole "the person serving me basically has no clothes on, which cannot be sanitary" thing. I'd come in every morning after the a.m. rush and every morning Richie would offer me a job. At first, I'd dismissed it as harmless flirting but Richie was serious. He'd extol the virtues of working for him. Dental. Vision. Even tuition reimbursement because, like strippers, the majority of bikini baristas were apparently just doing it to pay for college.

I'd always turn him down. I didn't care how great the 401(k) match may be, no way I'd ever reduce myself to being half naked for a paycheck. Being half naked for free? No problem at all. I did live for the beach, after all. But definitely not for a paycheck! Of course, after months of not receiving a paycheck totaling more than a couple hundred bucks from jobs that required you to be fully clothed, I'd suddenly seen the light.

Swallowing my pride, I texted Richie out of the blue to ask if the offer still stood. It did. He was opening a new downtown location and would be happy to set up an interview with the manager. Even though I was happy for the opportunity, I still had to give myself a ten-minute pep talk to walk in the door. Words like *self-worth* and *college degree* flew around in my head, but I banished them for the only two words that now mattered: *steady* and *income.*

Joey smiled again and this time it was actually genuine. Maybe this could actually work. "How much do you weigh?"

Or maybe not.

"Enough," I said.

He gave me a once-over and apparently was not too impressed. "Our biggest uniform is a size six."

"I'm a six." If it was really, really, really, really, really stretchy.

I'd kinda, maybe, sorta put on a few pounds since Richie had last seen me, blossoming from a size four to a ten. Not considered big in any state known to vote Republican, but in LA, I might as well have been fused to a couch and needing a forklift to help me get up. "I'd be happy to try on the uniform," I said.

Joey didn't say anything. Just looked at me. And then something changed. I knew that look. It was coming. The question I dreaded most, even more than the tell-me-about-yourselfs. He was going to ask if we'd gone to high school together.

People always knew I looked familiar but just couldn't figure out why. So they assumed they knew me from home. I'd been from places like Seattle, Omaha, and in one case Wasilla, Alaska. I've always said there is at least one black person everywhere. Folks all seem to think that lone integrationist is me.

"You look like someone I went to school with," he finally said.

There it was.

"Oh?" I said. "She must be beautiful."

I smiled, just so he'd know I was joking. He said nothing. Just stared some more. I waited.

It took a few seconds, but it finally hit him. "Don't think so, boo! You're the 'Don't think so, boo' girl in those commercials."

"Was," I clarified. "I *was* the girl in those commercials."

I had been considered famous once upon a time. But unlike Cinderella and Snow White, my fairy tale had not ended with happily ever after. Instead, it came crashing down a year and a half ago, and I had joined the rest of the mere mortals.

Having had fleeting fame, I was not recognizable as much as familiar. The familiarity was courtesy of the Chubby's Chicken chain. For almost two years, I would somehow end every situation — and commercial — with the catch phrase "Don't think so, boo." If the scene called for me to be really upset, I'd even give a quick little finger jab, a long neck roll, and a sophisticated sucking of my teeth. Rosa Parks would be so proud.

Eighteen months ago, Chubby's had abruptly ended my contract with the all-too-standard "we're going in a new direction" spiel to my now-former agent. Silly

11

me had been under the impression Chubby's would be just the beginning, not the end. I knew there was more in my future than just chicken wings. I was wrong and now officially unofficially retired from acting.

"You gotta say it. Just once." He looked at me, all goofy-like — a complete 180 from the wannabe-grownup of a few minutes before.

I shook my head. I hated that phrase even more than I hated my life at that moment.

"That was a lifetime ago." A lifetime and an almost-repossessed Lexus. "I don't act anymore."

"Oh come on." He was practically begging. "We love those commercials. 'Don't think so, boo.' Just say it one time."

I was tempted to tell him I'd say it every time I brewed a freaking XXXpresso if he would just give me the dang job already.

"Wait," he said, as if I was actually about to do it. "Bobby needs to be here." He turned in the direction of the counter and screamed at the top of his lungs, "Bobby get out here." The bleached blonde at the register barely blinked.

Before I knew it, a tall redhead was in front of me, his uniform staring me smack-dab in the face. It was obvious he didn't have a clue who I was, which was fine by me.

"Dude," Joey said.

"Dude," Bobby responded.

"Dude!!"

I could tell by the inflection that each *dude* had a different meaning, but it was a language I didn't know or care to learn.

"Dude, it's —"

"Don't tell me!" Bobby said. "I wanna guess."

I sat there while Bobby and Joey both stared. And stared. And stared. Like I was some kind of exotic tiger. At least they fed the animals at the zoo. All the Chubby's Chicken talk was just reminding me I'd skipped breakfast. I needed out of there. Unfortunately, I could only think of one way to make my escape. "Don't think so, boo."

I even added a neck roll.

Joey really didn't give me the job. Instead, he made some joke about how I obviously preferred my two-piece to be chicken orders, not bathing suits, and sent me on my merry little way. He was lucky I didn't curse because he surely would have gotten a mouthful.

Twenty minutes later, I sat at a stoplight on Vermont Avenue staring longingly at an

Original Tommy's Hamburgers. At that moment, I wanted a chiliburger almost as much as I wanted world peace. It was almost lunchtime, after all. I went for my purse, hoping to scrounge up enough cash for at least some fries.

My retirement from acting had only been official for about six months. Each and every second of those six months had been used to make up for every meal I'd missed in the three years of my *illustrious* acting career, hence my aforementioned hypothetical size six status.

I checked my wallet. Three dollar bills. I was counting my change when the light turned green. It took the guy behind me all of .00013 seconds to honk. I hit the gas. Nothing happened. So I hit it again. Still nothing. I looked down. The gas gauge was *past* E.

Fudge.

The guy behind me pulled around me with one hand while still blowing his horn with the other. I casually gave him the finger. Like I said, I never cursed. Hand gestures, however, were fair game.

Putting on my hazards, I got the gas jug out the trunk. A station was a couple of lights up the road. I made it with no problem and just stood there. The cheap stuff was $4.89 a gallon. My new-to-me pale pink Infiniti was twelve years old, had a cracked windshield and a temperamental horn, and was nearing 200,000 miles. The gas was worth more than the car.

There went the French fry fund. Since I didn't have my emergency credit card with me, I rooted around in my purse and found a stray nickel and a penny. That upped my disposable income to $3.56. I was about ten miles from home in Beverly Hills. Was it enough? I was attempting to do the math when curiosity got the best of the gas attendant. "Help you?"

"I ran out of gas," I said, motioning down the street, where the Infiniti was causing quite the traffic backup. Eek. We walked over to an empty pump.

"Pretty car," he said, then looked me over as I removed the nozzle. "Pretty girl."

Not to sound too conceited or anything but I actually *was* pretty. Of course, this was Los Angeles. Everyone was so pretty — the men even more so than the women — that you had to resort to a sliding scale, on which I was closer to cute than beautiful.

My skin was what Maybelline dubbed Cocoa and L'Oreal deemed Nut Brown, while MAC had bypassed all food groups to call it NC50. I had straightened black hair that was just long enough to get caught in stuff. My nose had been on the receiving end of many a nose job recommendation. But I'd gotten my boobs done first and the pain was so bad I swore off any further surgery. When I was little, I was as bug-eyed as a Bratz doll. But now that I was grown and the rest of me had had a chance to catch up, my eyes were my pièce de résistance. I didn't even own a pair of sunglasses.

I used them to look at the attendant.

"Smile," he said. "It's not that bad."

And with that, he walked away. I wanted to scream after him that I'd just been turned down for what was probably my last chance at steady income — a bikini barista job at that. So yes, it was in fact that bad. I was ready to have a full-out meltdown in the parking lot of an Arco. I needed a distraction. Pronto.

I found it on a billboard. It was your typical high school graduation photo, complete with a hand awkwardly holding a graduation cap tight to the chest. The girl was blonde and young. On the pretty scale, she'd definitely be considered beautiful.

The copy was straight to the point. *Wanted: Information on the hit-and-run murder of Haley Joseph. Tuesday, August 18th, 11:30 p.m., Vermont Ave near Hillside St.* And across the bottom, right over her press-on French manicure, *$15,000 reward.*

I peered closer at the billboard, looking for a hint this was a brilliant marketing scheme for some new movie. I was tempted to call the number, sure I'd hear some prerecorded message letting me know what time and day it would be airing on Lifetime. But I realized this was real. The address was right up the block. They wouldn't put the cross streets on there if it was for some silly movie. Haley Joseph had died.

I stared back at her, and then my eyes moved to the date. It was familiar. Too familiar. I realized why.

That was the last time I'd seen *him.*

Two

August 18th had indeed been a Tuesday. I was in my friend Emme's car trying to stop my skirt from hiking up to my privates and wondering why I'd had that fourth Whiskey Sour. My excuse was that we were celebrating and I wasn't paying, so down it went.

Yes, I was drunk on a weeknight. It was a Tuesday, but it was also Hollywood. Anywhere else, being drunk on a Tuesday would've gotten you a pamphlet extolling twelve steps. In the land of the nine-to-five, Tuesdays were for watching *Law & Order* and calling your parents to babysit. In the land of make-believe, it was for auditioning for *Law & Order* and calling your parents for money. So my being drunk was no biggie. Besides, I wasn't the only one.

Sienna had somehow commandeered Omari's cell phone and was using it to record herself giving a "newscast." "This is Sienna Hayes reporting live from Omari

Grant's celebration party."

Sienna also was drunk, but then she was slightly better at it than I was. Probably because she had much more experience. She was riding shotgun because of one slip-up when she had to throw up but was stuck in Emme's backseat. After Sienna paid for the car wash, she'd been granted lifetime front-seat privileges, which meant Omari and I were squeezed into Emme's sorry excuse for a backseat.

We'd dubbed it the Black Hole, because once in, you were lost in a sea of darkness and it practically took the Jaws of Life to get out scratch-free. Emme's car was the size of a closet — a Manhattan studio closet, not a Beverly Hills one. Those things were bigger than a tour bus and had just as many compartments.

Emme was driving and ignoring Sienna as usual, so Sienna turned the phone to face us even though she couldn't see a thing. Her faux-newscaster voice was in full effect. "Mr. Grant, anyone you'd like to thank for this lovely evening?"

"Jack," he said.

"Nicholson?"

"Daniels."

He was in a good mood, but then he should have been. He'd learned he'd be playing Jamal Fine on the new CBS show *LAPD 90036.* The role had needed to be quickly recast a month before its premiere when test audiences found the previous actor's nose unlikable. His loss had been Omari's gain. He was scheduled to start filming in two days, the same time his predecessor was probably visiting a plastic surgeon.

I was happy for him. I needed some good news — even if it was once-removed. "Any particular highlights tonight?" Sienna asked.

"There were so many . . ."

He started naming them, but I wasn't paying attention. I was too busy wondering about the hand that had suddenly appeared on my thigh. I looked at him, but he was still facing the window and talking to Sienna.

I shifted, figuring maybe he'd mistook my thigh for the seat, since it was also brown and smooth. I expected him to remove it as soon as he realized his mistake. It moved all right, but not the whole thing. His thumb made the slightest circular motion on my thigh. *My* hands, in turn, got sweaty.

The seventeen-year-old in me was having a conniption. She was the one who had crushed hard on Omari in high school, when he'd transferred from Brooklyn and provided her first kiss courtesy of our high school production of *Guys and Dolls.*

Back then, I would've given anything to be in the backseat of a car with Omari Grant feeling me up. But that was almost ten years ago. He'd moved to the friend zone — mainly due to a seeming lack of interest on his part — almost as soon as I moved to Los Angeles. I was glad he had. At least I thought I was, but then this.

The shock finally wore off and I realized I was not upset about the hand's sudden presence. I just wasn't sure what to do. Put my hand on his leg? Put my hand over his? Cross my legs, thereby holding it hostage? I selected none of the above and just sat there while the hand moved an inch north. I was excited and nervous and several words rappers have yet to invent. Luckily, Sienna and her interview skills moved on to Emme. She turned to face her. "Ms. Abrams, what was the highlight of your evening?"

"IDK. Probably beating Chazmonkey69 for the eight kabillionth time on Trivia Crack."

We continued like this for another minute. Them talking. Him feeling. Me freaking. Then Sienna suddenly turned around. "You guys are awfully quiet back there. If I didn't know better, I'd think you were both up to no good."

Busted. Fudge. Omari didn't say anything. Unfortunately, I did. "Please. Who knows what he has."

I regretted it as soon as I said it. It was meant in a playful way, something silly like cooties. As usual, in my nervousness it came out wrong. And just like that, the hand was gone. I missed it instantly. "I was joking," I said.

But he didn't hear me because at that moment, Emme suddenly slammed her brakes. "WTF?" She leaned hard on the horn.

I tore my eyes away from my hand-less thigh in time to see a car crossing the street not even three feet in front of us. It had to have come from a cross street, slicing across the four lanes of traffic with zero regard for the fact we were also on the road.

It happened so fast all I noticed were the custom-tinted windows that had recently become so popular with the a-hole set, AKA seventy-five percent of Hollywood. This particular productive member of society had gone for an etching of a rose. My heart would have started beating fast if it hadn't been already. Why couldn't anyone in Los Angeles drive? Sienna rolled down the window and waved Omari's cell phone. By then the car had disappeared down the side street, but that didn't faze her one bit. "We got you on tape, buddy!"

Then we were all silent. I looked at Omari as Emme continued driving, but it was too dark to see his expression. I willed him to look at me. That way I'd know we were okay. I got nada. A few hand-less minutes later, Emme finally spoke. "Something's up."

Ahead of us, a small crowd had gathered on the opposite side of the street. Everyone was looking down at something or someone. They all blended in with each other, save for the one with a shock of pink hair. We got closer. I still couldn't make out much, but I did see a pair of jeans-clad legs attached to heels lying on the ground. We did the obligatory rubbernecking. It didn't look good at all.

My nervousness kicked in. Again. "She probably couldn't hold her liquor and passed out. Amateur."

I regretted that one as well. Not as much as the first, but still. I really needed to learn to shut up. If I was hoping no one would acknowledge my bad taste, I was in for more disappointment.

"A girl's passed out. On the ground. And you assume she can't hold her liquor." It was the first time Omari had spoken since

Handgate. "Real nice."

I didn't appreciate his tone. At all. So I refused to admit he was right. "It was a joke."

He kept his eyes trained on the window as he spoke. "I know. Everything's a joke with you, Dayna."

My full name. He was really mad. "Better to laugh than cry," I said.

"Sometimes it's better just to be quiet."

His being pissed off made me really pissed off. "Now it's my fault you can't take a joke?"

Sienna and Emme were quiet, but I knew they were listening. Did they know what we were really arguing about? He started to speak again, but I cut him off before he could get out half a syllable. "How about you stop talking to me? I'd hate to offend you with any more jokes."

"Not a problem."

We dropped him off that night and he gave me his usual quick hug and promised to call me tomorrow. Except, he didn't. And so I didn't. And we both *didn't* for six weeks now. He was obviously mad. He had a right to be, but still.

Being a glutton for punishment, I mentally replayed everything a couple more times. And just when I thought I couldn't feel any worse, I realized something else. Haley Joseph was the girl on the ground that night. Omari was right. I'd seen her dying and I'd made a joke. A horrible joke.

It was a slap in the face but one that I desperately needed at that moment. Talk about putting your own problems in perspective. I gave the billboard one more glance and said a quick prayer that the police caught the a-hole who'd hit her, and soon. Then I got in my car to see if I could make it home on three dollars' worth of gas.

It turns out three dollars is in fact enough to get you to Beverly Hills. I was sure that knowledge would come in handy the next time I ran out of gas. Considering my tank was already back on E, it probably would be sooner than later.

Sienna and I lived in a two-bedroom condo off Burton Way, a few blocks west of the Beverly Center shopping mall and Cedars-Sinai hospital. The button in the elevator claimed we lived on PH, aka the penthouse floor, but that was just a fancy way to say "five."

Sienna wasn't home when I got there so I went straight to the "bloset," my nickname for where I slept. It was a combination closet and bedroom. A month earlier, I'd

25

temporarily moved into Sienna's spare bedroom. Two years ago, she'd turned it into a shoe closet. Three walls featured shelves upon shelves of shoes. Imagine if Foot Locker only sold stilettos and you'd get the picture.

No sooner had I plopped on the bed and turned on the television for the early afternoon showing of *Judge Judy* than my cell rang. I sighed. The only people who still used a phone for anything besides texting and photoshopping pictures for Instagram were my parents and bill collectors. And my mom and Visa's representatives were neck and neck when it came to people I just wasn't in the mood to deal with.

Luckily, it was Daddy. "Hey, baby girl, you're looking beautiful as ever," he said, despite the fact that he couldn't see me.

I instantly felt better. "Thank you, kind sir. You like my dress? I wore it just for you."

"Sure do," he said. "I don't know what that eye doctor is talking about saying I need glasses. I'ma let him know I got 20/20,000 vision."

"I'll be happy to be your reference," I said. "Amazing vision aside, how you feeling?"

He'd suffered a stroke the year before that had left him temporarily paralyzed on his left side. Scariest time of my life. It took him longer to recover than either of us would've liked but he did, finally getting full use of the left side of his body. I was so proud of him.

"Can't complain. I don't want to keep you long, baby girl. I just wanted to tell you how beautiful you look today."

"I appreciate it. I love you, okay?"

"I know you do, baby girl."

"I'm glad your memory is just as good as your vision," I said. "Talk to you soon, Daddy."

I was about to hang up when he spoke again. "Oh, forgot to tell you, I heard from the bank."

"Oh great. Did they say they spoke with NorthWest?"

"They said they're foreclosing on the house. Plan to sell it by Thanksgiving unless we catch up on our payments." His voice was so casual he might as well have been saying that he was out of milk.

I was nowhere near as cool. I felt my heart drop to the first floor. "That can't be right! I just spoke with David over at the firm. He said everything was on track!"

"Probably a mistake, then."

"Has to be. I'll call him right now."

I hung up and forced myself to breathe. Daddy was right. It had to be a mistake. No way was the bank foreclosing on the house. Daddy's stroke had forced him into early retirement from his job as a city bus driver. Unfortunately, it was six months shy of his pension kicking in, leaving him struggling to keep up with the house payments and not telling a single soul. My parents had me in their forties and my father was the epitome of an old school Southern black man. He'd have rather sold his kidney on Craigslist than ask his only child for help.

Even when I'd been pulling in serious bank from my Chubby's gig, he still sent me "spending" money on the first of each and every month. I'd told him I didn't need it. In fact, I'd even begged to give them money, going so far as to mail each of them checks. My mother cashed those suckers within thirty minutes of the mailman dropping it off. My father, on the other hand, just sent his checks back to me.

So when he called a few months ago to ask for "a little something" for that month's mortgage, I knew things had to be dire. Considering I'd been living off savings for almost a year at that point, I wasn't in much of a position to help. Of course, I didn't tell him that. Instead, I went straight to the bank and took out what was left in my savings account.

Knowing that would only buy us a couple months at most, I found NorthWest after googling loss mitigation firms that specialized in foreclosures. Their website was filled with client testimonials and pictures. Their clients all looked happy and, more importantly, non-homeless. I spoke with a David, who promised me that for the tidy sum of $2,500 they'd work a miracle and save my parents' house. I borrowed the money from Emme. To her credit, she didn't ask any questions.

I was happy that my parents were taken care of, but unfortunately I was a completely different story. Without any savings to fall back on, my finances looked worse than someone doing the walk of shame after twenty-four hours of straight tequila shots. I didn't regret giving the money to my dad, though. Instead, I turned in my Lexus .02 seconds before it was repossessed, broke the lease on my beachfront Santa Monica apartment, and took any and every nine-dollar-an-hour temp job I could get. It still wasn't enough. I'd started speaking to bill collectors more than I spoke to my own mother.

As soon as I calmed myself down, I called NorthWest. David picked up on the first ring. I quickly explained the mistake and waited for his reassurances. They didn't come. "I've been meaning to call you with the bad news," he said.

Um, I didn't pay him $2,500 of Emme's hard-earned money to have bad news. "I'm a bit confused, David. Last time we spoke, you assured me that my parents' house would be fine."

"And I thought it would, but unfortunately this may be one of those rare instances when we came in too late in the process. If only you'd contacted us sooner."

I wanted to barf. David obviously didn't hear me start to gag because he continued on. "Of course, I'd be more than willing to speak with the bank again."

Thank. Goodness. "Can you call them now?"

"Sure thing," he said. "I just need an additional $1,500."

That's when it hit me that good old David was running a good old scam. You'd think I'd have really lost it but instead I was remarkably calm. I even made a mental note to give myself a pat on the back later. "How do you sleep at night knowing that you're taking advantage of hard-working people when they're at their most vulnerable?" I asked. "Lying to them. Taking their money."

David must've heard that spiel before

because all he said was, "I'm sorry you see it that way, Ms. Anderson."

"You'll be hearing from my lawyer."

My threat was as fake as my boobs. David knew it, too. "Please be sure to point out to him the part of our contract where it clearly states there are no guarantees."

He hung up and that's when I lost it. So much for that pat on the back. I threw the phone across the room, knocking over one of Sienna's prized Louboutins. Then I ran over and grabbed my cell so I could call him back and break my no-cursing rule.

This time the call rang once and went straight to voicemail. I'd dealt with enough lame dudes to know what that meant: he'd blocked me.

The tears began to fall, enough to end the Southern California drought. I knew I had to be upset because I didn't even care that I was messing up my makeup. Instead, I slid down to the floor and forced myself to count my breaths. It took me to 146 before I was finally able to regain control. I needed to fix this. Immediately.

There had to be a way to get my hands on a big amount of cash. But how? I didn't possess the inner-thigh strength needed to work a stripper pole and didn't even have enough physical money to buy a lotto ticket. Not to

31

mention that it'd be mighty tough to make a bank robbery getaway with less than three dollars' worth of gas in my tank.

My rapid descent into the depths of depression was interrupted by a commercial for *LAPD 90036.* It was one of those cookie-cutter shows where beautiful people delivered clichés while solving gruesome murders in sixty minutes or less. The ad ended with a close-up of its biggest star: Omari Grant.

He slapped cuffs on an anonymous baddie and said his catch phrase. "It's time to pay for your crime."

Seeing Omari made me think about *that* night. Which made me think about poor Haley Joseph. Which made me think of the billboard. Which made me think of the $15,000 reward.

THREE

As soon as Sienna got home, I immediately convened her and Emme for a pow-wow. The way I saw it, the police wanted information. I had information. Probably. We'd been too late to see the actual accident, but since we'd been coming from the opposite direction, we had to have seen the car making its getaway. If I could just remember any details of cars that passed us — color, number of doors, if the driver was a he or she — it might be enough to lead the cops to the killer and me to the reward money. Haley's killer would be in jail and my parents would not be on the streets. A win-win situation if there ever was one.

Still, I had to admit it sounded crazy. But I reasoned that this was Hollywood. Trying to get the reward money for a hit-and-run you witnessed definitely wouldn't be the craziest thing an actress — or in my case, an ex-actress — had done for cash around these parts.

Billboards aside, actual info on the accident was scarce and went like this: Haley worked at a small consignment shop off Vermont Avenue. The area was mostly commercial, housing the type of shops more likely to be open at 7:00 a.m. than 7:00 p.m. On August 18th, she stopped by work after hours to help with inventory and didn't leave until approximately 11:30 p.m. There was a marked crosswalk right outside her job. Like many crosswalks in LA, it wasn't accompanied by a stop sign or a light. I don't know if the LA City Council was on a tight budget or just on crack when it came up with that idea.

Haley used the crosswalk to get to her car on the other side of the street. It was unclear whether the driver was drunk, texting, or just didn't see her. What was clear was that he or she hit her and didn't bother to stop. There was one witness who arrived minutes after the accident. Police had no leads but believed the car to be a Rolls Royce.

I'd hoped reading up on the accident would jog a memory. It didn't, besides a few bits and pieces: That a crowd surrounded her. That one of them had bright pink hair. That someone else was gesturing wildly while on his or her cell phone.

34

Unfortunately, Emme and Sienna didn't seem to remember anything about the car either.

"It's LA," I said. "You're more likely to see a Rolls Royce than a drop of rain. We had to have seen at least one that night, if not two or three."

"It's not LA. It's Silver Lake," Sienna said. We were on my bed in the bloset. "Hipster central. You're way more likely to see a hybrid than a Rolls."

She had a point, but still.

"What about license plates?" I asked, not willing to give up on remembering the car just yet. "Any vanity plates?"

Emme spoke up. She wasn't in the room but rather on the screen, her eyes constantly roaming between illegal poker games, IM chats, and us. "BigOne6969, you cheating SOB."

She loudly banged on her keyboard, sending what I could only guess was an all-caps tirade. If you didn't know better, you'd swear Emme's jumping eyes were a result of going through withdrawal from some illicit substance that had entered her body through a vein between her toes. But she was probably the only person in Hollywood who didn't do drugs.

"What do you remember, Sienna?" I asked.

"Seeing MC Ghetto Ghet at that club downtown. His girl's boob job was horrid."

"He drive a Rolls?" I would not let her get me off topic.

"Porsche."

"And you?" I asked Emme. "What do you remember?"

"Wanting to go home," Emme said, her voice laced with her Valley roots.

All righty, then. "Thank you," I said.

"NP," Emme said. No problem.

"A girl was hit by a car," I said. "Maybe if we just focused, we'd realize we know something."

"Why?" Sienna asked.

"I don't know why. Honestly, I only care about who."

"Why are you doing this?"

I didn't want to get into it. They'd just offer to let me borrow money. Again. I was sick of using my friends. Even if they didn't mind, I did. So I settled for a partial truth. "I saw a billboard asking for information and it just reminded me that we'd driven by."

Sienna still looked confused, so I kept talking before she could ask another question. "What about anyone driving erratically? The guy had to be drunk, right?"

But they both just shook their heads. I silently read an article about the accident for the 50 bajillionth time on Emme's old *old* iPad, not to be confused with her old iPad that had displaced it and was succeeded by her new iPad, which would be replaced when the new *new* version came out. She'd let me permanently borrow it after I sold my own tablet a couple months ago.

The article still wasn't much help. Neither was my piss-poor job of rallying my friends. The Rolls was a bust. I needed to do something else. Maybe if I actually went back to Vermont Avenue, it would trigger something. I got up and grabbed my bag.

"Where are you going?" Sienna asked, her voice still dripping with accusations.

"Vermont."

"Shopping? I'm in."

"Great," I said. "You'll have to drive."

I still didn't have enough gas.

By the fourth crosswalk drive-by, Sienna began to suspect she'd been bamboozled and wanted to go home. As a compromise, I suggested she shop while I stared at the crosswalk some more before the sun disappeared completely behind the store.

The word "shopping" to Sienna was like "abracadabra" to a magician. Say the magic word and stare in amazement as things magically appeared in her closet. Ready to begin that evening's performance, she dropped me off right in front of Clothes Encounters. No way was I using the crosswalk.

I was standing there trying to will even the slightest memory when I heard someone behind me. "Hey, are you from Jersey?"

There it was.

She was Asian and looked like she still needed a fake ID. Her face was as wide and round as my grandmother's fancy plates. Her body looked just as delicate. It barely looked strong enough to hold the maroon and gold University of Southern California book bag she'd slung on her back. She smiled, showing off old school braces, the metal connected with lime-green rubber bands.

I guessed she had come out of the consignment store. What tipped me off was the store name tag. *Marina* was written in a font designed to look like handwriting. I'd never understood that. Why not just use actual handwriting?

"Georgia," I said.

Her smile faltered a bit. "Sorry. It's just

38

you look like someone . . ."

"You went to school with?" I finished the thought for her. "I get that all the time."

Six months ago, I would have explained how she knew me. But after the bajillionth "Oh, what are you doing now?" I had halted that practice. Now I just smiled and let them figure it out, preferably well after we parted.

"Okay, well, have a good day," Marina said and disappeared into the yonder.

I went back to staring at the crosswalk and trying to conjure up an image of that evening. Instead, images of chicken nuggets danced through my head. I would have preferred them in my mouth. I was hungry, but what else was new?

Sienna strolled up in her four-inch platforms and gasped. I knew that gasp. She'd seen something that would be in her closet by night's end. I used to gasp like that myself. "Those pants are to die for," she said.

Considering the circumstances, it was not the best word choice. In the display window of Clothes Encounters was a pair of the ugliest, reddest, sequin-iest pants I'd ever seen. Not my style, but if anyone could pull those off, it was Sienna.

She was inside before I could stop her. I

didn't want to go in *there,* the place Haley Joseph worked. I was tempted to not follow her, but I knew the best course of action was to get her out of there as soon as possible. Left to her own devices, Sienna would be there until next week.

I walked in, trying to be as inconspicuous as possible. The bell attached to the front door had other plans. "Welcome to Clothes Encounters!" a pack-a-day raspy voice called out, all *Wizard of Oz*-y. "I'm Betty. Let me know if I can help you with anything."

I couldn't tell where the voice came from. The place had two rooms, each packed solid with old school round racks. Someone, Betty perhaps, had strategically left a winding path about a foot and a half wide. I plunged inside the forest of clothes, wishing I could leave bread crumbs in case I needed to find my way out.

The clothes were beautiful. Every era was represented from the last fifty years. They'd even managed to find nice clothes from the eighties. I kept going until I found Sienna adding clothes to a pile an employee was holding. An employee with pink hair.

She was younger than her voice would lead you to believe, but older than the hair would make you think. I pegged her for late forties. She'd had the decency not to go the plastic surgery route, instead looking for youth in layers of foundation the color of unbaked biscuit dough. I expected the lipstick to match the hair. Instead, she'd gone for a deep red, which turned her lips into thin red lines when she smiled at me. Her teeth were perfect. "I'm Betty."

The last time I'd seen her, she was leaning over Haley's dying body.

Seeing her immediately made me want to abandon my plan to get the reward money, but I literally couldn't afford to do that. Instead, I shook off any doubts and looked for a distraction. I found it in Sienna, who was holding up a dress. I glanced at the price tag: *1208*. "That's $1,208!?"

Sienna shrugged. "That's reasonable."

"That's not the price," Betty said. "It's the seller. We're a consignment shop, so we don't actually own what we sell. We're more a middle man. All our sellers are assigned four-digit numbers. So if you find someone you like, you can specifically ask for their clothes."

I didn't know what to say to that, so I just kind of nodded and smiled. Luckily, Betty left me alone while Sienna grabbed one thing after another. It wasn't until she had Sienna settled in a fitting room that she gave

41

me a second glance. She smiled. I smiled. She smiled. I smiled. It went on like this for longer than I cared for it to.

Desperate to end the world's friendliest staring contest, I examined a vintage wrap dress. "That color would be gorgeous with your skin tone," Betty said. "Go look."

She motioned toward a mirror near the check-out counter. I walked over and set my phone on the counter while I held the dress against me. She wasn't lying. The dress and my skin didn't go together as well as, say, peanut butter and jelly. But it was close. I handed the dress back to her. "Maybe next time."

We had another awkward few minutes of smiling silence before she came up with another topic. "You guys come to this area often?"

Sienna had told her we lived in Beverly Hills. I shrugged. "Not really. The last time was August."

Betty glanced off to the side, remembering what happened in August. Why did I say that? Since I'd already been dumb enough to inadvertently bring up the subject, I decided I might as well go all in. Maybe I could ask her a few questions, learn something that could finally trigger my memory and help figure out who hit

Haley Joseph. "We, uh, happened to drive by the hit-and-run."

As soon as it was out, I got scared she'd wonder how I knew she was related to it. So I tried to clarify. "I remember seeing your hair. I read somewhere the girl died. I'm so sorry."

"Me too," Betty said. "That was one of my employees. Haley. She'd only been in town for nine months. She came out here to act, naive enough to think she could move out here Monday and be famous by Tuesday. I feel for these poor girls so desperate to be famous they actually believe that it'll be easy, which is complete BS. I can't understand why these girls waste their time and their talents."

She looked at me then, as if realizing exactly what she was saying and that she may have offended me in the process. "Oh, you're not an actress, are you?"

"Oh, no! I came out here for business school," I said, which was the truth.

"You graduate yet?"

"One more semester." I didn't mention it'd been one more semester for the past three years.

"We had a viewing party the other day for this show she was on," Betty said. "Something on USA. And she was . . . What's it called when your character doesn't talk but you're still important in the scene?"

"Featured extra?" Extra work was a rite of passage for any and every acting wannabe, except for me. I'd gotten my Chubby's gig on my third audition.

"Yes!" Betty said. "She was 'Hooker number 2' in the credits. She was so excited, which is why I was surprised when she came in that night and told me she was leaving LA. Said it wasn't what she'd thought. I was so distracted with the inventory I barely paid her any attention. She realized it too and left. I was going to text her to do lunch the next day . . ."

Haley getting killed right before she planned to move made it even more tragic. "I'm sorry for your loss," I said, meaning every word. Then I dragged Sienna out of there before she had a chance to make a single purchase. She was not a happy camper.

I couldn't stop thinking about Haley, even after we were back home later that night. Like Haley, I'd been a kid who wanted to act. I just hadn't had the balls to come out here with nothing but the clothes on my back. I'd gone the more roundabout, and expensive, way of b-school. Because of that fear, I admired the Haleys of the world who weren't afraid to go for what they wanted.

This was not just someone on some TV show. This was a real person with real dreams and real friends — exactly like me. Of course, I was also a person with a real problem. I'd already called my dad back and told him that I was working on getting the money. I had to keep at it, but I made sure to make a new vow: no more personal info about Haley until I had something for the police tip line. It would just make me feel horrible.

Sienna sliced through my thoughts. "God, I look good."

And she wondered why some people hated her. Not that she was lying. She did indeed look good, which just made people hate her even more. She was at my mirror, primping. It was Monday night, and for Sienna, that meant club night. But then so did Tuesday, Wednesday, Thursday, Friday, and Saturday. On Sunday, she rested. She gave herself one final once-over and spoke. "Ready for my close-up."

She'd read that the stylist for singer/rapper Kandy Wrapper always took pics of her client to ensure her outfits looked good in photos. Since then, I'd spent a good portion of my waking hours taking pictures of Sienna on the off chance she got caught in the background of a paparazzi shot of a celebrity leaving a club.

Sienna placed one hand on her tiny hip and smiled with her eyes. She topped out at five feet tall, but we were eye-to-eye if you counted her ever-present stilettos. I didn't know her exact weight, but it was nowhere near triple digits. She'd drunk too much once and needed me to carry her to her apartment. I'd had grocery bags that weighed more.

Sienna was an itty-bitty thing, but her appeal wasn't her height. It was her look. Her eyes and skin were almost the same light caramel color. Both looked store-bought. They weren't, though the jet-black hair most certainly was. She wore it stick straight, midway down her back. Tourists were always asking her directions in their native tongue. She could have been Italian, Indian, Dominican. The list went on and on. But she was black.

I think.

She never explicitly said, and there wasn't a single family photo to be found, not even a shot from her wedding to her rich ex-husband. You only really have a three-month window to ask those sorts of things and I'd missed it. So I resorted to context clues. She said weave, not extensions. Ashy, not dry. Thick, not plus-sized. And last Thanksgiving, she'd made the most amazing sweet potato — not pumpkin — pie.

I thought fondly about the pie as I snapped a final full-length shot with my tablet and examined my handiwork. "You can tell you're not wearing a bra."

"Good! I wish you'd come, Day."

She'd asked me to hang out every night since I moved in, and every night I refused. Tonight was no exception. I wasn't in the mood for any party that didn't have the word "pity" in front of it. "I'm too tired."

I wasn't anti-club. In fact, Sienna and I had met in a club bathroom right after my first Chubby's commercial. She'd yelled over the stall that she was my biggest fan. I was flattered. By the time I figured out that she said that to everyone who got a paycheck for stepping in front of a camera, we'd already bonded over a mutual shoe size and bladders the size of a pin prick.

"You know the rules," I told her. "Call if you think you've drunk too much to drive. I'll come get you." Of course, I still had no gas in my car, but that was a problem for Future Dayna.

"Yes, Mom," she said.

I didn't answer. I was too busy looking for my phone. Curiosity morphed into panic as

Sienna and I searched the entire condo. Sienna tried calling it to no avail. I was wedged halfway under my bed when I remembered I'd last seen it at Clothes Encounters. Fudge.

People survived for centuries without cell phones. Today, however, lose your phone and you might as well have chopped off your right hand. It was like you'd suddenly forgotten how to talk.

It wasn't that I thought I'd have tons of missed calls. Sienna never called when partying, Emme would rather give you a kidney than a phone call, my parents were both snoring by nine, and the bill collectors all got off at five. But what about tomorrow morning?

With my luck, one of the temp agencies I'd signed up with would call with a job paying a million dollars an hour and requiring three semesters of business school and the ability to juggle while speaking in a German accent.

I remembered from reading about Haley's death that someone sometimes stayed late at the store to do inventory. I looked up the number and called on Sienna's phone. No one answered, but it was after hours. Why would they? I hung up and grabbed my keys.

Looked like I was going out after all.

■ ■ ■ ■

The only smart thing I'd done the last three years was not open a kajillion credit cards. I had one for emergencies. But everything qualified as an emergency lately, like the gas I put in my tank before heading back to Silver Lake. I took the 10 freeway so I could drive north on Vermont like we did the night of Haley's death. I figured it might trigger something. It didn't.

I got back to Clothes Encounters a touch before midnight. The light was on, but otherwise the place was deserted. I wasn't scared. It wasn't that type of neighborhood. It could be 2:00 a.m., my doors unlocked, all four windows down, and a thousand dollars in untraceable bills in the front seat. No one would touch it. If anything, someone would probably thoughtfully roll up my windows, lock my door, and leave me a gift-wrapped wallet.

I knocked. And waited. Then I cupped my hands around my eyes and peered inside the store. Lots of clothes. No people. I headed over to check the other half of the store.

And that's when I noticed him.

FOUR

He just appeared in the middle of the crosswalk. He was bending down but looked up when I broke my no-cursing rule and loudly took the Lord's name in vain. He was only about fifteen feet away, so I could tell it had been a minute since he'd owned a razor. Wisps of blond hair covered his cheeks. I pegged him for five foot seven, short enough to be an action star. His body type was "to be determined" because he was wearing some weird plastic one-piece outfit. Definitely a fashion don't.

We stared at each other, me hoping this wouldn't one day be the basis for some horror movie that spawned a plastic blood-spattered Halloween costume. He was either a serial killer or homeless. Maybe both.

He only stopped staring at me when he heard a car approach. It was moving as fast as you'd expect of a car hitting a stretch of street with no traffic lights or other vehicles.

Neither of us moved, which was fine for me. I was on the sidewalk. He, however, was still in the middle of the street.

I was preparing to provide some insight along the lines of "Move, you idiot" when I was distracted by the sudden burst of light. The car's headlights hit him, lighting him up like Times Square. His fashion no-no was actually a reflector suit. That explained his confidence.

Instead of slowing down, the driver blared on his horn. The homeless serial killer not only refused to budge, but the look on his face was lackadaisical, as if playing chicken with speeding cars was an everyday thing. He stayed. The car honked. I almost peed my pants.

When the car was about two car lengths away, he casually strolled toward the sidewalk. Within seconds, he was next to me and the car was disappearing down the road. He stuck out his hand. "Hello, I'm Aubrey S. Adams-Parker."

He spoke to my back. I booked it to my car and was half a block away before I remembered to breathe. When I looked in my rear-view mirror, he was still there.

Sienna and I were back at Clothes Encounters bright and early. I was there for my phone. She was there for the red pants. We both must have done something right in the ensuing eight hours because it only took three tries and a quick prayer to the Parking Gods to parallel park.

The bell announced our entrance, but no one greeted us from the clothing-covered abyss. Sienna made a beeline for the pants, leaving me to fend for myself. I was halfway to the counter when the voices drifted over from the other half of the store. "And you saw the car, Ms. Miller?"

The voice was deep. Not Satan-deep. More like "taking love dedications on the radio after the kids are put to bed" deep. It was also slightly familiar. Like maybe he was one of the investigative reporters from a local news station. "Yes," another voice said. It was Betty. "The Rolls Royce."

My ears perked up, primed for some good old-fashioned eavesdropping. The male voice continued. "What color was this Rolls Royce, Ms. Miller?"

"I don't know. It was dark."

"It was dark out?" the man asked. "Or the car was a dark color?"

"Dark color."

"Did this alleged Rolls Royce have two or four doors?"

"Four. What are you getting at?"

I was thinking the exact same thing.

"Here is my problem, Ms. Miller," he said. "I have canvassed this neighborhood the past two days. No one else saw a Rolls Royce anywhere in the vicinity the night of Ms. Joseph's death."

I noted the formality in his tone. Barely any contractions. Not Miss, but Ms. He *had* to be a news reporter. Who else spoke like that?

"It was definitely a Rolls Royce," Betty said. "I saw it."

Her voice was not only insistent, it was closer. They were coming to this side of the store. Fudge. You'd think a place like that would have a million places to hide. It did. It just didn't have a million places to hide for anyone with thunder thighs. The garments were packed tighter than freshly done cornrows.

"I am not saying you did not see a Rolls Royce," the man said. "What I am saying is no one else saw one."

I took a page from my inner two-year-old, where your idea of hiding was just covering your eyes. If you couldn't see them, they couldn't see you. I pretended to admire a particularly foul polka-dot dress that was not the eighties' greatest creation.

They were so caught up in their conversation, they walked right by me without a glance. I chanced a look at them. The voice belonged to Aubrey S. Adams-Parker, the homeless serial killing fashionista who loved playing in traffic. He wore the same orange reflector suit as the night before.

Betty was not a happy camper. Her words tumbled out like a gymnast on floor exercise. "Haley saw it too. She said so right before she died. She saw a Rolls Royce. We both did."

"I believe that you believe you saw a Rolls Royce," Aubrey said.

I gave up all pretense of pretending to shop and trailed behind them. Neither noticed. "I was there," she said. "You weren't."

He said nothing. They both stopped. I didn't know what to do, so I just sort of stood there. They were at an impasse, staring each other down. Neither saying a word. The silence stretched. After a minute, even I started to feel uncomfortable. Never one for awkward silences, I spoke. "Betty has a point. She was there."

What I didn't say was Aubrey had a point too. Just because you *think* something was a Rolls Royce doesn't mean it actually was one. It would explain why Sienna, Emme, and I couldn't remember seeing the car.

If either was surprised by my random intrusion, they didn't say anything. I took that as a sign to continue. "There's a way to settle this."

I got out my tablet and googled cars. Once I found what I was looking for, I extended the tablet to Betty like a peace offering. "This was the car, right?" I asked.

Betty glanced at it and quickly nodded. "Yes! That's the car. Like I said, a Rolls Royce."

Her telephone rang. She handed the tablet back to me, glared at Aubrey, and practically stomped off to answer it. "I'm glad that's settled," she said.

But it wasn't. The photo I showed her wasn't a Rolls Royce.

It was an Infiniti. Not mine, but a new-and-improved version. I turned to Aubrey. "You were right. She only thinks it's a Rolls."

"Of course I am right."

His tone wasn't cocky, just matter-of-fact. I wasn't expecting him to catch the Holy Ghost, scream Hallelujah, and give me a high five, but dang. He walked out the door. I followed, walking beside him in silence past two storefronts. "I showed her a picture of an Infiniti," I finally said, as if we were actually having a conversation. "Of course,

I doubt the car was actually an Infiniti. I just wanted to make sure that she doesn't know what a Rolls Royce looks like and it was the first thing that crossed my mind."

I thought it was brilliant on my part. I was the only one, because Aubrey didn't even give as much as a grunt. As was becoming his trademark, he said nothing. "She's an unreliable witness," I added. I'd heard the term once on *The First 48*. "I'm Dayna Anderson, by the way. Sorry I didn't introduce myself last night, but it was late." And you were creepy as heck.

"I am pleased to meet you, Ms. Anderson."

He stopped long enough to shake my hand before continuing on. I struggled to keep up with him. He had to be a private investigator. He definitely wasn't a cop in that getup. "You're investigating Haley's murder?"

"Yes." Thought so.

"Haley's family hired you?"

"No."

"The boyfriend then."

"No." He smiled. "It is a bit more complicated than that."

Did that mean no one hired him? "You're doing it for the reward?"

"No, Ms. Anderson."

If he wasn't investigating because he was hired or for the reward, that didn't leave many options. "Because it's 9:00 a.m.?"

That one made him pause. I thought maybe he'd laugh. Instead, he checked his watch. "It is actually 10:03 a.m. Pacific Standard Time."

We'd gotten to our destination: a bike rack. He went to the ugliest one — a lime-green number — and unlocked it as he spoke. "I would never dream of getting paid to solve a murder."

Me neither, but then David from North-West had entered my life. Aubrey continued on. "I want to know who thoughtlessly killed a young woman without even stopping to see if she was okay."

"Well, I do too!" I knew I sounded more than a touch defensive. He picked up on it, too, because he took me in for a moment before speaking.

"How long have you had your license?"

Huh? "Driver's?"

"Your private investigator's license."

"Oh, I'm not an investigator. I don't even play one on TV." I smiled and got no response.

"You are an amateur detective, Ms. Anderson?" He made it sound like the equivalent of a serial arsonist.

"No, but I was there the night Haley died."

"Did you see the car that hit Ms. Joseph?"

"Yes. No. Maybe."

I probably *had* seen the car. I just didn't remember.

He put on his helmet. "Ms. Anderson, I am not sure if you just want money, but I can assure you this is not fun and games. You should leave the investigating to the professionals."

Of course, he didn't bother to explain how he was any more of a professional than I was. Instead, he rode off, leaving me and my guilt to battle it out. I won and my guilt was banished. It was quickly replaced by anger. Didn't he know that vigilante crap was only in comic books and movies based off comic books? In real life, people did things for money. People like detectives, who also happened to investigate crimes — for money. And they did it every single day. At least I was doing it just this once.

I trekked back to Clothes Encounters, managing to push evil thoughts of Aubrey S. Adams-Parker out my head and replace them with thoughts about the car. The sooner I figured it out, the sooner I'd be done with all of this. Then I could go back to looking for jobs and probably being turned down.

"You come back for your friend?"

I was too busy thinking about Betty to actually see her standing there. She was placing merchandise on a display case right outside the door. I've never understood that. Aren't they afraid someone is going to just run away with their stuff? "I left my phone here yesterday," I said.

"The old iPhone?"

"I prefer the term 'classic.' "

"I like 'retro' myself. It's inside."

I followed her into the shop. "Nat," she called out as soon as we entered. "Can you bring out that old iPhone?"

As we waited for Nat, Sienna walked by us, zeroing in on a rack a few feet away. It looked like she'd been reunited with the pants and apparently saw some dresses she liked just as much, if not more. While she shopped, Betty and I had yet another in a growing series of uncomfortable silences. I spent most of it thinking about the car. Why would Betty mistake the car for a Rolls Royce if she had no clue what one looked like? Finally, I had to blurt something out. "What if the car wasn't a Rolls?"

Betty looked like the question came out of nowhere. Since she wasn't a mind reader, it probably did. "Not that I don't think it was a Rolls, but what if it wasn't?" I asked.

She stared at me like I was crazy. "What's your interest again?"

Sienna walked over to us. "Day, are you still talking about that car?" I shook my head at her, but she'd already turned to Betty. "She's been driving me crazy about that freaking car since yesterday. Ever since she saw that billboard."

Betty looked me dead in the eye and spoke. "The one offering the reward?"

I didn't know what to say. I did know that whatever I said, it wouldn't be the truth.

"This your phone?" a female voice said from somewhere to my left. I was happy for the interruption. "Aren't you the Chubby's girl?" she continued. Make that *unhappy* for the interruption.

She was holding my phone in her hand, so she had to be Nat. Even in heels, she was just average height and weight, which in LA meant five foot eight and barely 110 pounds. Her blonde hair wasn't happy to be that color. In protest, it had staged a walkout. Jagged, broken-off parts jutted out of the crown of her scalp. If she were black, we'd call it baby hair. Nat and Betty were both staring me down. Nat had a bit of wonder in her eyes. Betty's eyes, however, were saying something else.

"Did you just call me chubby?" I asked, then smiled.

"Chubby's. You did the Chubby's Chicken commercials." Nat rolled her neck, stuck up her finger, and said the phrase that had become the bane of my existence. "Don't think so, boo."

Her inflection was pretty good for a white girl. I blamed hip-hop.

"Wrong person," Betty said. "She's in business school."

"No, she's not," Nat said. "Her name is like something with a D."

"Dayna," Betty said. Even her bright pink hair seemed to be glaring at me.

"Yes! Dayna Anderson. She was on the Super Bowl."

"Dang right she was!" Sienna's voice dripped with pride. "And it was the second-most popular commercial that year. Not to mention the two million-plus YouTube views!"

She raised her hand to me for a high five. Needless to say, she was left hanging.

"You lied to me?" Betty asked as a cell phone began to ring. "You're not a grad student. You're an actress. And you were asking all those questions about Haley because you saw the billboard offering a reward. You really don't care. You're just looking for money."

That wasn't true. I did care. I just happened to also be looking for money. Of course, that wasn't something I could easily explain, so I focused on the part I could easily answer. "I *did* act. But I'm retired."

The phone rang again and I realized it was my cell phone, which was still in Nat's hand. She made no effort to give it to me. Instead, she asked, "Why would you give up being famous?"

My phone rang yet again. "I should probably answer that," I said.

Nat looked at the phone like she'd forgotten she had it. A picture of Emme had popped up to let me know she was calling. It was the one photo I had where Emme was actually looking at the camera. Nat's attitude did a complete 180. "You know Toni Abrams?"

Toni was Emme's twin sister. She was also *People*'s Most Beautiful Woman Alive last year and a double Oscar nominee. It was good to be Toni Abrams. What it wasn't good to be was someone who looked exactly like Toni Abrams. At least that's what Emme said, and I had to take her word for it. She'd know.

"Is she doing a movie about Haley?" Nat asked. "Is that why you're here?"

"No." I practically snatched the phone out her hands and put Emme on *ignore*. "That's not who you think it is."

"Oh, I get it. You can't talk about it until the deal is signed."

"I can't talk about it because it doesn't exist."

"Right." Nat actually winked at me. Twice. "Will we be in it? Can I play myself?"

I turned to Betty, hoping to talk to someone with an iota of sense, but even she looked impressed. She opened her mouth. I expected her to ask about my teeny, tiny, completely inconsequential, no-big-deal white lies. "I saw the car" is what she said. It was amazing how even the hint of being famous made people much more cooperative, not that you'd find me complaining. "Well, I saw the back headlights."

"What's a back headlight?" Sienna asked. "Oh, you mean tail lights. Yeah, you really know nothing about cars."

I shook my head at Sienna again. She really wasn't helping matters. At all. I attempted to turn the convo back to the subject at hand. "The photo I showed you wasn't a Rolls. It was an Infiniti. Was the car an Infiniti?"

Betty seemed genuinely surprised. "But that's what Haley said it was."

I'd already forgotten that she'd mentioned that. It meant Haley had seen the car coming. I couldn't imagine what must have gone through her head when she realized it wasn't going to stop. Geez. I shook those feelings off and continued my *Law & Order* impression. "Those were her direct words? A Rolls Royce hit me."

"She just said, 'Rolls.' Kept repeating it. Rolls. Rolls. Rolls. She was pretty banged up at that point, so it was all she seemed able to say."

Like I said, I couldn't even imagine. "Was she a big car person?" I asked.

"She lived in LA. She knew a Rolls," Nat said, more to not be forgotten than to actually help. "Why say it was a Rolls Royce if it was something else?"

Good question.

FIVE

Besides a one-day gig filling in for a receptionist at an investment firm downtown, the next few days amounted to a whole bunch of nothing. I spoke to Daddy a couple of times, but the bank hadn't called again. I chalked the Rolls misunderstanding to Haley being delusional. There were also no new revelations about the night she died. Not wanting to waste even a drop of gas, I barely left the condo. But then I had to. Emme was actually planning to leave her house. It was a joyous occasion. And it was all thanks to something called Call to Action 5.

When I promised I'd go with her to buy it, I didn't realize we'd be going at 3:00 a.m. to some place called Claremont so Emme could be among the first to buy the game. It was a bit too inland for my taste, but Emme claimed there'd be less people than in LA proper. Sienna tagged along, coming straight from the club. Even that early, we were about fiftieth in line. To say we were out of place would have been an understatement. Sienna and I weren't the only ones with breasts, but we *were* the only ones with breast implants.

Emme, however, was completely at home *and* completely natural. The lack of makeup made her angular face even more pale. Her blonde hair was kept long solely to make it easy to put in a ponytail. She was skinny, mainly because she was always forgetting to eat. Even in her ever-present Converse, she towered over us. She wore her usual uniform — jeans that managed to be skinny and loose at the same time, a T-shirt that read *The Princess Saves Herself,* and, of course, her necklace.

The diamond on it had been on her grandmother's favorite pair of earrings. Grandma Bess had gotten them when she was sixteen and wore them until she died. She only took them off to let her twin granddaughters play dress-up. Unfortunately, she only had one pair of earrings and two granddaughters. Right before she passed, she had each earring made into a pendant necklace — one for Emme and one for Toni.

Although she never said it, I think Emme

loved the necklace so much because it was the last time someone had treated her and Toni as equals. She played with it as we began Hour Two of our wait.

"They claim that Kandy Wrapper had piles of cash lying around," Sienna said. "In garbage bags."

She and I were discussing a recent string of celebrity home break-ins. The cops had nicknamed the robbers "The Rack Pack." The most recent target was Kandy Wrapper and her slam-dunking boyfriend. "I wonder who they'll hit next," I said. "They're —"

"Toni Abrams."

The stranger's tone was familiar, like he and "Toni" went back to sandboxes and Seven Minutes in Heaven. Emme looked at him and even managed to smile. "Not her. Sorry."

"Yeah, you are."

"— due to hit up someone else," I said, like I had never been interrupted.

I'd been friends with Emme long enough to know the best way to handle the situation — politely say no, then if they still didn't get the hint, continue what you were doing. Normally, they'd realize how awkward it was and shuffle away. "Fab started a pool to see who was next," Sienna said.

SNAP!

The guy took a photo of Emme with his phone. Since it was still dark, the flash nearly blinded us. She didn't say anything, just shifted her head slightly so she was blocked by Sienna. Not bothered in the least, he snapped another pic. A woman a few feet away noticed, then did a double take when she saw Emme. "Is that Toni Abrams?!" Her voice was one of those annoying stage whispers that is always louder than using your regular voice.

"Yeah," the guy said. "Major attitude problem."

I broke protocol and glared, wishing him a venereal disease. Not that either of them noticed. The woman spoke. "Ms. Abrams, I'm a huge, huge fan."

Obviously not huge enough to know Toni wasn't even in town or that she had a twin sister.

"Can I have an autograph?" she continued.

Emme smiled at her. "I'm not who you think I am. Sorry."

"You can have my autograph," Sienna said. She was joking. I hoped.

The woman looked at Sienna and tried to figure out who she was, then gave up and just handed her a piece of paper. It was an old receipt. "Okay."

Emme and I exchanged a look. "Who should I make it out to?" Sienna asked.

"Stephanie Dimsey."

Sienna narrated her writing. "To Stephanie. Keep shining. Love always, Sienna."

She finished with a flourish and a dotting of the *I,* then handed it back. I don't know who was cheesing harder, Sienna or the woman. I glanced away and noticed a crowd was forming, and not for Call to Action 5. The news had spread a star was in their midst.

"Toni, give me your autograph!"

"Toni, I called my sister. Talk to her."

"Toni, marry me!"

Those who weren't talking were taking pictures. I was surprised. This was LA. Folks were supposed to be used to seeing famous people getting coffee or buying groceries, but that must not extend to parts east of Los Angeles proper. In the excitement, someone shoved someone else. Someone shoved back. Everyone turned, scared — or excited — a fight might break out.

Emme used the distraction to walk to the car. Sienna and I followed suit. No one else did; an autograph wasn't worth losing their place in line. Thank you Call to Action 5.

"I can stay," I said to Emme. "Get the game for you."

She shook her head. "I'll order it online."

We got in and pulled off. We drove in silence the first full minute, digesting what had happened. Finally, Emme spoke. "You can have my autograph."

Her voice was a perfect imitation of Sienna. Just like that, all three of us started laughing. "You should've charged her," I said.

"I could never do that to my fans," Sienna said. "Though I'm not as friendly to my fans as Joseline's latest fiancé was to his last night."

I was about to ask for more details when we drove past another tip line billboard. It wasn't about Haley's death, but it was enough to remind me about it. I had to be the only person on the planet who knew less after investigating than more. Blurg.

"Day, did you hear me?" Sienna asked. "He got her at least ten karats."

I heard "carrots" and couldn't figure out what she was talking about. "For a salad?"

"Joseline's engagement ring! You stay with food on the brain."

"Amen," I said.

A light bulb went off over my head. And it illuminated Haley's face. "What if Haley wasn't talking about a car? What if she was talking about a rose?"

Emme and Sienna had no clue what I was yammering about.

"Haley," I said. "Her last word was 'Rolls.' It doesn't really make sense, unless she wasn't talking about a car at all. Remember the car that was coming from a cross street and would've run into the side of Emme's car if she hadn't stopped? It had those gaudy roses etched into the window tint. That had to be the car. Haley must've seen it."

They both looked doubtful. " 'Rolls' and 'rose' don't necessarily sound alike," Sienna said.

"If you're enunciating," I said. "Haley had just been hit by a car. She was probably slurring her words, and Betty misinterpreted what she said."

"Shouldn't he have been coming down Vermont toward us if he'd hit her?" Emme asked.

"Not if he was trying to get away," I said. "That area has a bunch of dead ends. People always get screwed trying to take a short cut to Normandie."

"So we did see the car." Sienna sounded as surprised as I felt.

I actually had information that could help the cops find Haley's killer. Of course, I still had to remember what kind of car it was. I drew a blank. "So what kinda car was it?" I finally asked. One of them had to know.

"An Audi." Sienna sounded pretty confident. "Sedan. Definitely dark-colored."

Yes! I imagined myself writing a check, sticking it in a stamped envelope addressed to my parents' bank, and putting it in a big blue mailbox.

"Wrong," Emme said. Wrong? What the heck did she mean by wrong? "Two doors. Something American like a Chrysler. It was dark-colored, though."

Why couldn't anyone remember this car? Me? Sienna? Emme? Betty? My check-sending fantasy was replaced with a nightmare of a foreclosure sign being stuck in my parents' front yard while Ms. Jenkins from across the street looked on with glee. "At least we've established it had doors," I said.

"There's a way to find out what it was, FYI," Emme said.

"I can't call every mechanic in LA," I said.

Sienna looked at me. "She's talking about Omari, Day."

I drew a breath. No one had actually dared say his name to me in weeks. He was like Voldemort, except with a nose. Both my best friends knew we'd gotten into an argument, but I'd been too embarrassed to tell either of them about Thumb-gate. I had no plans to tell them either. Just like I had no desire to talk to him. Yes, I missed him, but part of me felt if I called at this point, he'd think I was another person trying to leech off his success. If I wanted to see Omari, I could just turn on CBS like everyone else.

"He's not going to remember anything," I said. "He has the worst memory of anyone I know. I'll just have to fig—"

Sienna interrupted me. "His phone. I was recording with it. I caught the car."

I figured Omari would have already erased all elements of me from his life, deleting my number from his phone and my photos from his Facebook and petitioning the government to remove "Day" from America's vocabulary. "No way he kept that video."

"One way to find out," Sienna said.

No way was I contacting him. No way at all.

SIX

Sienna had made Anani Miss's blog again. And by "made the blog," I meant she was in the background of someone else's photo. This time, it was A-list actor Luke Cruz. She had her own version of photo bombing down to an art form. She stood close enough that she couldn't be cropped out and never looked directly at the camera, instead wearing the same oh-so-serious "I don't see you even though you're standing two feet in front of me loudly screaming my name like a bad porn actress" expression Luke wore himself. They almost looked like a couple.

"This is going on my wall," she said, hitting the print button.

We were in her living room, the shades fully raised in an effort to catch the late morning sun. She handed me the laptop and scurried to the printer, running past a wall with a collection of similarly themed photos. I had dubbed it "Sienna's Wall of (Background) Fame."

Anani Miss was our all-time favorite gossip blog, so I clicked the back button to see what other celebs she was skewering and found Omari's face staring at me. He had a Trader Joe's bag in his hand and was walking with some bottle-blonde white chick who had a bigger booty than I did. I didn't recognize her. I did recognize his shirt, the result of a joint shopping trip after he'd gotten to the age where there was no excuse not to own a shirt with buttons.

Omari was all pretty boy, though he'd kill me for describing him like that. It's hard to be called anything else when you have dimples and eyelashes so long I'd once been tempted to rip them off to give to my eyelash lady for my next appointment. He also had curly hair but kept it close to the scalp so no one would find out.

"OMG," Sienna said, sneaking up on me.

"What?"

"OMG! That's his nickname on Anani. He's officially big-time."

In Anani's world, being bestowed a nickname was the equivalent of winning an Oscar. I willed myself not to be impressed. "OMG, though?"

"His initials. Omari Michael Grant. I

should call him. OMG, it's OMG!!! He'd curse me out so bad."

"You *should* call him," I said. "And then you can ask about the cell phone video." So I wouldn't have to.

Sienna was already shaking her head no. "No and thank you. You got in a silly little argument. Big whoop. Call the boy."

I sighed. Then finally decided to come clean. I patted the couch next to me. "Sit."

There must have been something in my voice, because she sat immediately. No questions asked. I launched into my tale, sharing every single sordid detail about what had happened in the backseat of the Black Hole, even yanking up my dress to show her the *exact* spot where thumb had made contact with skin. The entire thing took five very long, very painful minutes. I was mentally exhausted by the time I was done. So I sat there, waiting for Sienna to say something. Hoping she'd finally understand.

It took her a beat but she finally spoke. "Girl, are you serious? He hit on you."

I nodded.

"And you panicked," she said.

I nodded again.

Her face was even more somber when she spoke again. "You know what this means, right?"

76

Once again, I nodded. It meant I could never talk to him again.

"It means you guys are finally at the end of Act Two!"

She broke out in the biggest you-know-what-eating grin I'd ever seen. If she smiled any wider, I could have made out the coffee she'd drunk for breakfast. I was not amused.

In screenplay speak, the end of Act Two is the main character's lowest point. In action films, the star's been captured. In romantic comedies, the couple has had a big fight. In horror movies, all her friends are dead and she's been stripped down to just a bra and panties. Sienna had already been convinced that Omari and I were destined to walk hand-in-hand into the sunset while the credits started to roll. Nothing I said could convince her otherwise, even apparently Thumb-gate. "You need to call him," she said.

And with that, she went to hang up her celeb photo and I went back to the bloset, where I didn't call him. Instead, I got on my tablet and googled "Tricks to trigger memory." A ton of hits came up. All of them were for how to remember things in the future. That would be fine and dandy for the next hit-and-run I witnessed but was not helping me now. I typed "How to remember something you forgot."

The first hit was a video link about self-hypnosis. My first thought was, I'm not that desperate. My second thought was, Well, yes, I actually am. I clicked the link. It promised Brother Mo would be my guide to help trigger my memory. It suggested I find a comfortable place and "let the Brother do his thing." What in Blaxploitation heck . . .

Against my better judgment, I hit play, immediately pausing the video to let it load. The last thing I needed was to be in the throes of hypnosis and have to buffer. I nestled in bed next to my tablet and prayed this would work. I hit play again.

"Welcome." Brother Mo spoke over a slow, mesmerizing beat. It was so spoken word that I resisted the urge to snap my applause. Though he had gone all-out with the music, he'd skimped on the visuals. I was expecting squiggly lines moving hypnotically like a belly dancer, or at least something that required a warning it might cause seizures. The screen was just black. Boo. I was also hoping he'd at least give me a "You are getting very, very sleepy." Instead, he said, "Are you comfortable and relaxed with your mind open to this experience?"

He paused just long enough that I wondered if I should answer him. I compromised and nodded. "Good," Brother Mo finally said. "It's important you clear the brain. Repeat after me, slowly, surely, 'I am open, I am ready, I am free.' Repeat now. 'I am open. I am ready. I am free.' I can't hear you."

I felt stupid, but since that was nothing new, I repeated it. "I am open. I am ready. I am free."

"Continue with this mantra as you concentrate on your breathing. In. Out. Up. Down. Feel me next to you. Feel me inside you."

Why was this reminding me of bad phone sex with my ex? Nevertheless, I was mantraing my butt off when my cell rang. I jerked up like I'd been hit by lightning. Brother Mo would have to wait.

It was Daddy. I knew something was wrong when he didn't go through his usual spiel about how pretty I looked. "Hey baby girl, have you talked to your mama?"

I hadn't. Mainly because I'd been avoiding her. He didn't need to know that, though. "Not today," I said. "You on lunch break?"

His doctor had forbid him from doing anything strenuous, so he'd picked up a job working as a cashier at the drugstore around the corner from the house. It paid nowhere near what he'd made working for the city. But he had too much pride not to do something, even if it was just for minimum wage.

"Sure am. Your mama told me the bank called while I was at work."

Fudge. My father and I had a strict "Don't tell, seriously don't tell" policy when it came to sharing things with my mother. It was especially true for the foreclosure situation. There was more of a chance of aliens coming from space and both Will Smith and Tom Cruise *not* being able to save mankind than her handling that piece of information well. Although at this point, I was more than ready for someone or something to come take me away. Another galaxy seemed like the perfect place, too. "She didn't say what they wanted?" I asked.

"Sure didn't. All she said was that the bank called."

"She probably doesn't know, Daddy." I tried to sound reassuring. "Mama isn't one to play it cool."

He didn't respond, so I continued. "Everything's going to be fine. Mama won't know a thing. I told you I have a plan. I just need a few more days."

I could hear him sigh through the phone.

"I never shoulda gotten you involved. This is my problem. Not yours. I don't want you to worry about it anymore. Okay, baby girl? I'll handle it."

"Not a problem, Daddy."

Then I hung up and immediately decided to call Omari.

The fact that the number wasn't even in my phone was a testament to the state of our relationship. I'd been forced to downgrade to one of those pay-by-the-month no-contract deals right after our argument. Luckily, he'd kept the same 706 number from Augusta since he'd moved out here. It was one of the few numbers I knew by heart.

Of course, I didn't have the slightest idea what to say. I figured texting would be easier, but I was still hesitant. I wasn't scared of what to write as much as I was scared of his reaction. It felt abrupt to send a "Hey, what's up? I need something from you," text, especially after I hadn't heard from him.

You wouldn't believe the number of "Hey, girl! Just wanted to catch up even though we haven't spoken in five years" messages I got the day after my first Chubby's commercial aired. Everyone who'd ignored me in high school now claimed to be a close friend. It was like I was retroactively popular. Omari and I would joke about how pathetic it was.

Then there were the Hand-Outs, strangers who wanted to be your best friend only because they had their hands out, looking for you to help their come-up. Read their script. Invest in their business opportunity. Hook them up with your agent. LA had more Hand-Outs than plastic surgeons. It was one of the few things I didn't miss about my brush with fame. I didn't want Omari to think I wanted something from him just because he was famous. That was not the case. I wanted something from him because I was broke.

I decided to go the simple route. *Hey, stranger,* I texted. I put my phone down and, of course, went to the bathroom. As I washed my hands, I could hear the phone vibrating on the desk. A million thoughts raced through my head as I walked back into my room, and they all boiled down to one thing: What would he say? I read his response. *Who's this?*

Was he being funny? I responded, *Very funny,* even though it wasn't. His response was instantaneous. *I'm not playing. Who is this?*

He was serious. Had he deleted my number? When? Right after our argument?

Because he was that mad? Because we hadn't spoken? I decided to play it light. *OMG!!! Someone's come a long way since Guys and Dolls.*

I waited for a response. And waited. And waited. After an hour of pretending not to stare at my phone, I wrote again. *It's Day.*

He didn't respond to that one either, which pissed me off. Omari knew I hated being ignored. It was one thing to be mad at someone. It was another thing to be just plain rude. I sent another text, *Glad to see success has made you an a-hole!* Then I decided that wasn't enough and dialed his number.

Despite the fame and despite the argument, we went back to high school. I had enough on him to anonymously sell a story to the *National Enquirer*. The phone rang four times before the voicemail picked up. "Hi, you reached Charlotte. Sorry I couldn't answer your call right now."

Oops. I double-checked the number. It was Omari's. Key word being *was*. I needed to talk to him, but how? He'd never been good at checking his email, even before he was super busy being hot and rich and famous. And I didn't have time to waste. I immediately put on my shoes and grabbed my purse. If I wanted to talk to him, I'd have to do it in person. Sigh.

Omari brought three things with him when he moved to Georgia from Brooklyn our junior year: a New York accent, a sneaker addiction, and a hatred of driving. Even in LA, he stuck close to home when it came to his favorite places, and home had been a studio off Pico a few blocks west of Fairfax.

That area is three miles from Hollywood, but it might as well be in the South Bay. It's filled with large two-story duplexes and single-family homes occupied by people with jobs they got through interviews, not auditions. You can do breakfast at CJ's, which holds the title for the best — and possibly only — soul food/Mexican spot in So-Cal. For lunch, you can get garlic chicken at Versailles, a Cuban spot on the corner of La Cienega. It's so no-frills they don't take reservations. You wait in line outside until a table opens up. The area doesn't even have a single Starbucks. If you want coffee, you have Paper or Plastik, where you're actually allowed to use words like *small* and *large.*

I hit them all to no avail. Omari wasn't at any of them. It took me all afternoon — if you accounted for both lunch and dinner breaks. I even went by his apartment building, but a quick glance at the directory told me he'd moved. Depressed as all get-out, I hit Sienna up on text to see what she was up to. Of course, she was shopping.

I got in my car, took La Brea up to Melrose, and parked on a side street right next to a sign that warned me I only had two hours to park there unless I had a permit. Sienna was at a shoe store a couple of blocks away. As I walked to meet her, I passed by Platinum Motorsports.

It was the only auto mechanic shop on the street. Melrose was known more for fashion than auto mechanics. But even though it seemed weird to put an auto detailing place there, in reality, it made sense. Platinum was basically fashion for your car.

It was well after seven and the place was pretty deserted. I went inside and was greeted by a six-foot-five behemoth. He was black, had to weigh at least three hundred pounds, and looked like he'd make a great pillow. He smiled when he saw me. "Welcome to Platinum. I'm Jay."

"You're just the person I needed to see, Jay." I pushed my boobs out slightly. If you bought them, you might as well use them.

I may have been setting the women's movement back fifty years, but I needed every distraction I could get for the tale I planned to weave. He nodded, so I continued. "Can you believe this idiot hit my car and didn't bother to stop?"

"That's horrible."

"Isn't it? I ran after him, but hello, I was in five-inch heels, no way I could catch him. And so he got away. But he did have, like, this rose etched in his window tint, and I know you guys do that, *soooo,* I thought maybe you could help me out and like maybe look up what cars you did that for?"

I smiled wide and waited to see if he bought it. After a brief pause, he spoke. "So you think your man is cheating on you with some chick with roses etched in her windows?"

What a chauvinist . . . said the girl who'd just tried to trade her boobs for information. If he wanted to believe that, it was fine by me. "That obvious, huh?" I asked.

"You know I could get in trouble for giving out clients' information." My smile tightened. What a waste of a boob job. "Lucky for you, they don't pay me enough to give a crap," he continued. "What kind of car was it?"

Good question. I decided to use the fact he thought I was a dumb girl to my advantage. "There are different brands?" Then I giggled. I hated myself for it.

He grabbed a pen and scribbled down a number. "Do some more spying, find out what kind of car it is, and call me when you have it."

Blurg. I was never going to remember anything about the car that hit Haley. My parents' house was about to be seized by the bank. And Omari had truly moved on with his life while I shared a bedroom with about fifty pairs of shoes. Nice pairs of shoes, but still. I said goodbye, took the number, and moped all the way to the shoe store.

When I got there, Sienna was admiring herself in one of the store's full-length mirrors. She was wearing the red pants from Clothes Encounters. She'd finally bought them during the disaster that was our last trip there. They were paired with a black ribbed fitted tank top. "Aren't they gorgeous?" she asked.

They were a pair of red suede platform stiletto booties. "They're gorgeous," I said, but my heart wasn't in it.

Sienna picked up on it immediately. "Okay what's wrong? You're obviously depressed, because shoes always cheer you up."

So true. She handed her credit card to the sales girl. Much like a five-year-old going school shopping, Sienna loved wearing her shoe purchases out the store.

"I spent all afternoon looking for freaking Omari," I told her. "I hit all his spots on Pico, and I couldn't find him anywhere."

"Of course, you didn't find him," she said. "You're looking in the wrong places."

"He practically lived in Paper or Plastik."

"That was before his show. He's gone Hollywood."

I couldn't see Omari pretending to be shocked to be caught by the paparazzi while shopping on Robertson Boulevard. "No way."

"He wouldn't be the first," she said.

She was right. Four years ago, I couldn't see myself pretending to be shocked by the paparazzi while shopping on Robertson either, but I had. My bank account balance proved it.

"You need to go above Wilshire if you want to see him." Sienna grabbed her cell phone from her purse and tapped the screen a few times. "Let me look up his Twitter. If I don't find anything there, I'll check Instagram."

Omari having a Twitter page was proof enough she might be right. He'd refused all my efforts to get him to sign up. I peered over her shoulder. He had almost 300,000 followers. Not bad for six weeks' work. His Twitter feed was mostly retweets of fans who just couldn't wait for *LAPD 90036* to come on!!!!! He did occasionally tweet himself. Sienna read his most recent entry out loud. "Excited for *Man in Danger 2: Man in More Danger* premiere tonight."

That was all the confirmation I needed that Sienna was right. Omari really had gone Hollywood if he was attending premieres for movies he wasn't even in. The only reason people did that was to get their red carpet pictures on blogs and in magazines. Blurg.

Sienna left the Twitter app and hit another button. There was a beep. "Siri, what time does the *Man in Danger 2* premiere start tonight?"

There was another beep and then Siri's mechanical voice. "I found some information that may help you."

It did. The premiere was at the ArcLight, with the red carpet happening from 7:30 to 8:30. I glanced at the phone's clock. It was 8:02.

"Let's go," Sienna said. "We have a movie to catch."

SEVEN

Hollywood is high school with prettier clothes and better lunch options. You study scripts, not textbooks. Try out for roles, not varsity. Take screen tests, not math exams. And you vote for Oscars, not prom king. Movie premieres are like a school dance, an excuse to dress up and take pictures, except you don't have a school dance every week. You do have a premiere.

Between the premieres, openings, award shows, and other honors, Los Angeles rolls out the red carpet at least three times a week. You'd think Angelenos would be over it, but we live for this stuff, even if we pretend we don't. A premiere produces more rubberneckers than a three-car pile-up on the 405. And, yes, it's always called *the* 405. We're even pretentious about our freeways.

God was among those anxious to witness my encounter with Omari because the roads were practically empty. The ArcLight was on Sunset Boulevard, not that far from where we were on Melrose to begin with, and Sienna breezed along side streets at fifty-five miles per hour. Part of me wished she would pass a cop. Not that I wanted her to get a ticket — Sienna always managed to talk herself out of those, anyway. I wanted to buy some time because I wasn't sure I wanted to see Omari. And what if he didn't want to see me? That would be even more embarrassing.

The ArcLight hosted many a premiere because of its location and the Cinerama Dome, which looked like a giant dirty golf ball wedged halfway into the ground. Fox must not have had high hopes for the film because it hadn't sprung for the Dome. The premiere was in the regular ArcLight building, set a couple hundred feet back off the street.

We avoided Sunset and took Ivar to the parking garage. Perhaps because of the premiere — the D-level folks often drove themselves — the line to get into the garage stretched half a block. "Go," Sienna said. "I'll park and meet you."

Nodding, I jumped out the car. I immediately heard screaming photographers being drowned out by screaming fans. I cut through the parking garage — it was much quicker on foot — and came up to the red carpet the back way. No one stopped me. The theater didn't close for a premiere. The ArcLight was about its money. So if you wanted to get up close to your favorite celeb, you just needed to buy a ticket to another movie and kind of hang out in the lobby or right outside until said celeb got tired of smiling for the camera.

Getting on the actual red carpet, however, was akin to getting into Fort Knox. There were security guards galore, but they weren't the scary part. That was the publicists. No way were you getting on that red carpet if you weren't on the list.

After you finished the red carpet, official invitees had to walk the two hundred or so feet to the actual building. My plan was to linger outside the building and let Omari come to me. If anyone asked, I'd just say I was waiting for a friend. And I was. He just wasn't expecting me.

The walkway was surprisingly empty, but I wasn't complaining. It gave me a good view. I immediately saw Omari as he wrapped up the press line. He looked great in a yellow blazer that he'd paired with a pair of yellow high-top designer Nikes.

The same white chick that was in the

Trader Joe's pictures was waiting for him. So was a short white guy wearing a suit tailored within an inch of its life. I immediately pegged them as publicist and manager, respectively. Omari ran out of carpet and she grabbed his elbow to lead him away from the cameras. As soon as she did, the smile slid off Omari's face.

He hated every moment. That made me feel better. Maybe he hadn't changed and gone Hollywood after all. The aforementioned publicist and manager anchored him on both sides, forming a protective barrier as they came right toward me. I inhaled and waited for him to see me and say something. I just hoped it would be something nice.

They were a few feet away. I waited. They were right next to me. I waited. And just like that, they passed me while I still waited. Omari hadn't bothered to look up from the ground. The not-making-eye-contact was new.

I'd have to approach him. Great.

After a moment, I finally willed myself to follow him, staying a few steps behind. "Omari," I said.

Either I wasn't loud enough or he purposefully ignored me, because they continued their trek. I tried again but got the same non-response. Contemplating my next move, I almost walked into his back. A fan had put herself right in his path. "Omari," she screamed, so loud he had to look up. "Marry me."

She attempted to kiss the groom. He dodged her but laughed as he did. "I thought I was supposed to kiss the bride, not the other way around," he said, smiling.

Not invited to the impromptu wedding, I continued on. I walked to the theater and stopped. What now? I hovered, expecting Omari to be behind me any second. I planned to look back, do a double take, and pretend to be surprised to see him. Except when I looked back, he was still talking to his intended. His publicist and manager stood a few feet away, at the ready in case they were called into action.

A security guard approached me. "You can't block the doorway."

"I'm waiting for a friend." Thank God I practiced that one.

"You can't block the doorway."

"Fine." I noticed a cement stoop a few feet away and sat down. The security guard's eyes narrowed, but he didn't say anything. I wasn't blocking the door, after all.

I formed a plan of attack. I wouldn't speak first. Just let him lead the convo so I could judge his tone and determine how to play the rest of our conversation. Heaven forbid I play nice if he was still mad. Or even worse, go all Angry Black Woman when he was fine.

He and the entourage were where I left them, his back to me. The woman fan had been replaced by a man. I couldn't hear what the man was saying, but from his hand motions, he believed every word of it. Omari nodded, managing to look equally as interested.

As they talked, Omari put his hands behind his back. It looked like he was doing some weird gesture. I narrowed my eyes so I could see better. He made a fist, then released it. Then he did it again. I wasn't the only one who noticed. His publicist and manager quickly ran over. The publicist took Omari by the elbow and led him off. The man went with them. As they got closer, I could hear what she was saying: "I hate that I had to interrupt, but Mr. Grant's going to be late if we don't get a move on."

So that wasn't a fan, it was a Hand-Out. Omari had developed a foolproof system of getting away from one without coming across like an a-hole. Impressive. The man slunk off, and before I knew it, they were walking past me, Omari having resumed his stare-at-the-ground routine. I popped up and followed behind.

They got to the door. Omari held it open as both his publicist and manager went inside. I was right behind him. We'd finally make eye contact. I was about to ask him to hold the door when the security guard stepped in front of me. "Ma'am, I know you're very excited, but we can't have you harassing our guests."

Fudge. Omari disappeared inside without so much as a glance back. I turned to the guard and decided to figure out what he was talking about. "We have a strict no loitering policy," he said. "If you aren't buying a ticket, I'll have to ask you to leave the premises."

He thought I was stalking Omari. I was instantly offended. Yes, I was stalking Omari, but not for the reasons he thought. "I told you I'm waiting for my friend," I said.

"A friend in your head?"

I was about to tell him where he could stick that attitude when his eyes shifted behind me and he was off. I don't know what or who caught his attention, but I didn't care. I used the opportunity to sneak inside. Omari and Co were gone. I'd missed him. Fudge.

I texted Sienna and headed to the bathroom. It was tucked behind the ticket counter, an area you had no reason to be in unless you had to pee or were a perv.

I quickly did my business. After washing my hands, I examined myself. I was wearing a pair of tight jeans — there weren't any other kind at this point — that I'd paired with a bright yellow, loose-fitting top that played nice with my skin tone, and my favorite pair of heels. I looked great. Too bad it was all for nothing.

Then I exited the bathroom and ran smack-dab into Omari.

His publicist whispered into her cell phone a few feet away. His face screamed surprise. My face called his bet and raised him one to alarm. Then he smiled.

God, he looked like home. He pulled me in for a hug and I breathed him in. He smelled like home. He squeezed me. He felt like home, mainly because his stomach was as hard and rippled as aluminum siding. But I stepped back, because just like home, I'd messed everything up. "You got the memo," I said, then almost covered my hand with my mouth like I'd said a naughty word.

So much for not speaking first. I was referring to us both wearing yellow. Would he get that? Should I clarify? Gesture to my shirt. Point to his shoes. While I thought, he spoke. "The one Big Bird sent?"

I should've known he'd get it. "Go Team Yellow," I said.

"We are a movement, no doubt."

"School buses."

"Cabs," he said.

"Lemons."

"Bananas."

"The most disgusting Skittles flavor," I said.

"But the best traffic light."

"You'd think it'd be green, but yellow does give you an option. You can stay or go. It's up to you."

We paused to look at each other and smiled. What had I been so scared about again?

"I drove past your place the other day. I thought about stopping by," he said.

Oh, that. He didn't know I'd been forced to move. I didn't want to tell him.

"How's —"

I cut him off, afraid of what he might ask next. "I'm glad I ran into you. I need your help. Remember that girl we drove past the uh, last time we saw each other? She died from a hit-and-run. The police are looking for any info on the car. And they thought it was a Rolls Royce, but it's actually not. It's that car that almost hit us, the one with the roses etched in the windows. The problem is we don't remember what type of car it was. And so I thought maybe you might. Do you?"

He looked shocked when I stopped long enough to let him speak. He shook his head no and opened his mouth to say something. I didn't let that happen. "I figured. Sienna was recording on your phone. It would be nice to look at that video. I can look at it, right?"

Another pause. Then he finally spoke. "I don't know."

"Don't know if you'll help?"

"Don't know if I still have it."

"Right. Why would you keep that? Or even remember if you kept that? It's not really that important to you, not now with all the stuff you have going on." It was getting awkward, yet I couldn't shut my mouth.

"No, I just got a new phone."

That also made sense. "Oh well. I just figured if I could see it, maybe it'd jog a memory or we could give the video to the police or something."

I waited for him to answer. Instead, his publicist appeared. "Sorry to interrupt," she said, but it was clear none of us, myself included, was sorry. "Mr. Grant's going to be late if we don't get moving."

It was only then that I realized Omari had his hands behind his back. Did he just do what I think he did?

EIGHT

She began to lead him to safety, away from the crazy stalker chick with her hand out. As she did, he glanced back and said, "I'll call if I still have the video."

Like I'd ever hear from him again.

As soon as they were gone, I booked it outside to find Sienna. She hadn't answered my text, but I knew she was around somewhere. Knowing Sienna like I did, somewhere was in close proximity to the cameras, so I headed in that direction. The movie had already started, but there were still a few stragglers on the red carpet.

And one of them was Sienna.

She was posing like Victoria had shared her secret. The photographers were eating it up. She looked in her element, which cheered me up a little bit. I was glad someone's evening was going well.

The only problem was her outfit. She still had on the red pants and her newly purchased red booties. That wasn't the issue. The problem was that she'd chosen to wear a coat over her black tank top. A coat that she had zipped all the way up. A coat that belonged to me and happened to be made of a similar red leather as the pants. She must have felt cold when she'd gotten out the car and grabbed it, not thinking she'd actually make it onto the red carpet. Rocking red from head to toe, she kind of looked like a Twizzler. Eek.

I tried to get her attention, even making wild motioning gestures for her to take the jacket off. In her excitement she must have forgotten she had it on, but I knew she'd be so disappointed when she searched for the photos the next day.

She didn't see me. I could only watch in horror as she continued down the line, her fashion faux pas captured again and again. I was waiting for her when she finished. "How'd I look out there?" she asked as I hugged her.

She looked so excited, I didn't dare bring up the jacket. "Amazing!"

"I can't wait to see the pictures tomorrow," she said. "So did you talk to Omari?"

"Unfortunately."

I regaled her with every moment as we made our way to the parking garage. Once we got in the car, we used her phone to FaceTime Emme, where once again I went over every painful moment and even gave her an abbreviated version of Thumb-gate. "He signaled her," I said after I'd wrapped up.

"You're probably right," Sienna agreed. What? Wasn't it your friend's job to lie to you when you can't even lie to yourself? "But only because he was still embarrassed. Think about it from his perspective. He made a move. Was rejected —"

"I didn't reject him! I panicked."

"And he sees you again and you act like nothing happened. He needed out of there and he had an out. You guys are now in Act Three. You have to make a big gesture to proclaim your love. It has to be someplace crazy, like in the pouring rain."

"We're in a drought."

"Girl, aren't we?" she agreed, not acknowledging I was being literal. As usual, Southern California was on drought watch. Folks could only water their lawns on certain days. Of course, she also wasn't lying. The grass wasn't the only thing not getting none.

Emme finally spoke. She was splitting her time between listening to us, playing some online poker, and editing a video. It was one of the ways she earned money since she had another year until her trust fund kicked in. "Ever think maybe he was late to the movie?" she asked.

I had not. Nor did I want to. I glared at her, but it was less effective through a small chat box. Sometimes I questioned whether Emme had lady parts. The only people who took things at face value were men. It was women's job to analyze and overanalyze. It was part of the fun of being female, not that it made up for periods and labor, but still. "So why blow me off with that whole 'I'll call if it's still on my phone'?" I asked.

"Because he plans to call you if it's still on his phone?" Emme said.

I wanted to throw something at her, when *my* cell phone rang. Even Emme stopped what she was doing. We all looked at each other. "Who is it?" Sienna asked.

I checked the ID. "Don't know. It's a 323 area code."

Local number. It could be Omari. We all stared as it rang. No way was I answering it. Just before it headed to voicemail, Sienna grabbed the thing, hit accept, and thrust it in the general direction of my ear. I had no choice but to speak. "Hello?"

"What's up with the Y?" The voice was male and definitely not Omari.

I shook my head at Sienna and Emme and

said, "Who is this?"

"The Y in your name," the guy said. "It's completely unnecessary."

"The Y's for Yolanda, my grandmother." I was going to say more but realized I was explaining myself to a stranger. "Who is this?"

"Haley's boyfriend. Victory."

At first I thought he'd won something, but then I realized Victory was his name. Yet he was giving me crap about my parents' spelling choices. "Betty gave you my info?"

He ignored that. "I know what you're doing, Dayna with the Y. I won't let you do it."

If I were a cartoon, my eyes would have literally bugged out of my sockets. Blurg. Another person had realized I was using Haley's death to get $15,000. A much needed $15,000, but still. I was all set to explain everything and name-drop Emme's sister if need be — the connection had worked with Betty, after all — when he spoke again. "You need to pay me." I was confused. He wanted to split the reward money? "My dad's in the biz. He said if you use my likeness in a movie, you gotta pay up."

At first, I had no clue what he was talking about, but then I flashed back to Nat thinking I was shooting a movie about Haley. Someone must have told the boyfriend, and he wanted to make sure to get a paycheck. What a sweet one this guy was.

Having an attitude about someone profiting off Haley's death was a bit pot-and-kettle of me, but still. I hadn't even known the girl. He'd dated her. I was tempted to judge Haley's taste in men, then remembered a few of my exes and switched to feeling bad for her. Victory was still talking, but I did something I'd always loved doing to the aforementioned boyfriends. I hung up and wondered how long before he realized he was talking to a dial tone.

Twenty-four Omari phone-call-less hours later, I decided I didn't care anymore. By the time I got to hour forty-eight with no phone call, I'd been reduced to kinda, sorta, maybe cyberstalking him. I checked his Twitter and Instagram while that night's new episode of *The First 48* played in the background. There hadn't been any new tweets or photos since the premiere. So I'd resorted to checking his @s on Twitter for any mention of Omari sightings. Maybe he'd not gotten back to me because he'd taken an impromptu trip to Mars.

I was checking his page for the fourth time

that day when there finally was a tweet. It was "from" him; in other words, his publicist. *Almost at 300,000 followers. When I get there, I'm giving $10,000 to the United Way.*

I hadn't the slightest clue what the United Way did, but I suddenly wanted to help them. If that meant signing up for Twitter and following Omari, so be it. I'd deleted my own account about six months earlier. I didn't want it back. Twitter was much more effective as a stalking tool than a sharing one. Or so I'd heard.

I needed a new name. DaynaTheStalker seemed a bit too obvious. I decided on Boop618, my birthday and my mother's nickname for me. I'd wanted to be Betty Boop for Halloween when I was five. My mother was too Southern, too black, and too traditional to even think of letting me live that dream. I ended up being Strawberry Shortcake, but the name stuck. I had family members who didn't know my real name was Dayna.

I signed up and immediately followed Omari. United Way, you're welcome. I was going through his photos when Sienna burst into the room. "Whatcha doing?"

The three-year-old in me resisted the urge to scream, "I wasn't stalking Omari's Twitter." Instead, I played it more like I was thirteen and went on the defensive. "Don't you knock?"

"Sorry! I just wanted to show you something."

I barely had enough time to hide the evidence, AKA the tablet, before Sienna was squeezing next to me on the bed, her cell phone showing the mobile page for Anani Miss. I recognized the photo. It was a picture of Sienna on the *Man in Danger 2: Man in More Danger* red carpet. Uh oh.

The post read: *Behold, boys and girls, I have found a new shero. Not since Michael Jackson retired his Thriller ensemble has someone made all red look all good. She just has to cross her legs and she could be mistaken for the world's longest piece of Red Vine licorice. Isn't she just delish? Let's all worship at the altar of the Lady of the Red Vine.*

I got pissed. I'd thought practically the same thing, but still. Not even my beloved Anani could talk about my friend like that. I was about to start a rant stating such when Sienna spoke. "Isn't it the most awesome thing in the world? Anani gave me a nickname. I'm famous, Day. I'm famous."

I had to smile. I loved her too much not to.

He finally called.

When he did, I didn't even pick up the phone because his number came up private and so I thought he was a bill collector. It took almost another twenty-four hours before I checked the message. When I did, I was surprised to hear his voice.

I listened to his message four straight times, but only to make sure I'd written down his number correctly, I swear. He sounded rushed. "It's me. Found the cell. Hit me back." He left his new cell number.

The call started off well. "Hi," I said.

"How are you?" he asked.

"I'm great," I said.

And that's when it went downhill. There was a long, awkward pause. It lasted fifteen seconds. I counted. "So," I said. "The video."

"The video," he repeated.

This silence lasted eleven seconds. "You have it," I said.

"I have it."

"Can you email it?"

I thought he was going to repeat my question. In that case, I planned to throw the phone out the window so it disappeared into the dark inky abyss. Instead, he said, "File's too big."

"Oh," I said, not sure what that meant. Was I just out of luck? "Is it super long or something?"

"Don't know. I haven't watched it. I'm off tomorrow," he continued, unaware of my crazy girl thoughts. "We can meet up. You can take a look."

He actually wanted to see me? I got excited, then realized he might want to come to my apartment, an apartment I no longer lived at. "We can do Southern Girl Desserts," I said, naming a dessert place off Pico.

"Sure. I could use a sweet potato cupcake."

We agreed to meet at noon and I got off the phone as quickly as I could.

Sienna offered to let me borrow something. I thanked her for pretending I could fit into a size double zero. While she went through my closet, she filled my head with how the file thing was just Omari's excuse to see me and I better not put her in any ugly bridesmaid dress when he and I got married. By the time I finished my makeup, she was naming our children.

Sienna did such a good job with the

110

clothes *and* the pep talk that when I slipped out the door, I felt more confident than I had in months. After all the house drama, I needed something to go right in my life. Stat. It didn't help it had started to rain. Was the drought over? I spent the car ride going over different scenarios so I'd be prepared. I went through everything, from Omari standing in the middle of Pico proclaiming his love for me to him bringing up that night and what had happened. In each one, I didn't panic or throw up. Go me.

I got there early, but Omari still beat me. He stood when he saw me come in. "You look great." He sounded like he meant it. He really did seem happy to see me.

"You too," I said.

He slid out my chair, waited for me to sit, and then did the same. A sweet potato cupcake was already waiting for me. He'd opted for the red velvet for himself. It almost kind of sort of felt like a date. We both spoke at the same time. "So how did you like the movie?" I asked. "I have to go," he said.

I wasn't sure what to make of that, so I didn't say anything and he continued. "They rewrote a scene and so I have to go to work."

Oh. Make that a speed date. "We could've rescheduled."

"Yeah, but you need the video," he said. "I know it's important to you."

I smiled. He cared about what was important to me. "Then let's have at it," I said and he handed it over.

I hit play and Sienna popped up on the three-and-a-half-inch screen. She shakily turned the camera to the backseat and there I was. She "interviewed" Omari, then moved on to Emme. I didn't pay much attention, remembering what wasn't caught on camera. His hand on my leg. I looked at him out the corner of my eye, wondering if he was thinking the same thing, but he had no expression.

Then we got to my joke. I couldn't believe how rude I sounded. No wonder he'd stopped speaking to me. Maybe Sienna was right and I'd bruised his ego. I stole another peek at him, but he refused to look in my direction. I wondered if he was embarrassed. I felt horrible.

After a few minutes, it finally got to the car. I didn't see headlights, but then there were no headlights to see. The driver hadn't bothered with them. The car crossed in front of us. I could hear Emme slam the brakes as Sienna and the cell phone instinctively turned to watch the car make its getaway.

I couldn't make out any details, including the custom tint. The screen was too small. The video would need to be blown up, which luckily fell within Emme's realm of expertise. I abruptly looked up to find Omari watching me. He looked away quickly. Was he staring at me? I hoped so.

"I replayed it a couple of times. The screen's too small to see the exact make, but the car's definitely luxury," he said.

"So you did watch it?"

"Figured it might trigger some memories."

"Did it?"

Then I waited. This had been one of the scenarios I'd practiced in the car. If he brought up what happened with us, then I'd be honest. No jokes. No freak-outs. No big gestures. I would simply tell him I'd crushed on him since high school and I was game if he was. I was tempted to blurt it out first, but I held back and just smiled for him to go on. He looked at me a couple of seconds longer than necessary, then finally spoke. "I was drunk."

I didn't plan for that. At all. I didn't say anything, and maybe he thought I didn't hear him because he spoke again and the knife went deeper. "I'm really sorry."

Yeah. I was too.

NINE

She didn't even hesitate, just raised her gun, aimed, and got off a quick round. The guy fell, blood spurting out of him in fits and starts. She must've not hit any major arteries because within seconds he was back up without a scratch on him, so Emme raised her gun again. "4COL."

"What is a forcal?" Sienna asked.

"Some new fork?" I guessed, missing the good old days when you could just sound out a word to figure it out.

"Something to do with a snorkel?" Sienna guessed.

"For crying out loud," Emme said.

At first I thought she was annoyed with our guesses, but then I realized she was telling us what it stood for. "Thanks," I said.

"NP," she said.

We'd brought Omari's phone to Emme's apartment in Los Feliz that afternoon, in hopes she could enlarge the video. Sienna and I were sprawled on the floor. Emme had no room for a couch. She didn't have a living room. She had a control room.

A huge desk with three large monitors dominated the room. All the monitors were filled with what could best be described as stuff — the Call to Action 5 game she was playing, a website where she grocery shopped, a few IM sessions, and Omari's video. She controlled it all from the comfort of a steroid-injected office chair twice her size. Her ever-present headset — complete with a high-tech microphone that would be the envy of switchboard operators everywhere — caressed her right ear. It was amazing to watch.

"Alcohol's practically a truth serum," Sienna said.

I threw her some serious side eye. It'd been more than a day since I'd left Omari, and I still felt foolish for misunderstanding his intentions. The convo after his apology had been mercifully short. We'd agreed Emme needed to look at the video. What we didn't agree on was what to do after she had. I was too embarrassed to see him again, so I figured I could just keep the cell. He insisted the stupid phone be returned. Why? I don't know. It wasn't like he didn't have a new one or anything.

The only good thing was, it had made me even more focused on identifying the car. Video shot on a postage-stamp–sized screen didn't exactly translate to larger proportions, and Emme was using some computer program to sharpen the images, but it was slow going. I would rather have fixed each pixel myself than keep talking about what had happened. We'd gone over it four times already. "He only did it because he was drunk," I said.

"And harboring a crush on you." Sienna played on her cell as she spoke. You have to love twenty-first century interactions. No one looks at each other anymore. "Omari hit on you for a reason."

"Jack Daniels hit on me, with the help of his friend Coca-Cola."

"I don't care what you say, we're still in Act Three," she said.

"Yeah, just not of my movie. I'm the clueless best friend."

I expected Sienna to respond with some more glass-half-full mumbo jumbo. Instead she said, "I'm a hussy!"

Emme glanced back, decided it was too easy, and returned to her screen. Sienna held her cell like it was an Oscar and said, "I'm nominated for Hussy of the Week."

Whoa.

Every week, Anani Miss nominated two people for Hussy of the Week. It wasn't exactly something to brag about. It was her code for the week's biggest idiot. Readers had the weekend to vote and a winner was crowned on Monday. "Congratulations," I said. I knew that's what she wanted to hear.

"We need to get out the vote," Sienna said. "Maybe I can take out an ad on the site? That's what they do with the Oscars. Take out ads in the *Hollywood Reporter*. Emme, can't you, like, create a program that can vote for me a million times?"

As a response, Emme said, "Video's done. I've already jumped forward to the car."

I smiled at Sienna and then got up to look. Emme had been able to convert the video to a clear, enlarged file. It didn't look as great as HD, but it beat VHS. When the car crossed in front of us on the screen, Emme hit pause.

It looked like it was either black or, maybe, dark blue. Unfortunately, the tinted windows were too dark to see the driver. I couldn't see a license plate but was able to make out a dent in the hood. I shuddered to think that Haley had left her mark. The camera followed as the car cut across Vermont. The back license plate was covered with dirt. Not very helpful. But I did make out a decal on the trunk.

It was a BMW. "Am I blind or does that look like a BMW decal?" I asked, just to be sure.

"It's a BMW," Emme said.

I decided I wanted a second opinion, so I asked Sienna. "That's a BMW, right?"

She glanced up from playing with her phone. She was no doubt already voting for herself for Hussy of the Week. "Definitely a BMW."

I would have done a cartwheel if there was enough room. There wasn't, so I settled for smiling real big. "We figured out the car," I said.

"So what now?" Emme asked.

Good question. Maybe part of me hadn't thought I'd ever figure the car out because I hadn't planned what to do after I did. "Call the tip line?" Sienna asked, messing with her phone.

That sounded like a good idea, except for one thing. "Is a dark blue or black BMW too vague?"

"You can give them a screenshot of the roses," Emme suggested.

"I could, or I could give them more information," I said. "I might be able to find out the owner."

They both looked suitably impressed,

which was what I was going for. I went to my purse and pulled out the piece of paper I'd gotten from Jay at Platinum Motorsports. It was the hottest auto mechanic shop in LA, and I felt more hopeful than ever that the tint had been done there. I dialed, making sure to put it on speaker so Emme and Sienna could listen. My luck continued, because it was Jay who answered.

"Hey, this is Dayna. I came in the other day . . ." I trailed off.

"The one trying to catch your man's jump-off," Jay said.

I smiled. "Glad I was memorable. I found out the car for you. It's a BMW, either black or dark blue. And it has a rose etched in the tint in all the windows."

"Everyone's getting those," Jay said. "Idiots."

He paused and I figured he was typing on his computer because he then said, "We got twenty-four black or dark blue BMWs with rose-etched tint. Like I said, everyone's getting them."

Fudge. No way could I read off a list of twenty-four cars to the tip line.

"The dent in the hood," Emme whispered.

Right! Unless the driver was still cruising around town with Haley's indentation on his car, he had to have gotten it fixed. "How many of those twenty-four came back the week after August 18th with car damage?" I asked.

After a brief silence, he spoke. "Montgomery Rose." He rattled off a few more details about the car and a Miracle Mile addy as Emme, Sienna, and I exchanged excited glances. "Came in on August 22nd to get his grill replaced. Paid $1,322.33. Looks like your boyfriend's jump-off is also cheating on her boyfriend."

"I'm not surprised. She looked like a complete and total slut," I said. "Thank you so much, Jay."

"Don't beat the chick up too bad."

"I can't make any promises."

I hung up and did one of the things I hate most in this world: a fist pump. I, Dayna Olivia Anderson, with the help of my trusted allies, had done something the cops failed to do. Something that Aubrey guy failed to do. That everyone else in the entire world failed to do. I'd located the guy who'd killed Haley Joseph. And his name was Montgomery Rose.

We wasted no time looking him up. His website was the first hit on Google. Mr. Rose ran his own talent management firm.

I'd had a manager once. I supposed I technically still had a manager, just one I hadn't spoken to in over six months. All managers were afraid one day you'd become the next Julia Roberts and wanted to leave the door open in case they needed to leach off you in the future. That meant instead of outwardly rejecting you now, they just stopped returning phone calls.

There was no doubt in my mind that if I hadn't quit acting and got myself booked as the lead in the next Will Smith movie, my manager would have been calling me before the article about the casting news was fully uploaded to *Deadline*'s website. I was so glad to be done with the BS.

I clicked on Montgomery Rose's bio and stared at the accompanying half-body shot. He was standard-issue okay-looking white guy. His teeth were whiter than a Klan rally. His brown hair was close-cropped, but I could tell it probably curled if he ever let it grow longer. He was wearing a suit tailored to cover any body imperfections, though I doubted he had any. He spent too much time on presentation not to go to the gym on a regular basis.

The bio itself was three paragraphs. A tip-off he was nowhere near the top of his field. The longer the bio, the less relevant the person. It was as if the person had to convince you of his importance. The actual important people took for granted that you already knew everything about them and kept their bios to a minimum with statements like "Oprah is human."

Emme read and I translated. "Montgomery Rose is the Founder, CEO, and Chairman of the Rose Agency," she said.

"Three titles," I said. "He has no other employees and works out of his house."

"Rose has an office in the heart of Beverly Hills."

"He rents a P.O. box on Wilshire," I offered.

"At just thirty-five, he has spent half his life learning every aspect of the business."

"It took him a long time to finally get that position in the mail-room at the Creative Artists Agency."

"He has worked with some of the biggest names in the business," Emme continued.

"He once waited on Steven Spielberg."

It went on from there. After we finished, Emme gave me a copy of Omari's video and Sienna and I headed home. I drove so Sienna could continue to vote for herself as Hussy of the Week. When we got back to our place, I went into my room and looked at the piece of paper where I'd written down Montgomery Rose's address and vital information. Haley's killer, summed up in a couple of lines.

All I needed to do was to share this information with the police. I couldn't remember the tip line number, so I dialed 311 and kept hitting buttons until I reached the LAPD. The voice was female, but I couldn't decipher anything else regarding its owner. "Hi!" I said, with a bit more energy than I'd intended. "I'd like to report a tip!"

There was a pause. If it weren't for the incessant chomping of her gum, I would have thought the call had dropped. I thought maybe she was blowing a bubble, but I didn't hear the telltale pop. The voice finally spoke. "Congrats."

Not exactly what I'd expected from LA's finest. "The billboard said I should call if I have information, so here I am."

"Oh, you're trying to get a reward," she said. Snap.

She didn't have to be so judgmental about it. "I guess."

"You need to call the tip line," she said. Crackle.

"Can't I tell you and you pass it on?"

"Not if you want your money." Pop. "And I know you want your money."

I did indeed want my money.

"If you went to our website, you would

have seen that in order to be eligible for a reward, you have to use the tip line," she said.

"Budget cuts that bad?"

She didn't laugh. "I don't make the rules, ma'am. Call the tip line if you want to be compensated."

I was impressed how she could make a good deed sound so rude. "What's the tip line's nu—"

But I was talking to a dial tone.

I googled the LAPD Tip Line and clicked the link to make sure I didn't miss any other fine print like having to sacrifice my first child if my tip turned out to be wrong. I read: *"Crime prevention cannot be achieved by the police alone. Together professional law enforcement officers must work hand-in-hand with the public to fight crime and neighborhood disorder throughout our communities. As such, we depend heavily on your assistance in reporting crimes to the police."*

After that reassuring introduction, it explained the process. All tips were submitted anonymously, and prospective tipsters should not fear being pressured to provide their names or contact information. Each tipster was given a code number. If the information resulted in the arrest and subsequent filing of criminal charges, the tipster would receive his or her reward in cash, using his or her assigned code number to make arrangements to receive it.

Sounded good to me. Information in hand, I called again. "Tip line." The voice sounded familiar.

"Hi, I want to report a tip."

A smacking of gum, followed by a pause and then, "Congrats."

"Did I just talk to you?"

"Ma'am, this is a busy office. Do you expect me to remember everyone's voice?"

All righty. I decided to ignore that. "I have information on —"

"I need to ensure that you are aware of your rights before you provide any information."

"Um, okay," I said.

" 'Crime prevention cannot be achieved by the police alone. Together professional law enforcement officers . . .' "

I realized she was reciting the information I'd just read on the website. What's more, she didn't even bother to pretend like she wasn't reading. I interrupted. "Ma'am, I'm aware of my rights."

More gum smacking. "I need to ensure that you are aware of your rights before you provide any information."

"I read them on the website."

126

"I need to ensure that you are aware of your rights before you provide any information."

Realizing this was a lost battle, I surrendered. It was almost five, quitting time. Maybe she was just ready to go home. I reminded myself the woman was my key to keeping my parents off the street. I needed to play nice. "Ensure away."

"Where was I?"

Having read the website, I could have told her, but I kept my mouth shut. I heard her clicking her mouse, trying to find where she had stopped. Smack. Click. Smack. Click. Smack. Click. She finally spoke. " 'Crime prevention cannot be achieved by the police alone. Together professional law enforcement officers . . .' "

Geez. I admired Sienna's shoe collection as I half-listened to her recite the website copy. I didn't fully tune back in until I heard her say, "Now what is your tip regarding?"

"The hit-and-run murder of Haley Joseph."

I waited, prepared for her to type something or ask another question or smack her gum some more or something. I got nothing. She finally spoke. "I don't have all day, ma'am." She made "ma'am" sound like a very specific word for a female dog.

"I have reason to believe the driver of the car was one Montgomery Rose. He drives a year-old black BMW. It was fixed at Platinum Motorsports four days after Haley was killed."

I spelled out his name and gave her his contact information. She didn't ask any more questions, nor did she thank me for the information. She didn't say anything at all, in fact. "If you need to reach me, my name is —"

"Ma'am, this is an anonymous tip line. *Anonymous.*"

Right. "Don't I get a secret identification number? I'm hoping it's 007."

I waited for her to at least laugh. She did not. Maybe she'd heard that one before. Because I'm a glutton for punishment, I continued on. "That one's already taken, right?"

Again, no laughter. Instead, she said, "1018."

"Not as sexy as 007, but I'll take it," I said, then laughed for her.

"If this information leads to an arrest and conviction, please call this number back and provide your code number," the voice said.

"Just call and say '1018'?"

But she'd hung up on me. Again.

TEN

After phoning the tip line, I did two things. First, I called Daddy and told him my plan had worked. Hearing the relief in his voice hit home how scared he really was. The second thing I did was celebrate. Sienna and I hit PF Chang's in the Beverly Center. I sprung for an appetizer and quite a few drinks. My body woke up at 8:00 a.m. the next day. My brain didn't wake up until noon.

Once operating at full capacity, I checked my email. I'd created a Google alert for Haley and fully expected my inbox to be overflowing with articles about a suspect being apprehended. There were none. Either Google was broken or there hadn't been an arrest. I was disappointed, then reminded myself these things took time. Montgomery Rose would be in police custody by the end of the business day.

I didn't think Betty should have to wait

that long to find out. I jumped in the car and drove across town to Clothes Encounters. She was alone when I got there. She also seemed a bit wary about seeing me, but I knew how to change that. "Did you hear the news about Haley?"

Her expression said she hadn't. I was about to share when the door banged open. It was the Asian woman I'd met the first time I came here. She carried her USC book bag. "Sorry," she said. "Class ran a bit late."

"No problem," Betty said. "Marina, this is Dayna. Dayna, this is Haley's roommate. Dayna was telling me there was some news about Haley."

I sure was, so I launched right in. "I found Haley's killer!"

Their reactions were just as I'd hoped. Marina squealed and immediately pulled me in for a hug. Betty soon joined us. "Wow," Betty said when they finally both let go.

She kept repeating that single word, giving it different meanings each time. Excitement. Disbelief. Shock. I gave a quick version of how we'd ID'd the car and wrapped it up by saying, "He'll be in jail by tonight."

Betty hugged me again, patting my back as she gently rocked me from side to side just like my mom used to do. "You don't know Haley from a can of paint, so for you to go above and beyond . . . It's amazing," she said. "Thank you."

It felt so good to hear her say that. I just smiled and decided not to remind her about the reward money.

"We probably should tell Victory," Marina said. She sounded like even she knew this wasn't one of her best ideas.

"He still badgering you about Haley's stuff?" Betty asked.

Marina nodded. I was surprised. "You still have her things?" I asked. "What about her parents?"

"They've been meaning to come get it," Marina said.

"Meaning to for the last six weeks," Betty added.

"You don't sound like their biggest fans," I said. Now that I'd found the killer, my "no personal info" ban on Haley was lifted. I was more than ready to be nosy.

"They weren't the most supportive. They wanted her to be a bank teller. In Kentucky." Marina made Kentucky sound like outer Pluto. "They're super conservative and felt she was living in sin. My one convo with them after she died, her mom told me she was praying Haley wasn't in Hell."

Wow. And I thought my mom was bad.

When I got home, Sienna was on the couch playing with her phone and there were a load of shopping bags littering the front hall. Her therapy of choice was the retail variety, and it cost her at least $150 per hour. "Audition go well?" I asked hesitantly.

The bags made me think that maybe it hadn't. Luckily, I was wrong. She lifted her eyes from her phone long enough to squeal excitedly, "They gave me a note!"

"Nice," I said, relieved the bags were the result of happy shopping.

A note is when a casting director asks you to redo a scene a bit differently. They're a good thing. It means they like you and want to see if you can take direction. You have no chance in Hades of getting a callback if, when you finish a scene, you just get a "Thank you."

Sienna motioned to the bags. "I already bought an outfit to wear to the callback. I got you a little something-something as congratulations for the whole Haley thing."

"You didn't have to." But I was sure glad she did.

Finding my gift wasn't hard. It was the only thing in the bags that wasn't red. Sienna had bought herself five dresses, four pairs of pants, three shirts, two jackets, and quite possibly a partridge in a pear tree. All in varying shades of red. "Thanks for the blouse," I said.

She smiled but barely looked up from her phone. She had to be voting for herself on the Anani Miss site.

"Sienna, what's up with the red?"

She shrugged like it was no big deal. "The stuff I liked happened to be red."

Or it just happened she was hoping the more red she wore, the better chance someone would recognize her from Anani's site. I just nodded and vowed that if she came home with a package of Red Vines tatted barbwire-style around her arm, I'd stage an intervention.

We spent the rest of the evening cooking (her), eating (me), and voting on Anani Miss (both) while watching reality TV. I checked my email again before bed, but there was no news. Sunday was more of the same. Lots of voting and email checking and wondering about the lack of an arrest. I was pretty sure detectives didn't take weekends off. On *Law & Order,* they never even went to sleep.

When I woke up Monday morning, I was not a happy camper. I checked my email while hiding under the covers. Not a word.

What the fudge? I needed there to be an arrest. Not just for me, but for Betty and for my father. I didn't want to disappoint either of them. Not again. I stomped down the hall, hoping to be greeted by French toast. That was the only thing that would make me feel better. I found Sienna at the kitchen table, looking as sad as I'd ever seen her. "I lost."

She showed me her phone. Hussy of the Week was already posted, and it had gone to something called Dopey Cat. I was appalled. "There is no way a dopey cat is more of a hussy than you. Today already sucks! There's still no arrest."

Sienna immediately went from sad to angry. She snatched a carton of eggs out the fridge and slammed it on the nearest counter. "After you handed them that guy's name *and* address? You need to find out what's going on!"

She was right. "I'm gonna call the tip line and demand answers!" I said.

"Use my phone."

The tip line rang three times before someone picked up. I immediately heard gum smacking and knew it was *her.* The Voice. "Tip line."

"Yes, ma'am. I'm calling to follow up on a tip I submitted a few days ago."

"Code number, ma'am?"

"1018, ma'am."

The clacking of keys joined the symphony of smacking gum. "We received your tip, ma'am."

"I know you received it because I spoke with you, ma'am. I wanted to know the status."

Sienna gave me a nod of approval as she cracked eggs into a bowl. The Voice spoke. "The status, ma'am, was that it was received."

"Yes, ma'am." I made sure my ma'ams sounded as despicable as hers. "Three days ago. There has been no new information in the news. Ma'am."

"We don't work for the news, ma'am. We don't publicize everything we do."

"So you're saying an arrest is coming?"

"I'm saying we don't publicize everything we do, ma'am." Her last "ma'am" sounded like a metaphor for "Duh."

"How will I know if I'm eligible for the reward?" I asked. She didn't say anything. I took more pride than I care to admit in stumping her. "Considering it was my tip, ma'am, I have a right to receive an update."

"You do not, ma'am. This is an open investigation."

"Ma'am," I said. Translation: *Don't let me*

see you in the street.

"Ma'am," she countered. Translation: *Bring it on.*

"Ma'am," I said and slammed the phone down just to be sure I got the last word in. Then I remembered it was a cell phone. I would have had to hit the red icon to end the call. Not as effective, but too late for that now. I could hear her saying "Ma'am" as I hung up. Darn it.

"So?" Sienna acted as if she hadn't eavesdropped on the entire thing while starting breakfast.

"They won't tell me Sugar Honey Iced Tea," I said. "I gave them the name of the killer."

"And address!"

"And proof the car was fixed right after Haley died. And the stupid police are just sitting on that information."

"Doing absolutely nothing."

"Except not telling me anything. It's probably sitting there in some file while this Montgomery Rose is driving around."

"In his murder mobile," Sienna said.

We'd worked ourselves into a frenzy. She was beating eggs like she was in the third round of a UFC fight. Even the prospect of an impending meal did nada to make me feel better. "I'm going over there!" I said.

"Talk to this Montgomery Rose myself!"

Sienna slammed the mixture down. "Let's go!"

Montgomery Rose lived a few streets east of the Grove, this fancy-shmancy outdoor shopping mall off Third and Fairfax. The road was technically two lanes, but the planners of yesteryear hadn't anticipated a world of SUVs and minivans. With cars parked on both sides, the street was essentially one way. If another car was coming in the opposite direction, you had to play chicken and hope for the best. I idled my pink Infiniti in what was the general vicinity of Montgomery Rose's house. It didn't have the address listed, but then it didn't need it.

The lots were intended for small one-story houses, and that described every house on the block except for Montgomery Rose's. He'd shoved a sprawling two-story fiasco into his tiny lot. It was the equivalent of a size sixteen trying to fit into a size eight. I didn't know what had happened to the original house, but I guessed the new house probably ate it.

There was a spot open in front of the neighbor's house — that poor, poor man or woman — on his right. After two attempts, I parallel parked. We got out and I had to

137

wait for Sienna to catch up. She had on a newly purchased pair of red patent-leather pants. They looked great but were so tight she could barely move. These pants weren't made for walking, and neither were the boots. They were five-inch stilettos.

When we finally made it, I rang the bell and waited for someone to answer. No one did. "I lost to a dopey cat," Sienna said.

"At least you know you lost," I said. "I don't know anything."

Sienna took her anger out on the doorbell. There was no movement inside. "He's not home," she said. "We should wait for him! Maybe we'll see him get arrested."

Sounded like a good idea. What would make it a great idea would be some food. I'd skipped breakfast, after all. "Can we get snacks first? We passed a 7-Eleven."

She nodded. "I have to pee anyway."

We drove to 7-Eleven, where we loaded up on snacks and unloaded our bladders, then made our way back to Montgomery Rose's street. Our spot was still there. I parked and we settled into a comfortable rhythm. I opened my bag of chips. Sienna took out her Red Vine licorice. We asked the other if they wanted some. She said no. I said yes. I ate more of her candy then she did and then took a small sip of my Big

Gulp, making a promise to the bladder gods I would take my time.

"Candy. Oversized drinks. You next to me. It's like we're at the movies," Sienna said.

"I know! So exciting."

After forty-five minutes, I wanted to amend my earlier statement. It wasn't like the movies at all. It was like the commercials they play on a loop *before* the previews *before* the movie. Boring and repetitive. We tried listening to the radio, but after the same Kandy Wrapper song came on four times in one fifteen-minute span, we shut it off. Sienna caught me up on the latest gossip, but there wasn't much new to report.

Mostly, we just sat there willing something to happen. I didn't care if I just pointed at him and said "You, killer. Bad." I needed something. I was this close to literally twirling my thumbs when Sienna asked, "You want to run lines with me? I have another audition in a couple days."

She handed me the script pages. It was a crime drama. Sienna was up for the sassy minority female cop. She'd highlighted her lines in pink marker. I read the part of her gruff male partner. We were supposed to be interviewing a suspect. "Anything you want to tell us, creep?" I read.

Per the script, the creep had nothing to

tell us, so Sienna jumped in with her line. "Don't be shy now. Sharing is caring."

The next line belonged to said creep. Since there were just the two of us, I read the line in my best version of a deep male voice. "I swear, I was —"

"Save it," Sienna snapped. "Don't act like this is your first time at the rodeo. You know we gotta read you your Miranda rights."

The script called for Sienna's sassy minority to literally snap her fingers. I was getting Chubby's flashbacks. It only got worse from there. After we finished the scene, we did it again and again while Sienna tried to go "off book," AKA do it from memory. We were on our fifth go-round when her phone rang. Emme popped up on FaceTime. "You're in a car," she said by way of greeting.

"We're outside Montgomery Rose's house," I said.

Emme stopped her constant movement to look at me. "You're sitting outside the house. Of a murderer. WTF?"

When she put it that way, I immediately got defensive. "It's just a hit-and-run. It's not like he's a serial killer targeting broke black chicks trying any crazy way to get money."

"And what if he sees you?" Geez, she was

acting like we were the ones who'd killed someone.

I was about to say that when my back door suddenly opened. Sienna and I screamed, causing Emme to scream even though she was miles away. I looked back at our future rapist/killer and saw Aubrey slide into the backseat. He was the last person I wanted to see, here or anywhere else for that matter.

"You really should keep your doors locked at all times, Ms. Anderson," he said.

"What's going on?" Emme asked.

"Still alive. Gotta go, Em."

I hung up just as Aubrey was introducing himself to Sienna. "Hello, I am Aubrey S. Adams-Parker. That color is stunning on you."

Nothing like a compliment from a man to brighten Sienna's mood. "Sienna Michelle Hayes." She smiled at him and then noticed me glaring at her. I'd told her all about Aubrey. Traitor.

"What are you doing here?" I asked.

"The neighbor reported a suspicious car in the area. It was, and I quote, 'extremely old and the color of spoiled Pepto-Bismol.' "

Hmmph. "That doesn't even make any sense," I said. "Pepto-Bismol can't spoil."

He ignored that valid point. "I recognized the car description when I heard it over the scanner."

Scanner? Once again I found myself wondering, who *was* this guy? He clearly didn't have a day job. He apparently listened to police scanners for fun. And, once again, he had on that horrible orange reflector jumpsuit. If he was a vigilante, someone really needed to tell him that Bruce Wayne was doing it way better. He needed some tips.

Unaware of my internal diatribe, Aubrey kept talking. "Lucky for you both, the LAPD will not be able to send a patrol car for at least another two hours. So what is going on?"

Part of me didn't want to tell him, but a bigger part wanted to brag. "We found the car that killed Haley. This is his house."

"We're doing a stakeout!" Sienna piped in. She was staring at him, entranced.

"I see you are not going to take my suggestion to stay out of this, so let me give you some advice," Aubrey said. "Rule Number One of stakeouts: do not park directly in front of the house."

"Good thing we're next door," I said. That got me nothing. "What's Rule Number Two? Bring lots of donuts?"

"Drive an inconspicuous car. Sit in the backseat."

"That's actually two rules."

"Perhaps, but both equally important," he said.

"Great. We're gonna get out of here."

"Where are you going?" he asked.

I had to pee, but he didn't need to know that.

"She probably has to go to the bathroom," Sienna said.

Really, Sienna? Really?

"You did not bring a bottle to use?" There was an incredulous tone to Aubrey's voice.

I was going to ask if that was Rule Number Four when Sienna suddenly punched me in the arm. "Look!"

A black BMW with a rose insignia was pulling into Montgomery Rose's sliver of a driveway. He was home.

"Let's go," Sienna said, already halfway out the car. She took rapid-paced mini-steps up the driveway. She was quicker than I expected.

I had no choice but to follow her. Aubrey tried to come with us, but the child lock was on. Oops.

"Hey, you!" Sienna screamed. She literally banged on his driver-side window.

"Sienna," I said. Suddenly this didn't

seem like a very good idea.

The door opened and Montgomery Rose jumped out. He was not pleased. "What are you doing?" he asked as both Sienna and I took a step back. "I'll call the police!"

Technically, they were already on their way, but that didn't seem like helpful information to share at the moment. I wasn't sure what to say, so I opened my mouth, fully expecting something genius to come out that would completely save this situation. Instead, I blurted out, "We *are* the police!"

I could tell he didn't believe us. Can't say I blamed him. There was a moment of awkwardness, and then I said the first thing that came to mind. "Anything you want to tell us, creep?"

After a brief pause, Sienna jumped in. "Don't be shy now. Sharing is caring."

"What are you talking about?" Montgomery asked. That wasn't in the script, but I could forgive him for not knowing his line. He was coming in cold.

"They are not cops, Mr. Rose," Aubrey said, having somehow made it out of my car. "I'm Aubrey S. Adams-Parker. I am a former cop turned private investigator. This is your black BMW, correct?"

Montgomery looked suspicious but answered anyway. "Yeah."

"Where were you on the night of August 18th?" Aubrey asked.

Montgomery visibly relaxed. "This is about the robbery."

Huh? All three of us must've looked lost, because he continued on. "The Rack Pack stole my car and used it to rob Kandy Wrapper."

ELEVEN

"Oh my God! He knows Oscar Blue!" Sienna said.

Sienna, Aubrey, and I were on Montgomery's couch. She was referring to Montgomery's personal Wall of Fame, pictures of him with celebrities — next to them, sometimes even touching them. Not behind them like on Sienna's Wall of Fame.

The anger I'd felt when Montgomery wasn't arrested was now replaced with confusion. I'd thought I'd solved the thing. Now I was at Square Negative One. Again. I hadn't the slightest clue after all about who had killed Haley. I not only felt bad for myself, but for Marina and Betty. I'd gotten their hopes up for nothing.

Most of all, I felt bad for Haley. She'd been in the wrong place at the wrong time. She happened to step into the crosswalk a few short moments before some a-hole careened down the street, desperate to get away from robbing someone's house. It could have happened to any of us.

I was getting angry all over again when Montgomery came in with a tray of bottled water. He still had his suit jacket on. The only thing that kept him from looking like a butler was the lack of white gloves.

His place was as put-together as he was. I doubted he'd picked out a single item, but he'd done a good job picking out the decorator. He or she had made the home look masculine yet not overbearing. Montgomery sat down across from us and waited expectantly. I couldn't wait to tell him about Haley, but Aubrey got the jump on me. "When was your car stolen, Mr. Rose?"

"Same day as the robbery," Montgomery said. "Completely my fault for deciding not to valet. I was at the Americana. I met a friend at the Cheesecake Factory for lunch."

"What time was this?"

"Guess we finished up about two-thirty, but I didn't report it until four. Thought I just forgot where I parked. I walked every floor of that place twice before I realized it was gone. So who are you guys working for? Kandy?"

Aubrey sidestepped his question and countered with one of his own. "When did the police find your car?"

147

"Couple of days later in South Central somewhere. Or was it Compton? I get them confused."

"And the automobile was in good shape?" Aubrey asked.

"Except for the grill and hood. They really messed it up. They must have hit something."

I spoke up. "Yeah, like a hum—"

Aubrey let me get in three and a half words before he talked over me. "I didn't notice any dents on your car," he said.

"It was fixed right away!" I said, then realized I wasn't supposed to know that. They all looked at me. "I'm assuming. You don't seem to be the type to be riding around with a messed-up grill for very long."

Montgomery bought my awkward save. "I'm not. Couple of days after I got it fixed, the police were at my door, saying my car was used in the robbery at Kandy Wrapper's. Thank God I had the police report on the theft, 'cause for a second there I thought they were gonna try to pin it on me."

He looked at all three of us before stopping at Sienna. She smiled. He smiled. I grimaced. "Where do I know you from?" he asked her.

Sienna smiled some more. "I'm an actress, but you probably know me from Anani

Miss. I just came in second for Hussy of the Week."

He nodded, even though he didn't look like your typical Anani Miss reader. "That's it," he said. "Your name is . . ."

"Sienna Hayes, Ms. Lady of the Red Vine. I'm quite popular on the site."

"That's great. Building a buzz is all you need nowadays. We should get together. Discuss taking your brand to the next level."

Was he really hitting on her? We were talking about a murder here. Granted he obviously didn't realize we were talking about a murder, but still. "Your car killed a girl!" I blurted out.

Sienna looked shocked. Aubrey looked annoyed. Montgomery looked horrified.

"Your car hit a girl named Haley Joseph while she was in a crosswalk and the driver kept going," I said. "They must've been coming from the robbery."

"No," he said. "The police would've told me."

"They didn't figure it out. We did."

"This girl's dead?" Montgomery asked.

"You can imagine why it is so important to remember the condition of the car when you got it back, Mr. Rose," Aubrey said, like he'd been part of *my* investigation.

"They didn't leave anything. Didn't take

anything, either, not even my radio . . ." Montgomery trailed off for a moment, then finally spoke again. "I don't believe it."

"The police have no leads?" Aubrey asked.

"Not one. There were no prints. They don't even think the thieves lived in South Central. Just left my car there."

We were interrupted by the doorbell. Through the stained glass, I could make out a man in a uniform. The police had finally made it. Fudge.

"And the thieves ran out the house, jumped in the stolen BMW, and took off down the hill, taking $20,000 in cash with them!" Sienna finished with a flare.

It was later that day and we were back home. As soon as the police had arrived, we'd gotten out of Montgomery's place quickly, though Aubrey and Sienna made sure to get Montgomery's card. Sienna and I immediately drove home, where Sienna shared everything she knew about the Rack Pack with me and Emme, who was on Web chat.

The robbers — police estimated there were several of them — had struck three times in the past six months, averaging one robbery every six to eight weeks. The crew was dubbed the Rack Pack because of what they took: they bypassed heavy items like flat-screen TVs in favor of designer clothes and jewelry.

Their first target was Joseline, star of the reality show *Keeping up with the Jones-Miller-Smiths.* At one point, a fourth name had been added to the title, but it was quickly removed when the marriage barely lasted two months. The thieves had entered Joseline's house through an unlocked door and took off with a low six figures' worth of merchandise. Sienna claimed it took Joseline two weeks to realize anything was missing. It took her suitably less time to milk the robbery for all the press it was worth.

Perhaps press-shy, the thieves went for the anti-Joseline when they targeted eco-friendly actor Oscar Blue, who loved skinny, barely legal supermodels as much as he hated taking showers. The story had been big news, though Oscar had been mum on the matter. The third robbery was the night Haley died, at the brand-spanking-new Silver Lake home of Kandy Wrapper and her professional basketball-playing boyfriend, Ron "Stump" Matthews.

There seemed to be no footage of the thieves and no witnesses. The only cameras Joseline didn't seem to like were those of the security variety. She had none in her home, seeming to think a gate would be enough to keep the bad people away. Kandy had just moved in and hadn't found the time to get the cameras installed yet.

Oscar may have had security cameras but didn't seem to be cooperating with the police on the matter. His lone quote on the subject was to a paparazzo who'd caught him during one of his weekly recycling sojourns. He mumbled something about it only being stuff and claimed he was more concerned with prosecuting the people killing Mother Nature. He did so while covering his face with the sleeve of his $3,500 designer leather jacket.

In all, the thieves had made off with close to $500,000 in clothing, jewelry, and portable gadgets. They had to be selling it. Their best bet was the twenty-first-century equivalents of the car trunk — eBay or Craigslist. I said as much to Sienna and Emme.

"Can't you create something like a Google alert on steroids to see if any of the stolen objects showed up online?" I asked Emme.

"I could," she said. Could, not would.

"But . . ."

"Say I find something. You two plan to camp outside the robbers' houses?"

"You really think you could find where they all live? How?" She gave me a look, so

152

I quickly continued on. "Not that it matters. I'm done with stakeouts. From now on, I'm giving the info to the police." I actually was 99.9999 percent sure I was telling the truth.

Emme glared at me. The only thing that stopped me from offering to pinky swear was that I couldn't reach through the laptop screen. "I'll need to know what was stolen from Joseline," she finally said.

"The entire Louboutins Spring collection." Sienna sounded put out. "I covered this."

"Just searching Louboutins would be too many hits. I need details. Style. Color. Size. Same thing with what was stolen from Oscar Blue and Kandy Wrapper."

Sienna already had her phone out. "I don't know, but I can find out." She dialed and waited patiently a few seconds for it to ring, then spoke. "Fab! Hey, babe!"

Fab was Sienna's black gay male counterpart, from their love of gossip down to their source of income. Whereas Sienna was supported by a settlement from a much-older ex-husband, Fab's lifestyle was funded by his boyfriend, a Hollywood A-lister who was a much better actor than people gave him credit for since no one knew he was gay.

If there was anyone who could provide a

laundry list of stolen goods — complete with retail value, where they purchased it, and how many times they wore it and where — it was Fab.

Sienna gave him some BS excuse about why she needed the information. He must've bought it because she started furiously typing on her iPad, making the occasional exclamation at certain items. "Not the earrings her mom called tacky on episode four!"

They repeated the process — complete with shocked exclamations — for Oscar Blue and Kandy Wrapper. Afterward, Sienna got off the phone, emailed the list to Emme, and then got up. "Going somewhere?" I asked.

"Gonna meet Fab for a drink," she said. "How do I look?"

To put it nicely, she looked like a hooker, but at least a high-class one. She'd changed as soon as we'd gotten back and was now wearing the dress she wore last Halloween when she was a naughty devil. I had thought all devils were naughty, but Sienna informed me that I was wrong. The dress was made of a red pleather so shiny I'd used it more than once to check my makeup. The top was too low and the bottom too high, but that's what Sienna intended. She'd paired it with red feather earrings, though she'd bypassed the devil horns and pitch fork. I can't say I missed them much. "You look great," I said.

"You want my shoes?"

Sienna randomly offering me her entire shoe collection was the most exciting thing to happen in the twelve hours since Emme had created her program thing-a-ma-jig. Emme explained it to me after Sienna left, but I'd zoned out right after the word "autoresponder" and just smiled, nodded, and occasionally repeated the last word she said, Polly-want-a-cracker style. The basic gist was that Emme had plugged in the specifics of the stolen goods, and the program would alert her when select phrases came up online — together or in different combinations.

We hadn't had any hits yet, but as Emme pointed out, the Internet was a big place. It could take days. I didn't have that kind of time. I was getting antsy. I'd formulated a plan of action but now had gotten a bit sidetracked by Sienna's sudden offer.

"You're giving me *all* of your shoes?" I asked.

There had to be a catch. Sienna wasn't one to just give someone her shoe inventory, not even if it was last year's collection.

Not to say I wasn't excited. There was one pair of Louboutins I'd been stalking so long I was surprised they hadn't filed a restraining order with the Fashion Police. They were known as the Pink Panthers, a hot pink stiletto with panther spots that was the shoe of the moment. Everybody who was anybody had a pair.

No way would Sienna just give them up. This had to be related to the whole Anani Miss thing. To test out my theory, I grabbed a pair of red spiked heels. "Ooh, I've been eyeing these for a while."

"Not part of the deal."

Bingo. "What are you doing?" I asked. I knew. I just wanted her to say it.

It wasn't meant to be. As forthcoming as she was about other people's lives, Sienna was tight-lipped about her own. This was no exception. She finished removing all but her red shoes from the shelves and just smiled at me as she walked out the door. "Building a buzz."

And with that, she was gone, leaving me to wonder exactly what had happened last night with Fab. I knew exactly how to find out. My tablet was next to Omari's old phone. The only thing stopping me from returning his cell was that I had yet to develop a superpower that let objects go wherever I wanted by just snapping my fingers.

I logged on to Anani. Sure enough, there was another posting about Sienna, with pictures *and* video from the night before. She was walking out of a club with Fab trailing close behind. "And you are?" an unseen paparazzo asked in the video.

Sienna smiled, overjoyed to once again be in the spotlight. "Sienna Hayes, Ms. Lady of the Red Vine. First runner-up for Anani Miss Hussy of the Week."

She'd upgraded from second place to first runner-up. I'm not going to lie. It did sound way more classy. The paparazzo agreed. "Congratulations!! I'm enjoying the all-red."

"Thanks," she said. "Someone once told me it was my color."

"I'm sure every color is your color."

"Yes, but red's my favorite. I wear it and nothing but it every day. I'm aiming for a world record. Most days in a row just wearing red."

The paparazzi ate it up. One yelled out, "Even your underwear?"

"Who said I was wearing underwear?"

She smiled and the video ended. I looked at the practically empty shelves and the shoes on the floor. There had to be at least $25,000 worth of stilettos. If I had any sense, I'd have put them on eBay. But something told me Sienna would want them back sometime soon.

Until she did, they were mine. The question was where to put them. I glanced around. The mini shelves were still there, looking sad and lonely without Sienna's vast shoe collection. It was a perfect place for *my* shoe collection.

It took me about a half hour to return the shoes to where they'd been not more than an hour before. I stepped back to enjoy my handiwork, the early morning sun hitting it in such a way that it almost looked like a store display. To the untrained eye, it looked like nothing had changed. But the untrained eye belonged to someone with no sense of style. Sienna's shoes had been arranged by collection and then designer. *My* shoes were arranged by designer and then collection.

Satisfied with my work, I found Sienna in the kitchen. "World record? Where did that come from?" I asked. She just smiled. "What about your clothes?"

"Already donated."

"We'll now have the world's best-dressed crackheads," I said. They were the only non-actress types who could fit into size double zero. "Can I use your printer? I want to print out a few screen grabs of the BMW."

It was time to get back to work.

"Don't want any!" The woman shut her door before I even had a chance to explain I wasn't offering *any*.

This was the third time in my life I'd had a door slam in my face. I wouldn't have taken it so personal if the first two times hadn't happened in the last thirty minutes. So this was how people in this neighborhood treated folks coming to their door asking for a few minutes of their time to show them a photograph. I suddenly felt bad for Jehovah's Witnesses.

Even the people who lived on Kandy Wrapper's street hadn't been so rude. That had been my first stop on my canvassing tour. They had at least opted for not even opening the door.

Despite my promise to Emme, I just couldn't sit around and wait. Besides the ticking time bomb with my parents, Betty had left me a few messages asking why there hadn't been an arrest. I'd put off calling her back. I wanted what I had told her — that I'd found Haley's killer — to still be true. And it would be. The details would just be different.

Since Emme's program thing-a-ma-jig was not a definite, I devised a backup plan:

print out photos of Montgomery's car and head to Silver Lake to see if anyone recognized it. Maybe they remembered something about the driver. The plan seemed easy. Then I tried to enact it. Apparently everyone was in a collective bad mood. I couldn't even blame the weather.

It was in the seventies, sunny with just the slightest tickle of a breeze. Just like yesterday. Just like tomorrow. Just like three years from now, if the Big One hadn't taken all of Southern California straight to the bottom of the Pacific by then.

I decided to call it a day. My phone buzzed as I was walking back to my car. It was a text from Omari. Just freaking great. I read it. *How are you? Any word about the hit-and-run?*

I went for the short but sweet approach and wrote: *Good. No arrests yet. I'll get your phone back to you soon.*

Any guy who's ever been rejected by a girl knows "soon" is code for never. Omari obviously hadn't been rejected much. His response was almost instantaneous. *We should meet up on Thursday.*

Like that was going to happen. *I can just drop it off with your doorman,* I wrote.

No doorman. Let's meet on Thursday.

I can also leave it with a neighbor, I responded.

Only cool with one person. He works. So Thursday?

No prob. I can just ring all the buzzers until someone is dumb enough to let me in and then leave the phone outside your door.

I live in downtown. Everyone is too paranoid to do that. So Thursday?

All his neighbors were paranoid? I wasn't sure I believed that because he just said that he only spoke to one of them. How did he know they were all paranoid? Maybe he was paranoid that they were paranoid. I quickly wrote back. *Leave your window open & I'll throw the phone thru it.*

You and your jokes, he wrote. *So Thursday?*

I'm not joking. I pitched in high school.

I remember, he wrote. *So Thursday?*

He was a persistent one. It wasn't like he needed the phone. I finally wrote back. *How about we meet on Thursday?*

"I hate you," I said to the phone.

"Man problems?"

I looked up to see Marina, who was right up there with Omari when it came to people I didn't want to see. Earlier, I'd even walked four blocks out of the way to avoid Clothes Encounters and its staff. In my texting haze,

I'd forgotten to do the same on the way back to my car. She was standing outside the store and must've been heading to class because she had her USC book bag with her.

"Are there any other kind?" I asked. "I have something of his. He's insisting we meet up Friday, but I don't want to see him."

"If you can't control your peanut butter, you can't expect to control your life." She saw my look of confusion because she continued on. "*Calvin and Hobbes.* It was Haley's favorite quote. She would always tell me to control my peanut butter when she wanted to remind me I was in control of a situation."

I thought about it and decided I liked it. When I met with Omari, I just needed to control my peanut butter. "Haley was kinda brilliant," I said.

She smiled, showing off that mouth full of braces. "She really was. I've been checking the papers but haven't heard anything about the arrest."

I wondered if Haley had any advice for when you misinformed someone that you'd solved her best friend's death. I decided to be honest and control my peanut butter right then and there. "There was an issue.

We had the right car, but the wrong person. The car had been stolen."

Her face dropped. "So Haley's killer is still out there."

"Yes, but I'm working on it."

That didn't seem to reassure her. Thank God my phone rang. "I should probably take this. I'll let you know if something changes."

I answered my phone as I speed-walked away. It was Emme. "Got a hit on the robbers."

TWELVE

When I stopped by, Emme was in her usual spot at her personal command center juggling a simulation game called Second Life and two games of Hold 'Em. "You found them?" I asked.

"A GF." Girlfriend.

She bet the river, then motioned to the third monitor, open to a forum called Gossip Alley. The thread *My boyfriend loves me!* was written by a poster named PrimaDonna6969. I read, ignoring Emme as she won the Hold 'Em pot. PrimaDonna6969's boyfriend liked to show his love by giving her things, which she happily took photos of and posted online.

I pulled out the list of items stolen from Kandy Wrapper's house. Almost all were on the screen. Based on comments from other posters, PrimaDonna6969's boyfriend had done this several times before.

"Check the date," Emme said. Prima-

Donna had posted on August 21st, three days after Haley was killed. "She had two similar posts after the other robberies."

Geez. "What's her real name?"

"IDK." I don't know. I wasn't expecting that from Emme. "I pinged her IP," she added.

I had no clue what that meant. So I waited and got nothing from her. "And . . ." I prompted.

"IP addresses don't give names. They give physical addys."

"So where is she?"

"An apartment building in Echo Park."

Two hours later, I was across the street from the address. I'd already left a message with the tip line and somehow suckered Sienna into going with me. Per Aubrey's unsolicited advice, we'd taken her Mercedes.

I'd checked the building directory as soon as we pulled up. There were close to fifty apartments in there. None listed a Prima-Donna6969 as a resident. We were forced to wait and see who entered and left the building. Luckily, we'd stocked up on snacks again.

"We need a cover story," I said. I was determined not to repeat the Montgomery stakeout situation.

Sienna thought for a moment. "We're TV show hosts who stop people on the street. Ask them questions about who they're wearing."

"And do fashion trivia. And they can win a prize. A trip to Fashion Week."

"Paris? Milan? New York?"

That was a hard one. "All three. Based on the questions they get right."

"We're the fabulous hosts." Sienna looked at my outfit, Cavalli from two years ago. "Or I'm the host and you're the producer."

Valid point. "What about a camera?"

We both thought for a minute, stumped. Then it came to me. "It's hidden camera."

We spent the next thirty minutes giving our characters' back stories. I was a former *Project Runway* producer who'd been kicked out because my ideas were ahead of their time. My name was Carri with just an *I*. Sienna was an aspiring model who'd grown up rich but lost her trust fund in a Ponzi scheme. Her name was Samantha and she refused to answer to Sam.

As we spoke, no one came in or out of the building. At least, I don't think anyone did. We were too involved in our cover story to pay much attention.

Two hours and one and a half trips to the bathroom later, we were still in position.

The good news was that we'd sat through the evening rush hour. The bad news was that there was still no sign of anyone who looked like they could've just walked off a Fashion Week runway. Sienna was telling me about her lunch with Montgomery Rose. She'd taken the initiative and called him. I was surprised to learn they'd actually discussed business. I was sure he'd wanted to get in her red-colored pants. He probably still did. He was just biding his time.

We paused when a woman left the building. I squinted, because people always think squinting will help you see farther, and was sure it was a false alarm. She was dressed to the nines. Unfortunately, she was a three at the most. She looked uncomfortable, like a little girl playing dress-up. Even her shoes, a pair of Pink Panthers, looked like they'd been stolen from her mama's closet. No way was this PrimaDonna6969, the envy of everyone on Gossip Alley. "False alarm," I said.

Sienna shook her head. "That's her. There aren't many things I'm good at, but I can recognize Givenchy from distances up to a mile. I've tested myself."

I deferred to her expert opinion and we watched as PrimaDonna got into a lime-green Toyota Corolla she had to unlock by hand!

"She's going somewhere!" Sienna was darn near shouting.

"Follow her, right? She could be going to her boyfriend's. Or, better yet, to a robbery."

"That sounds good," Sienna said, but she didn't seem too sure.

I wasn't too sure myself. Neither the idea of her going to see gangbangers or to an actual robbery appealed to me. "What if she sees us?" I asked.

Sienna thought that over. "I'll google surveillance tips. You drive."

We quickly switched places and Sienna took out her smartphone. By the time PrimaDonna pulled out of her spot, she'd found tips for us. "Okay, make sure you stay one car away!"

I could do that! A minivan with a *My kid can kick your honor student's butt* bumper sticker pulled up behind PrimaDonna. I got in line behind it. So far, so good. Sienna was quiet for a few minutes while she continued to read. She finally spoke. "Would you call this heavy traffic?"

"I would call this LA."

"And LA has heavy traffic, right?" I took my eye off the minivan long enough to throw her a look. "If it's heavy traffic, you should stay on the car's bumper."

"So I need to be behind her?"

I got in the left lane, sped up, and then cut in front of the minivan without using my signal. It was okay because it was LA. You could do that here. Soccer mom, however, wasn't pleased. When I glanced in my rearview mirror, she and the toddler in the backseat were flipping me off. Mother of the Year.

We followed PrimaDonna onto the 5 freeway and merged into the traffic. Sienna got giddy. "This is the way to the Americana. Nothing like a little evening shopping. I can pick up that Gucci dress at Nordstrom. It's —"

"Focus!"

She rolled her eyes but typed something else. "There's no article titled 'Conducting surveillance at the mall.' "

"Maybe try 'Conducting surveillance on foot'? 'In a building'?"

She typed in it. "Found one. Apparently you need at least two people."

"Check!" Good to know we were finally doing something right.

"We should take turns following her so she's not suspicious. Whatever we do, we don't want to get burned."

"What the fudge does that mean?"

"No idea, but it can't be good. STDs. Forest fires. Freshly baked cookies. Burning is never a good thing."

Amen. We continued on our way, getting on the 16. Then PrimaDonna made a quick left. "What? No!" Sienna sounded heartbroken.

We weren't going to the Americana after all. PrimaDonna turned into a parking lot for an off-price department store chain called Bella's. "Oh hecks no," Sienna said. "I do not discount shop."

"You don't, but Samantha might. Cover story, remember?"

She glared but didn't try to push me out the car. I took that as a good sign. "You owe me," she said. I knew that was as good as I was going to get.

I continued down the street, then busted an illegal U-turn — an LA staple along with turning left on red — and doubled back. By the time we pulled into the lot, PrimaDonna had parked and was making her way into Bella's. I dropped Sienna off and went to find parking.

Bella's must have been having a sale because the lot was packed. It took me five minutes before I found an anorexic spot. I didn't know what was smaller in LA, the parking spaces or the women. I squeezed out the car, went inside, and found Sienna. She was dismissively rummaging through a rack of Donna Karan jeans.

"See, they have a lot of your old friends," I said.

"Last year's friends who I don't talk to anymore because I have new, cooler, prettier ones."

Touché. "Where's *you know*?"

"In that aisle over there." Sienna motioned to a long rack filled with different dresses. "They just throw all the different designers together by size." She sounded appalled.

"You should go check on her."

"Nope."

"She's in the two-to-fours. I'm a ten, there's no way I could be in that aisle without arousing suspicion. I'll follow her when she moves to the shoes or something."

As an answer, Sienna brushed by me. I looked down to see her red-bottomed shoes stomping down the aisle, then stopping a few feet from what I assumed was Prima-Donna.

After a few minutes, Prima's pumps moved away while Sienna's stayed put. I took that as my cue. I beat PrimaDonna to the next aisle and paused at a selection of horrendous print dresses so she could click-clack by me in her heels. I waited exactly ten clicky-clacks and followed, willing myself not to stare at her too hard in case she suddenly turned around.

After a few minutes, I felt in enough of a zone to think about my cover story. I mentally got into character. It reminded me of my acting days. I was focusing so hard I didn't pay attention to where PrimaDonna was going.

I followed her through a door where five sets of eyes, all attached to bodies in various states of undress, glanced at me. I was not expecting a communal dressing room. It took the women staring at me a beat too long to remind me that I had no clothes to try on. Since I was empty-handed, I looked like a perv. It didn't help that my mouth was hanging open.

I didn't come from a "naked" house. Other people's nudity made me uncomfortable. The last time I saw my mom nude was when I was breastfeeding, and even then I closed my eyes. Even when I get intimate, I make sure the lights are completely out. If I'm feeling adventurous, I keep the hall light on and crack the bedroom door, but no more than two inches.

I was contemplating slowly backing out the room when Sienna came up behind me. She at least had the good sense to bring in an item to "try on." She stopped short when she saw me and we just stared at each other for a minute. Then we both looked at PrimaDonna, already down to her bra and panties a few feet away.

Sienna, God bless her, shoved me toward the girl. PrimaDonna could see me standing behind her in the mirror. I had her full attention. It was now or never. Time to channel Carri with an *I*, reality show producer. I took a deep breath and finally spoke. "Anything you want to tell us, creep?"

Where did that come from? I didn't have time to think about it. PrimaDonna's eyes bugged out. I didn't even wait for Sienna to catch on. I just went right into her line from her audition, then added a bit of improv. "Don't be shy now. Sharing is caring. I'm Carri. And this is my partner Samantha."

I motioned to Sienna. "Don't be shy. Sharing is caring," she said.

I'd just said that, but PrimaDonna didn't seem to notice. She was too busy freaking out. "I don't know what —" she said.

"Save it," Sienna snapped. "We all know this ain't your first time at the rodeo. You know we gotta give you your Miranda rights."

I went off script. "We know about your

boyfriend and what he did."

"What are you talking about?" Prima-Donna asked. "What boyfriend?"

"The robberies. Kandy Wrapper. Joseline. Oscar Blue," I said.

"We know that's where you got that Givenchy you're wearing," Sienna said. "That he gave you."

"You know he killed a girl to get it?" I asked.

Prima's eyes bugged out even more, but she didn't say anything. The other women in the dressing room weren't even pretending to not be paying attention. One even got out her cell phone to record us.

"Her name was Haley Joseph," I said. "Your boyfriend and his merry gang of thugs killed her on the way back from robbing Kandy Wrapper."

"That Givenchy might as well be covered in blood," Sienna said.

Nice line! I threw her an approving look and we mentally high-fived. PrimaDonna took that time to finally speak. "That's impossible."

"Impossible?" I asked. "We have proof! You're in it up to your eyeballs."

"Unless you give us his name," Sienna said. "I can't make any guarantees, but we can talk to the DA and get you a deal."

We might as well be writing for *Law & Order.*

"You got the wrong girl," Prima said. "I don't even have a boyfriend."

"Oh," Sienna said. "You're gonna go that route."

"Help us help you." I'd always wanted to say that to someone.

"But I don't," she insisted.

"You're wearing the clothes he got you."

"I bought these," she insisted.

She was tougher to break than I thought. A true ride-or-die chick. I'd have given him up, gifts or no gifts. "We saw your postings on Gossip Alley," I said. " 'My boyfriend loves me so much. He surprised me with this Givenchy dress. Blah. Blah. Blah.' That's admissible in court, you know."

"I made that up." As she spoke, she looked at me and Sienna, then at the other ladies in the room as if they were a jury of her peers. "I just created this life on there because I wanted some excitement. I made up this boyfriend and then when I saw those clothes at the shop, I bought them and took those stupid pictures. I've never even had a boyfriend."

One thing she said caught my attention. It wasn't the lack of a boyfriend thing. They were overrated anyway. "Shop? Which shop?" I doubted she could afford the gas to even get to Robertson Boulevard, much less shop there.

"That secondhand store on Vermont. What's the name?" It took her a second, but it finally came to her. "Clothes Encounters! I bought them at Clothes Encounters."

THIRTEEN

All I could think was "wow." The Rack Pack was using Betty's store to peddle stolen stuff. At the risk of sounding repetitive, *wow*. Once I could conjure thoughts consisting of more than one word, I remembered that each seller was assigned a four-digit number. "Did you keep one of your tags?" I asked.

She shook her head. Fudge. I turned to Sienna. "We could've used it to find out the seller."

"6801," PrimaDonna said. "She's my favorite. The woman who owns the place even calls me when she gets something new from her."

So Betty knew the person who ran Haley down. Sienna and I exchanged a look. PrimaDonna took that to mean something — the wrong something. "Am I still in some kind of trouble?"

"No." I was impressed at how authoritative I sounded.

There was an audible sigh from the chorus. They'd been expecting an arrest and were getting boring conversation. If this were a movie, PrimaDonna would be cuffed naked on the floor. Disappointed, a few went back to trying on clothes. I wanted to scream, "Hello, she just gave us a big fat super-huge clue!"

I pulled a receipt and pen from my purse. "Write down your information in case we have any further questions."

Eager to please, PrimaDonna did. As she handed it back, she looked at me real close. "Did we go to high school together?"

"I want to help you. Trust me, I do. You guys know Toni Abrams. But Betty would freak if she knew I was giving out a customer's info."

Sienna had an open call audition right after our trip to Bella's, so we couldn't go to Clothes Encounters right away. We rushed there early the next morning, only to discover that Betty had taken an impromptu trip out of town with her boyfriend. Good for Betty. Not good for me. She'd left Nat in charge. A very hesitant Nat.

"Or she'd laud you for helping find Haley's killer," I said.

Nat considered that for a second, then went back to looking unsure. I motioned to the computer at the check-out counter. "Can't you just look it up?"

"I would, but what if you're wrong? I can't get fired. I'm only six and a half payments away from getting my new nose. I want the Jennifer Lopez."

"We're not wrong," Sienna said. "I can prove it." She held up a pair of stilettos. They had *6801* on the tag. We'd gone through the store before talking to Nat. Almost all of 6801's items matched the list of stolen things we'd gotten from Fab.

"You're a huge Joseline fan, right?" Sienna asked, reminding Nat about the reality star who was the Rack Pack's first victim. The girl nodded. "She wore these when she took her grandmother and ten-year-old sister to pole class during the third season."

Nat took the shoes and examined them. "Well, she is a 7 1/2 . . . but I bet there are a ton of women who wear 7 1/2's who wouldn't be caught dead in last year's Louboutins. Maybe if Joseline had auto-graphed it or something."

She handed them back to Sienna. Geez. I pictured Haley telling me to control my peanut butter. I took in a deep breath and tried another tactic. "Even if you don't tell us, at least give the name to the cops. Think how grateful Joseline, Kandy, and Oscar Blue would be if you helped them get their stuff back."

I could see her thinking it over and liking whatever it was that came to mind. I pushed harder. "They'd probably want to thank you personally."

Bingo. "Let me call Betty and make sure it's okay."

Nat grabbed the cordless phone and dialed a number from memory. After a second, she hung up. "It went to voicemail." Dang it. "How about you come back when she's back in town and I'll give you the name."

I wanted the name immediately, but I supposed I could wait a couple of days. "That's fine. When are you expecting her?"

"Two weeks," Nat said.

Blurg. Sienna looked ready to nail Nat with Joseline's stiletto. I needed to get her out of there before she went postal. Sienna wouldn't last a day in jail, and no way I could afford her bail. "Okay, thanks, Nat," I said, practically dragging Sienna to the front door. "We'll check back in a couple of weeks."

"No prob." Nat beamed as if she genuinely

thought she was helping.

Sienna spoke as soon as we got into the car. "You could still call the tip line."

"Nat had a point when she said the shoe could technically belong to anyone. It doesn't feel like enough information to go on. Or take seriously. We just need a name, then we can check it out ourselves. There's definitely no way I'm waiting two weeks."

"Let's not then."

"Doesn't seem like we have a choice. Nat won't help us."

"So we get someone else. What's the name of Haley's roommate again?"

"Marina. I don't want to tell her anything until I have concrete proof."

Sienna ignored me. Instead, she grabbed her cell. "Siri, call Clothes Encounters." By the time Siri found the number, Sienna had affected a thick Southern accent that would make Scarlett O'Hara proud. "Hi, is Marina in? No? When is she working next? This afternoon?"

I spoke as Sienna hung the phone up. "Want to clue me in here on your plan?"

"Marina knows you. She doesn't know me. After my audition, we'll go in at the same time, but separately. I pretend to be a shopper interested in 6801's clothes. Ask if 6801 has a particular item. Marina pulls up the information on the computer. And while I distract her . . ."

"I get 6801's real name and number from the computer."

It was perfect. I could get the name and not bother Marina about it until I had something definitive.

"Exactly," Sienna said. "Now let's work on my back-story."

Sienna dropped me off at our condo to pick up my car so she could head to her audition. As many times as we'd said those lines, I knew she'd nail it.

We met up again a couple hours later, choosing a location a block away from Clothes Encounters to go over final details. After Marina pulled up 6801's information, Sienna would take her to the area where the dressing rooms were located. I'd sneak behind the counter *Mission: Impossible* style, write down 6801's information, and be gone before Sienna tried on her second outfit. It was foolproof.

I went in first. The tinkle of a small bell above the door alerted Marina of my arrival. "Welcome to Clothes — hey, Dayna! Any word on the hit-and-run?"

I shook my head. "I'm still working on it."

And she was helping. She just didn't know it.

The bell tinkled again, alerting us we had company. "Good morning!" Marina called out. "Welcome to Clothes Encounters."

Sienna swept in with her sunglasses covering half her face, ponytail bouncing with each high-heeled step, and an oversized purse nestled into the crook of her bent arm. She glanced at us from over the top of her sunglasses before dismissing us as too inconsequential for a return greeting. She hit the racks of clothes, not even bothering to take the glasses off.

Marina could sense money was in the air, which made me no longer worthy of her attention. She made her way over to Sienna. "Anything I can help you find today?"

Sienna let her know that there was. I pretended to browse while I heard snatches of conversation as Sienna "discovered" 6801's clothes and demanded to see everything from this seller, including what wasn't on the floor. They glided past me on their way to the check-out counter. Sienna had affected an English accent. Her idea. Not mine. "Find out if 6801 has any vintage Louis. I need it today. I have no problem going to Out of the Closet."

Marina opened the counter door and went

to the computer, where she used the always effective pointer-finger typing method to look up 6801's information. She found it, then picked up the cordless phone and dialed. After a minute, she hung up and said something to Sienna, who was not a happy camper.

Sienna said something in return, then stomped off in my direction. Marina yanked open the counter door and scurried to catch up. By the time Sienna passed me, Marina was at her heels. I heard her tell Sienna, "We really do have some nice bags, you should take a look."

"I'm going to try on these dresses," Sienna said. "6801 better call back before I've got the first one unzipped."

"Okay." Marina stopped, perhaps thinking Sienna could handle changing clothes herself.

Sienna felt otherwise. She once again peeked over her sunglasses. "Chop chop. You need to tell me how good I look in everything."

They disappeared into the other room. Finally alone, I wasted no time running to the counter. I tried to pull the counter door. It didn't budge. I was afraid of making too much noise by yanking too hard. I pulled it again. No dice.

What would Tom Cruise do? He'd jump over the counter, even if he was wearing three-and-a-half-inch Pink Panther heels. So I did it, managing not to break the door or any vital body parts like my nails. As soon as I did, the bell rang.

A guy who barely looked old enough to drink came inside. His skin was pale and pasty, like he didn't get outside much. Judging from his size, his time indoors was probably spent shooting up. I pegged him at five foot seven and 110 pounds, tops, with stringy long brown hair that looked as dry and as dirty as a desert.

I glanced at the computer. 6801's information was still pulled up, but I was too far away to make it out. I glanced back at the guy, who was now directly across from me, staring at me as if waiting for me to say something.

"Welcome to Clothes Encounters."

That wasn't me speaking. Marina had heard the bell and come over. He turned around to face her. When she saw who it was, she didn't look happy to be of service.

"You bring my stuff?" he asked.

"You know the answer," she said, then glanced at me and did a double take. I was still behind the counter.

I said the first thing that came to mind.

185

Thank God it made sense. "I dropped my phone."

She nodded, seeming to buy it. They were a few feet away, which meant I couldn't go look at 6801's information. I bent down, as if pretending to look for my phone.

"How much longer you gonna keep my crap?" the guy asked. I could tell he was upset because his voice got higher and higher with each word. At this rate, he'd sound like he'd overdosed on helium by the time the convo was over.

"I'm not going to give you Haley's stuff, Victory."

Victory? That sliver of a thing was Haley's boyfriend? The name gods had a sense of humor because from looks alone, he was not winning. Anything. My first instinct was to pop up so I could get a better look at him, but I stayed focused. I crawled the five feet toward the computer screen, edging closer until I was just near enough to make out the name.

And that's when the computer screen saver came on. Fudge, squared.

"You bought it for Haley," Marina was saying.

Would they notice if I reached up and jiggled the mouse just a teeny, tiny little bit?

"It's not like she can use a cell phone

186

anymore," he said.

Did he really just say that? The only thing that stopped me from throwing *my* cell phone at his stupid face was that I was supposed to be looking for it.

"If you want her things, you'll have to talk to her mother."

"Or I can just come and take it."

He meant it to be threatening, but his voice had become too high-pitched to pull it off. I banged against the bottom of the counter, partly to diffuse the situation and partly to move the computer enough to get rid of the screen saver. They looked down at me from their side of the counter.

"Oops. Didn't see that. I'm fine," I said, even though neither of them asked.

Victory headed toward the exit. "I'll be back," he said. I'd rather see the Terminator.

Marina and I exchanged a look and rolled our eyes. No words were needed. Then I remembered why I was there. It wasn't to judge dudes who sounded like an angry chipmunk Alvin kicked out the group. I glanced at the computer. The screen saver was off, which would have been great — except the log on screen was on.

The whole thing had gone from *Mission: Impossible* to *Mission: Pathetic.* I was the only person in the galaxy who could mess up something as simple as getting a name and number off a computer. "You find it?" Marina asked.

I was about to say no, then realized she was talking about my cell phone, which was still in my hand. I held it up. "Yep."

At that moment, it chose to ring. I was so surprised I dropped the thing for real. I looked down. My phone was in what felt like a million pieces but was really just the phone and cover. By the time I bent down to pick them up, Marina was hovering over me, asking if everything was okay. "You can use our phone if you need to call them back."

She had the portable in her pocket and handed it to me. She might as well have been giving me one of Willy Wonka's golden tickets. If I couldn't get 6801's information from the computer, maybe I could get it from the phone she'd just used to call him. Best case scenario, 6801 wouldn't pick up and he was one of those uber-helpful types who gave their name and number on their outgoing message. Worst case scenario, he would answer and I'd hang up.

"Thanks." I took the phone and walked a few steps away.

I hit redial. The phone rang. And rang.

And rang. The voicemail kicked in and the familiar mechanical voice droned in my ear, asking me to leave a message for the telephone number.

It was the middle case scenario, which I gladly took. I hung up, handed the phone back to Marina with a lame excuse about having to run, and left the store. As soon as I got outside, I pulled out a receipt and scribbled down the number before I forgot it. We were in business.

Sometimes I wondered if Emme even knew what day it was, but then I remembered that Windows is kind enough to share the date and time on its desktop wallpaper. Emme was juggling two Hold 'Em hands, a sniper game, and looking up 6801's number. She did all of this with one hand while absent-mindedly playing with her grandmother's necklace with the other.

I sat there and wondered about Sienna's whereabouts. We'd agreed that if we got separated, we'd meet at Emme's house, yet Sienna was nowhere to be found.

After a few minutes, Emme finally spoke. "It's a Google Voice number."

"What does that mean?"

"It's basically untraceable," she said.

Things weren't supposed to be untraceable on the Internet. "How do we get by it?"

"We don't. We're SOL."

"That sucks," I said, because it did.

We sat there, her playing games and me trying to figure out what to do next. I could leave the phone number on the tip line. Maybe the cops would have better luck, though I doubted their computer skills were better than Emme's.

My thoughts were interrupted by a knock on the door. I could tell by the tentative yet quick taps it was Sienna. Emme made no movement to get it. She was not a fan of opening her front door. I'd once decided to drop by unannounced and stood outside her apartment for twenty minutes, listening to the sounds of her shooting folks online. Best believe I called before the next time I came over.

I answered the door and Sienna swept in with shopping bags. She noticed me noticing them. "Pretending to shop put me in the mood to really shop."

"What happened to you?" She'd stayed in the dressing room the entire time I was flailing around behind the counter. I could've used her help.

"No, what happened to *you*?" she asked. "You were gone when I came out. I tried calling. Nothing."

Oh. I pulled my phone out my purse. I'd been too excited to notice that my battery had died. Oops. It turned out Sienna hadn't even realized what was going on, spending the entire time in the dressing room blabbering away thinking Marina was still there. I gave her a quick summary of what happened, doing my best to make it sound like I wasn't a complete idiot. It was difficult.

"But you got this Smith person's address?" she said when I finished.

"No, it's a Google Voice number. Virtually untrace . . ." I trailed off. "Did you say Smith?"

"Jamie Smith. Marina said his name when she left the message."

Bingo. I ran over to Emme, but she was already searching for the name. "There are 1,321 living in Los Angeles proper," she said.

That was a lot. No way could I call all of them. I only had twenty minutes left on my phone card.

"Sigh," Emme said, which was as close to actually sighing as she got.

I opted for the real thing. "I doubt it's a real name anyway," I said.

"You tried."

That was true. What was also true was I

wasn't done trying. I thought about Haley's motto. Control your peanut butter. Before I knew what I was doing, I had Emme's house phone and was dialing the number. I waited for the voicemail to kick in.

"Yes, hi, this message is for Jamie Smith. I'm calling from Clothes Encounters. When Marina called earlier, she forgot to mention we sold a couple of your pieces, so we have a check for you. You can pick it up tomorrow at one o'clock. Thanks for choosing Clothes Encounters."

I hung up, all proud of myself. Then I noticed Emme and Sienna looking at me. Emme spoke first. "Okay, now I'm waiting for you to call the cops."

"Sienna's coming with me."

"I would, but I have my callback tomorrow," she said. "You should definitely call the police. I don't want you going alone."

I had no plans to call the cops, but they didn't have to know that. Everything I'd said to Sienna still held true. I wanted to get more information before I told anyone anything. "I'll call them tomorrow. Promise."

They didn't see my fingers crossed behind my back.

FOURTEEN

I attempted to leave the condo undetected early the next morning. I needed to drop off the phone to Omari and catch a killer. What did it say about me that I was equally anxious about both? I waited until Sienna was in the kitchen jabbering away on the phone to make my escape. I was halfway to freedom when she appeared behind me. "You call the police?"

"Yep! They'll have a patrolman in the area."

I hated lying, but there was no way I could tell her the truth. A Google Voice account and what was probably a fake name were not enough to find Haley's killer. These tips would be stuck in a box right next to the details about Montgomery's car.

"Yeah, Day thinks she got a lead on a number on the robber." Sienna clearly wasn't talking to me anymore. "Yeah, another one."

193

She motioned to the phone and mouthed, "Montgomery." They'd been talking a lot. Sienna had fixated on him being the person to guide her to fame, having decided it was fate that she'd literally wound up on his doorstep. I waved and got out of there.

I got into my car, ready to get this Omari exchange over with. He'd texted me an address for some restaurant I'd never been to. The last thing I wanted was to spend an hour eating and having awkward conversation with him. It didn't look like I'd have much of a choice.

I got there in less than twenty minutes, the LA equivalent of being able to fly. The first clue I wasn't meeting him for lunch was the four Star Waggons parked across from the restaurant. Star Waggons are fancy trailers studios rent for actors when they're shooting on location. Minus the blue Star Waggon logo, the outside looks like any other trailer you'd hook to the back of a truck. But depending on how soon the actor's name appears in the credits, the inside is nicer than 90 percent of our country's houses.

Omari had invited me to the *LAPD 90036* set.

I would have preferred the awkward lunch. I wasn't expecting this. When I saw him at the movie premiere, I'd been mentally prepared. Not this time. What if someone recognized me and asked what I was up to?

Since I'd already spent the gas, I parked. There were tons of people milling about, some with walkie-talkies. I could separate the extras from the crew by their clothing choices. The crew all wore sensible, closed-toe shoes and jeans. The extras were all female, cloaked in high heels and short skirts.

Even though I didn't know what her voice sounded like, I pictured Haley telling me to control my peanut butter. It made me feel better.

No one stopped me when I walked to the trailers. The name *Jamal Fine,* Omari's character, was listed on the third one. I tentatively knocked, then waited. No one came to the door. After the third knock, I accepted that he wasn't inside and ventured closer to the set to see if I could find him.

He was in the parking lot, wearing his patrolman's uniform and holding a gun aimed at some poor hapless "homeless" guy. I stood in the back and watched him work. I had to smile just a little bit. He always knew he would make it, and he had. In his element, he didn't seem to notice the hundred-plus people on the other side of the camera staring at him. He was the only one talking. No one else dared speak until the director said so.

"It's time to pay for your crime," Omari said, which made me giggle and the guy closest to me glare in my direction. I immediately shut up.

The director yelled "cut" and Omari was engulfed in a sea of makeup and hair people. I was so busy watching him, I didn't notice the woman until she spoke. "May I help you?"

Her voice held authority, which meant she was an AD, or Assistant Director. Judging from her location nowhere near the action, she must have been a second AD. The first AD was the director's right hand and always within a few feet of him.

"I'm here for Omari. He's expecting me," I said, since she obviously thought I was a fan, or worse, a groupie.

"And you are?"

I paused, not sure how to answer. I was still his friend, right? She must've took my hesitation as me getting ready to lie because she said, "I know you're not his girlfriend."

What exactly did she mean by that? Her tone was completely neutral so I couldn't tell. Did she think there was no way I could be his girlfriend because of how I looked?

Or did she mean she already knew Omari's girlfriend, which meant Omari *had* a girlfriend. He'd never been serious with anyone in the five years since I'd moved to LA. Had that changed in the last six weeks, along with everything else in his life?

I started freaking. Not only was I not controlling my peanut butter, it was spread all over the place. Talk about a giant mess. Geez. I looked up and remembered I wasn't alone. "No, not his girlfriend," I said. "A friend. I see he's busy. I'll just come back."

It wasn't until I got back to my car that I realized I was still holding his cell phone.

I headed straight to Silver Lake and parked on a side street, since I couldn't afford to pay the meter on Vermont. I pushed thoughts of the set visit aside and focused on my plan on what to do when Jamie Smith showed up. My idea was to covertly take some photos and get a real name, then pass it all on to the tip line. I wanted to solve this thing not just because of my parents, but for Haley.

I hadn't met her, of course, but based on everything I was hearing, I wished I had. She seemed like a cool chick. A chick who probably smiled at her killer, asked if she could help him, even called to let him know they'd sold a few pieces. And how did he repay her? By mowing her down in cold blood and then driving away like it didn't happen. It wasn't fair. Her life shouldn't have been cut short, especially not so someone could have the latest pair of Jimmy Choos. She deserved better. Much, much better!

I'd managed to work myself into quite a tizzy when 1:00 p.m. finally came around.

I started the car and pulled onto Vermont, finding a metered space more or less across from the store. Jamie Smith needed to be on time. I could only afford twenty minutes on the meter. I was so busy practically foaming at the mouth in anger, I didn't notice Aubrey until he was inside my car. Again. I really needed to remember to lock my doors.

"Are you following me, Ms. Anderson?"

I was not in the proper mindset to deal with him. Not now. Probably not ever. "You wish."

"Then why are we both here?"

"Because this is the scene of the crime?" It seemed pretty obvious to me.

"You need to stop with this so-called investigation of yours."

So-called? Was I not the one who found Montgomery's car while Aubrey was busy putting on his reflector suit? "And you need to get out of my car."

He didn't move. So I did. I got out, walked around the car, and yanked open the passenger-side door. Aubrey just stared at me.

"I will call the police." It was the second time I'd said this exact same lie in a twenty-four-hour period. "Out!"

"You need to calm down, Ms. Anderson."

There's nothing worse than yelling at someone and their response is to tell you to calm down. It only makes you angrier. "I'll show you how to calm down! Get out!" I yelled.

He still didn't budge, so I stomped over to his bike, which was tied to a tree a few feet away. I contemplated the best way to use my spiked heel to puncture a tire. He appeared next to me. "Do you not think you are overreacting?"

If he asked me if I was on the rag, I was going to choke him with the tampon in my purse. (So, I was on my period. Sue me.) "Take some deep breaths," he said.

It was only then I noticed Hollywood's equivalent of a minivan, a Range Rover, pull up outside Clothes Encounters and double park. The windows were tinted pitch black, so I couldn't see who was inside. I doubted it was a trophy wife. I was betting it was the robber, Jamie Smith.

I attempted to play it cool. Of course, I failed miserably. My eyes bugged out. It didn't help that I immediately looked away awkwardly, like one does when caught staring. Aubrey noticed and turned to the street. "Who is that in the car?" he asked. "Is that Ms. Joseph's alleged killer? Is that why you are here?"

Did he say "alleged" like he was talking to a jury? The killer wasn't going to leap out the car and threaten to sue for slander.

Aubrey took off across the street toward the car, managing to cross right in the crosswalk. "I am Aubrey S. Adams-Parker. I demand you exit this vehicle right now!"

The driver took off. It had to be Jamie Smith. Most people would have pretended to not see Aubrey while they subtly checked if their doors were locked. That's what we all did with the homeless. I watched my hard-fought lead disappear down the street.

It took Aubrey ten more feet to realize he was missing the six million in bionic parts needed to catch the car on foot. He ran back in my direction. "Give me your keys!"

He said it with such force, I handed them over. I barely made it into the backseat before he was busting a U-turn and taking off after the Range Rover, who now had a half-mile lead.

Aubrey made great progress. We roared down the street, then hit a red light. Aubrey stopped accordingly. We watched the Range Rover get smaller in the distance. "You're letting it get away!" I yelled.

"Call 911," he said.

I hesitated. "I'm gonna call the tip line."

He took his eyes off the road to throw me a shocked look in the rearview mirror. "You don't call the tip line, you don't get the credit," I explained as I took out my phone and dialed the 1-877 number.

The Voice picked up on the second ring, smacking away on her gum. "Tip line."

"We're chasing the killer!" I may have sounded a little too excited, but I had a good excuse. I was in an actual high-speed car chase. Well, I would be once the light turned green.

"Oh, it's you. 1018."

"Look, we're in a car chasing him —"

"Or her," Aubrey interjected. The light turned green and he took off.

"Or her down in a black Range Rover. I can give you the license plate."

"Or you can give it to 911," the Voice said.

I paused. "Are you telling me to hang up?"

The only answer I got was a dial tone. I

wanted to call her back to curse her out (without using actual curse words) but instead called 911. Thankfully, the woman who answered was *a lot* nicer. After I explained the situation, she promised patrol cars were on their way and we hung up.

We caught a break in the form of good old Los Angeles traffic. It was barely 2:00 p.m., but rush hour was an all-day thing in LA. I could see the Range Rover about seven cars ahead of us. "Drive on the sidewalk!" I ordered. I'd seen it in a movie once.

Aubrey didn't move. "He's not going anywhere."

"Neither are we!"

Aubrey stayed put. I couldn't take it anymore. In yet another of my well-thought-out decisions, I grabbed my cell, jumped out the car, and took off down the middle of the street. I always said I could run in four-inch heels. It was good to know I was right on that front.

I maneuvered through the traffic, even getting a few cat-calls and honks of appreciation. Jamie Smith saw me coming, because just when I was about to get to his car, the Range Rover made an abrupt illegal left turn, barely skating past oncoming traffic. It disappeared down a side street.

I glanced back to see if Aubrey noticed, but even if he did, the Infiniti was stuck in the right lane. No way would he be able to get over and make a left. It was up to me.

The Range Rover was already a block away. I could wait for oncoming traffic to subside or dash across the street, hoping drivers got the hint and stopped. I ran, eliciting honks *not* of the appreciative variety. But they did stop. I made it across just as the Range Rover made an abrupt right down a street about a block away.

I got to the cross street in good time, especially considering the heels. I turned, stopping when I saw the Range Rover parked about half a block down. Was it waiting for me? To do what? I went to redial 911, but when I looked down, I noticed I'd grabbed Omari's phone by mistake. Great.

I had no clue what to do. I couldn't help Haley if I was dead myself, yet I would never forgive myself if I was this close to her killer and let him (or her — darn you, Aubrey) get away. I spied a trash can chock full of empty glass beer bottles. Thank God for recycling. I grabbed one and held it out like a knife. "I have a weapon," I called out.

A weapon that would be much deadlier if it wasn't intact. I figured I could use a broken bottle's jagged edges to do serious damage. I'd seen that once on TV. I slammed the bottle against the curb to get it to break. It bounced up off the cement and hit my head. Ouch. So much for that. I slowly made my way closer to the car. "I called the police," I yelled.

For the first time all day, it wasn't a lie. My legs took me closer to the car while my brain wondered where the freaking police were. At that point, I would even have welcomed Aubrey showing up.

I got a few feet from the car but didn't hear any movement. I was cautious, waiting for Jamie Smith to pop up from somewhere. Anywhere. As a kid, I'd hated hide-and-seek. This was taking it to a whole new level. The driver was either hurt or hiding. Neither option was desirable. I tried to figure out the best method of attack. Not being able to do so, I decided to swing first, ask questions later.

I yanked open the door, squeezed my eyes shut in fear, and swung my unbroken beer bottle with all my might.

FIFTEEN

I hit air. When I finally got up enough nerve to open my eyes, I saw that Jamie Smith was gone. Based on the things still in the car, he'd left in a rush. McDonald's remnants and a crumpled receipt were thrown haphazardly in the passenger seat. Still breathing like I was Darth Vader's illegitimate black sister, I walked to the passenger side and opened the door. I was reaching in to grab the receipt when I heard a voice. "I know you are not about to disrupt a crime scene, Ms. Anderson."

I snatched my hand back like I'd gotten too close to a camp fire. "But there's a receipt," I said. "It could be important."

"That is for the police to decide. Did you see the man or woman?"

"He must've jumped out before I turned the corner."

We heard sirens. Aubrey went to flag down the officers. I glanced longingly at the receipt. "Do not touch anything, Ms. Anderson," he called.

I didn't. Instead, I used the much-needed alone time to get a few quick photos with Omari's cell phone. I didn't know what was important so I took pictures of everything, then examined my handiwork. The receipt was from a popular discount department store called T-Mart.

When Aubrey returned with the two patrolmen, I was sitting innocently on the curb. Both patrolmen looked like their bodies had been stretched. The red-headed Officer Murphy appeared to have been pulled by his head. He was tall and folding-chair-leg skinny. Whereas his partner, Daly, seemed like he'd been pulled by his sides. He was short and as round as a medicine ball.

We all listened as Aubrey described what had happened. His serious tone only made the entire thing sound even more ridiculous. Murphy looked like he was about to laugh any minute. Daly wasn't doing much better. He'd occasionally nod, making even that come across as condescending. When Aubrey finally wrapped up, Daly spoke. "And how do you know this was the hit-and-run suspect?"

Valid question.

"We were not sure," Aubrey said. "However, the driver took off as I approached him."

"Ever occur to you, Parker —"

"Adams-Parker," Aubrey corrected, but Daly acted like he didn't hear him.

"— that maybe the guy took off 'cause some crazy guy in a bright orange outfit was running toward him?"

Another valid question.

"I clearly identified myself," Aubrey said.

"As?" Murphy asked. "You're not a cop anymore."

That was enough of that. I got up. "I had good reason to think the killer would be in the area at that time. Based on the suspicious activity displayed, it seems logical to assume he was the killer. The guy's on foot now. He can't have gotten far. You should canvas the area."

I waited for them to see the light. Their faces remained as dark as a Haunted House at midnight. Desperate, I went with the old standby of name-dropping. "We also have reason to believe the killer is a member of the Rack Pack, the robbers who stole from Oscar Blue, Kandy Wrapper, and Joseline."

Murphy finally spoke. "Don't tell me Parker's got a partner. You must not know about his reputation."

I expected Aubrey to say something. He didn't, and I felt something I never thought I'd feel — sorry for Aubrey S. Adams-Parker. I wanted to say something to defend Aubrey's honor and put this a-hole in his place. "Reputation, smeputation." I definitely showed him.

"The car was probably stolen," Aubrey said.

I nodded in agreement. Murphy and Daly hadn't said as much, but drivers typically didn't abandon cars they actually owned on some random side street. It would be too easy to link them to the car, thereby negating the whole running-away thing.

"You should check with Robbery to see if anyone called in a missing Range Rover matching this description," Aubrey continued.

Murphy and Daly just threw each other a look. "You two, sit," one said. "This is now official *police* business."

In an act of defiance, I didn't sit. Neither did Aubrey. We stood to the side, watching as they examined the car and made unintelligible comments into walkie-talkies clipped to their uniforms.

"If those are the type of people you had to work with, I don't blame you for no longer being a cop," I said.

"It was not my choice." Aubrey actually sounded human and not like one of the officers from *The Matrix*. I wondered what that was all about, but I didn't want to pry. I could just google it later. So instead I decided to try and cheer him up.

"I got something," I told him.

"Please tell me you did not touch anything." *The Matrix* was back.

"No, but I did take pictures."

I handed him the phone. He threw a look at Daly and Murphy, then took it.

"I think it's a T-Mart receipt," I said. "It could belong to the car's owner, but it could also belong to Haley's killer."

Aubrey thought it over. "There is only one way to find out. There is an address on here, right?"

I peeked over his shoulder. The receipt only listed a few things, which made sense if it did belong to Jamie Smith. Why spend money on something when you can just steal it? He'd paid with a credit card, but the great folks at T-Mart hadn't been so kind as to include the person's name on the receipt. He'd also scribbled some numbers along the top, but I didn't pay them much attention. I was too busy searching for an address for the T-Mart. I finally found it. It was in the Valley.

"Maybe he went shopping right before he got to Clothes Encounters," I said. "Someone at the store could have seen something."

"The receipt is from July," Aubrey said.

Blurg. "No one's going to remember someone from three months ago."

"They have video cameras," he said. "I can talk to the security head and ask to look at the footage."

Great. He'd get the information and not tell me anything. Maybe I could just go in right after he left and say, "Tell me everything you told the guy in the reflector suit."

Aubrey interrupted my thoughts with a question. "What time can you pick me up tomorrow?" He saw my look of confusion. "I cannot bike all the way to the North Valley."

I smiled. Aubrey was actually asking me to help him. "I'll pick you up if you tell me one thing," I said. "What's the *S* stand for?"

We had to repeat our story, complete with its possible ties to the Rack Pack, for the detectives when they showed up. I took solace in the fact that they treated Murphy and Daly in the same dismissive manner Murphy and Daly had treated us. The detectives also confirmed what Aubrey and I already knew — the car was indeed stolen.

Once home, I filled Sienna and Emme in on what happened. I expected them to laugh about it. Instead, they both lectured me on how dumb it was to run after a murderer. They had a point, but everything had turned out okay, hadn't it? Still, they made me promise not to do anything else that could "put my life in danger."

Regardless, I was still in a good mood when I made my way to Aubrey's house the next morning. I was excited about how much progress we were making. Today could be the day Haley's killer was finally put behind bars.

Aubrey lived in the hills in the poor people section of Silver Lake. And by poor, I mean they made less than one million a year. I'd been in the car five minutes when my phone rang. I hit the answer button and put the phone to my ear without bothering to check the ID. "Make it quick. I got five minutes left on this phone card."

The person paused just long enough for me to regret my greeting. I immediately panicked, scared that it was the bank calling about the foreclosure. Maybe Daddy had given them my number. I was tempted to hang up so I could claim they had the wrong number when they called back, but I couldn't waste the phone card minute.

"Hello?" I said in my best Perky Black Girl voice.

"Why'd you leave yesterday?"

It was Omari. Fudge. Haley immediately popped in my brain, reminding me to control my peanut butter.

"I had another appointment. We really should have gone with my plan to throw it in your open window. I'll just have to mail it."

"You can give it to me. We can meet for lunch tomorrow."

Like that was going to happen. "A real restaurant or another set?"

He ignored that. "You know shows don't shoot on Saturdays. Two thirty too late? You try that new soul food spot yet? Anna Will's?"

No fair. He knew how much I wanted to try that place. Well played, Omari, well played.

I heard a beep signaling I had another call. I defied about seven laws to take a quick peek at my caller ID. "I gotta go, Aubrey's on the other line."

"Aubrey?"

"See you tomorrow." Best case scenario, Aubrey and I would find the killer courtesy of T-Mart's security footage and I'd be too excited to panic about Omari. Worst case scenario, I'd make some excuse about my body being abducted by aliens and not go. I switched over.

"Are you close, Ms. Anderson?"

I checked the clock — only ten minutes late. He'd clearly never heard of the concept of CP time. I was practically early. "Five minutes away." From the freeway that would take me another ten minutes to get to his house. "I really should go. I left my headset at home and I know you don't want me to break any laws."

"I will be expecting you in less than five minutes," he said.

Twenty minutes later, I pulled into his driveway. The house was cradled into the side of a hill and looked out on downtown LA, which held the distinction of being one of two places in all of LA County with tall buildings. It made for a beautiful view.

Judging by the two separate entrances, he also had neighbors. There was the main house, and underneath it was a door to a separate apartment. Aubrey must have been staring out the window because he immediately came out the door of the apartment. He got into the passenger side of my car with a very, very, very pointed glance at his bright orange watch. I ignored that. "How's it feel?" I asked.

"Pardon me, Ms. Anderson?"

"How's it feel to finally be in my car as an invited guest?" Of course, he didn't even crack a smile. "Nice place," I said as I pulled out. "It's one apartment plus the house?"

"Four. My studio, plus two more apartments around the side."

"How's your landlord?"

"I am the landlord," he said. "My grandparents built the house in the 1920s."

I suddenly understood why he could just roam around solving cases for free. Must be nice.

I spent the entire forty-minute drive attempting awkward small talk while Aubrey was more concerned with battling my phone's GPS over who could give better directions. At one point, I was tempted to jump out the moving car. I figured as long as I stopped, dropped, and rolled, I'd be okay.

After what felt like a millennia, we finally made it to T-Mart and parked. Once inside, I ran to the first security guard I saw — mainly to get away from Aubrey. "Hi," I said. "I'm looking for the security office."

"There a problem?" the guard asked.

Unfortunately, Aubrey had caught up and spoke before I had the chance. "We are not at liberty to discuss it with someone in an entry-level position." Entry-level? Why didn't he just call the guy's mother a ho while he was at it?

"I completely understand," the guard said. "Unfortunately, all the non-entry level people are busy at the moment, but I'll be glad to help." The guard had been trained almost as well as those poor customer service people who always claimed their manager was on another call.

"It's in regards to a burglary ring," I said.

The words *burglary* and *ring* were the abracadabra of T-Mart security, because the guard whispered something into his walkie-talkie and within minutes we were whisked deep into the bowels of the store. With a wall of monitors feeding video to four guards, the security office looked more suited for NASA than the Valley.

I didn't have much of a chance to marvel at it all. We were immediately ushered into the security head's office. She was one of those women I hated. Beautiful clothes, flawless skin, and, from the looks of it, she actually enjoyed eating stupid things like salads. She probably even took her dressing on the side. She was also tall for a man, much less a woman — easily on the north side of six feet. She stood when we entered, looking down at us both and making sure to give equal eye contact as she spoke. "Mika Bell."

"Aubrey S. Adams-Parker. And this is my colleague, Dayna Anderson."

She seemed to recognize Aubrey's name but didn't say anything about it. She just took a seat and motioned for us to do the same. "I hear you have some information about a robbery gang?"

Not wanting to risk a repeat of what happened with the first security guard, I spoke up. "We have reason to believe that at least one member of the gang was at your store on July 1st."

She hit a few buttons on her computer. "There's no record of any suspicious activity that day. You sure they stole from our store?"

"Oh, no," I took out Omari's phone and showed her the photo of the receipt. "The thief hits houses. He or she shopped here. See?"

Bell barely glanced at the receipt. "Forgive me for saying this, but we're not that concerned with the ones that pay."

"That was probably the only thing they did not do, Ms. Bell," Aubrey said. "Less than two months after they were here, they stole a car, robbed a house, and killed a young woman."

He must've said the right thing, because she took another look at the receipt. "And what would you like me to do?"

"We would appreciate it if you would check your security footage for the time of the purchase," Aubrey said. "It would be nice to have a photo to show the police."

"I'd love to. Problem is, unless there's something of note on it, we only keep security footage for thirty days," she said.

Figured. Bell got up then, the universal shorthand for "Get out my office. Now."

I started to do just that when Aubrey spoke again. "What made you leave the force?"

I didn't realize she'd been a cop, but once he said it, it made sense. For someone of her height, the career options were usually model, basketball player, or police officer. I couldn't see Mika Bell in a bra — either the push-up or sports variety.

"After I didn't make second detective for the fourth time, I figured my talents were better suited elsewhere," she said. "Plus this pays better."

They smiled at each other, sharing something I didn't or couldn't understand. She gave us a look that said she knew she'd regret what she was going to do next. "Do you know about our return policy? It's the best in the business. We give you six months to return anything in the store, even if it's been opened."

I figured I'd keep that in mind next time I wanted to buy a shirt. I reached out to grab Omari's phone with the photo, but she picked it up, looked at it, and started typing on her computer. "That means that every receipt, including the customer's information, is stored on the system for that length of time just in case there's a return. Your killer is Michael Mapother the IV."

I did not see that one coming. We didn't have a photo, but a name was just as good. I mentally jumped for joy as we thanked Ms. Bell and were on our way. The only thing that stopped me from skipping out the store was I didn't want any weird, judgy-looking strangers ruining my good mood. As soon as we were outside, I even hugged Aubrey. I thought he was wearing a bulletproof vest but realized I was pressing against his abs. Biking did a body good!

I let go and pulled out my cell phone. This was definitely worth sacrificing my minutes. "My friend Emme will have Mr. Mapother's photo, addy, and porn site password before I can spell out his last name."

She picked up on the second ring. "Go."

"I have a name for you. Michael Mapother the IV. Can you do a search?"

She grunted, which meant yes. I could hear her typing. Her fingers stopped but she didn't say anything. "Any hits?" I asked.

"Yeah, 698,131."

Huh? Michael Mapother the IV was not a Jamie Smith. There was no good reason for that name to be so popular on Google.

"Michael Mapother the IV is the real name of Oscar Blue," she said.

Oscar Blue wasn't our killer. He was one of the Rack Pack victims. Fudge.

Sixteen

I made my way to Anna Will's the next day. The drive was pretty quick when you spend it thinking about a murder investigation rather than who you have to eat lunch with. After Aubrey and I ID'd the card as belonging to Oscar Blue, we thought maybe it was his car that Jamie Smith had stolen. But luckily Sienna called Fab, who called his paparazzi contacts. Not only did Oscar Blue not own a Range Rover, he wasn't even in LA on July 1st — much less at T-Mart — which meant I was back at a dead end.

It took me three tries, but I was able to parallel park and find my way to the restaurant. The food at Anna Will's had to be amazing because the decor was as no-frills as you could get. It even had that barebones, black-and-white color scheme like the one you used to find on generic supermarket cans. I arrived at 2:29, but of course Omari beat me there.

He stood up when he saw me and smiled. He hadn't gained four hundred pounds and buckteeth in the forty-eight hours since I'd last seen him, which was unfortunate. He pulled me in for a hug, which I tried not to enjoy too much, and then we sat. We had the place to ourselves.

All I could think was "Control your peanut butter."

I'd been worried about making awkward small talk, but my fretting was for nothing. Our waitress didn't give me a chance to put my foot in my mouth. She shuffled over as soon as my butt hit the hard chair. She was older and looked like she kept a change purse in her bra. Her boobs were big, but then so was the rest of her. Her body type could best be described as fluffy. Her grand-babies probably loved stretching out on her. I know I'd loved to do that with my grandma.

She plopped two waters on the table and smiled like it was her good deed for the day. When she spoke, she had a touch of a Southern accent like most black people born in LA. "Name's Mae. Y'all know what you want?"

I'd barely realized there was even a menu on the table. It was one page and wilted like it had been on the wrong side of a spill.

"We'll need a minute," Omari said.

"Baby, you can take as loooonnnngg as you want," Mae said. "You single, sweetheart?"

My eyes jumped up from my menu to Mae. Not to sound too cliché, but she was looking at Omari like she wished he were on the menu.

He smiled at her. "Trying to hook me up with your daughter?"

"Trying to hook you up with me. Let her find her own man."

"Even better." He looked her dead in the eye and smiled. "As much as it breaks my heart to say this, I'm taken."

He moved his eyes from her to me, and Mae suddenly remembered I existed. "Oh, so this is you right here?" she asked me.

She lifted her right hand up for a high five. It was Omari's turn to be amused as I hesitantly brought my hand up. "I know that's right," she continued.

We slapped palms and she stood nodding at me and smiling, appreciation deep in her eyes.

I moved my eyes back to my menu, trying my best not to start laughing. Just when I thought I couldn't hold it in anymore, Omari spoke up. "We'll both have the chicken special."

"Coming right up, beautiful." Mae shuffled back to where she came from.

I burst out laughing. Omari stared at me, but he was struggling not to smile himself. "Did you really have to give her a high five, though?"

"You don't leave a woman like Mae hanging. She might spit in our food."

"*Your* food. I'm pretty sure I'm in her good graces."

We smiled at each other and it felt like it was supposed to, like I was with a friend again. "Before I forget." I reached into my bag and handed him his cell. He made a big to-do of inspecting it.

"I did take some pictures," I added.

As soon as I said it, he stopped and looked at me. I realized how that could be taken. Oh God. I'd been doing so good, too. "It's for the case." My words were rushed.

"Case? You sound like you're auditioning for *Law & Order*."

"I kinda, sorta started looking into who killed Haley."

"Besides just telling the police about the car we saw?"

"Yeah, that didn't work out so well."

I launched into what had happened, starting with finding Montgomery's car. I paused when Mae returned with food and some more sexual harassment but quickly picked up where I left off as soon as she was gone. I expected Omari to pull a Sienna-and-Emme and tell me that I'd gone mad, but he didn't. He didn't say anything at all. He just listened as he played with his cell phone.

"So then the Range Rover showed up and Aubrey and I —"

"Aubrey?"

"Aubrey S. Adams-Parker."

He smiled, no doubt finding the *S* as amusing as I did. "S. Adams-Parker," he repeated. "And who is that?"

"Former cop. Also looking into Haley's murder. We're now kinda working together."

"You have a partner?" I thought about it. I guess I did. "Who's Cagney and who's Lacey?" Omari asked.

"The prettier one's me," I said. "I have to say Aubrey —"

"S. Adams-Parker."

"Aubrey S. Adams-Parker is growing on me. We pursued a lead yesterday."

"The locker combination?"

"No, T-Mart." I realized what he'd said. "What locker combination?"

He showed me the cell phone photo of the receipt and pointed to the handwritten numbers: *9 31 14.*

I practically snatched the thing out his

224

hand. I'd been so focused on the receipt being from T-Mart that I'd hardly paid attention to what was scribbled on it. "How do you know it's not, like, a zip code?"

"Because I practically live in a gym. And because the guy also bought a Master lock. It's listed on the receipt."

I scanned it. What could only be an abbreviation for Master Lock was midway down, between a pack of Trident and a shower curtain. Did Omari just provide me with another clue? "What uses a lock?" I asked.

"A locker."

"Thanks, you solved the case." I got serious. "I doubt they're keeping stolen goods at LA Fitness. Train station, maybe."

"Or a storage facility."

That one made sense. The robbers needed to keep the stolen stuff somewhere. "Can you use your swag phone to look up the storage facilities in Los Angeles? Maybe I can call them all."

Omari rolled his eyes but did a quick search. "There are 208 listed."

"Or maybe I can't. What about the ones in Los Feliz?" It was a reach, but I had to start somewhere, and that somewhere were the ones closest to Clothes Encounters. I doubted the Rack Pack would want to drive long distances with stolen merchandise in their car.

"Twenty."

"Ten each for us to call," I said.

"Or twenty for you."

I stopped the busboy as he was passing. "Excuse me, can you get Mae? I need to tell her my friend here is single and ready to mingle."

The busboy nodded like he knew what the heck I was talking about while Omari put his hands up in mock surrender. "Ten, you said?"

We divided the numbers. I'd bought another phone card but was only able to afford fifteen minutes. Since it would have to last two more weeks, I needed a hit quick. I dialed the first facility. The bored employee answered on the fourth ring. He obviously didn't know about my phone card situation. "Stor-It-All Self Storage for all your storage needs. This is Devin."

"Hi Devin, I was wondering if you can tell me whether a Jamie Smith has a storage unit there?"

"We aren't allowed to give out that information."

No clue why I thought the honest approach would work. I could hear Omari spinning a long, twisted tale of a husband who believed his cheating hussy of a wife might be stealing furniture in anticipation of divorce proceedings. He could do that. He had unlimited minutes and steady employment. "It's for an investigation," I told Devin.

"Are you the police?" He continued speaking after I hesitated. "I can't give out that information unless you're the police or Jamie Smith."

He hung up before I could say anything further, but that was okay since he did give me an idea. I dialed the next number. "A-1 Self Storage, for all your storage needs."

"Hi, I need to pay my bill."

"What's your unit number?"

"I can never remember."

"Name?"

"Jamie Smith." I held my breath and waited.

"I can't find you under your name. What about a phone number?"

"Wrong place. Sorry."

I quickly hung up, impressed my plan had worked. I dialed three more facilities using the same story, and all three fell for it. I quickly learned two things. First, storage facilities were not creative when it came to their slogans. They all were there to "help with all my storage needs." Second thing I learned was that none of them had a Jamie Smith.

I was getting worried, more about my cell phone minutes than anything else. When I dialed number five, I launched into my spiel before she could even say hello. "Hi, I need to pay my bill and I can't remember my storage number for the life of me. Name's Jamie Smith."

I could hear the clacking. "Unit 8A?"

My eyes must have bugged out because I saw Omari smile. "Oh yes, that's me. I'm such a knucklehead."

"You're paid up until March."

"Okay. Thanks."

I got off the phone with two seconds left until I hit two minutes on my phone card. "It's StorQuest on Sunset," I told Omari.

He immediately threw some cash on the table and got up. "Let's go."

"Thanks, but you don't have to come."

"I know," he said. "Let's go."

I got up. "Okay, but I need to use your phone first."

He handed it over and I dialed Aubrey's number from memory. He picked up on the first ring. "Aubrey S. Adams-Parker."

"Hey. It's me."

"Ms. Anderson."

I walked a few steps away and filled Aubrey in on what we'd discovered. He promised he'd meet us there. When I hung up, Omari was standing by the exit pretending not to notice the two women pretending not to notice him. I handed him back the phone. "Aubrey's meeting us."

"Okay. You ready?"

I was. But first I had to use the bathroom.

As far as storage facilities went, StorQuest was not up there with the fancy-shmancy indoor ones. The place was surrounded by the standard metal fence and required a code to drive onto the lot. Once inside, it looked more like a junkyard. I bet it even had a hungry pit bull named Buster that its security managers let loose at night.

StorQuest's office was actually a double-wide trailer sitting on a block of decaying cement. Aubrey and his bike were waiting when Omari pulled into the lot and parked. He'd gone with a green color scheme under his reflector outfit. I jumped out the car. Omari took his time.

"Ms. Anderson." Aubrey nodded at Omari. "Ms. Anderson's friend."

"Omari Grant . . ." Omari trailed off, expecting something. Something neither of us provided him, because he spoke again as he offered Aubrey his hand to shake. "And you are?"

"Aubrey S. Adams-Parker, pleased to meet you. Do you mind if I speak with Ms. Anderson in private?"

Aubrey took me gently by the elbow and led me a few feet away. His hand rested there while we spoke. "I should speak to an employee to learn whether he or she encountered one of the killers. You said it was 8A, correct?"

"And what should I do?" I asked.

"You should stay outside."

I immediately saw red. "Are you really still on that 'leave the investigation to the professionals' BS? I thought we had an understanding!"

Aubrey sighed, as if mentally preparing for another of my freak-outs. "Ms. Anderson, I simply do not want the employee to know that we are associates. If I do not get the information I need, we can send you in using a different method."

Oh, in that case. "I'll be with Omari." I smiled innocently.

I watched him walk away, then joined Omari in his car. "He's going to take this one," I said.

Omari just nodded, staring at Aubrey as he made his way inside. After a moment, he finally spoke. "So Aubrey's a dude."

"Of course. Wait, you thought he was a girl?"

"Aubrey S. Adams hyphen Parker? Now why would I think he was female?"

He had a point. "His middle name is Steven."

"If I'd known that, I probably wouldn't have thought he was a girl."

"If he were here, he'd go into a spiel about gender neutrality."

"Good thing he's not here." We both stared at the double-wide in that comfortable silence that only comes when you're around people you've known forever and a day. It was nice. Omari finally spoke. "You must talk a lot to know his middle name. And his number."

"You mean, by heart?" I used my pointer finger to draw a heart on my chest, then started laughing. I cracked myself up sometimes.

"And what's with his bike?"

"I never asked. He probably cares about the environment or something like that. He bikes everywhere. His abs are like steel, though. You gotta feel them."

"I'll pass." Omari finally looked away from the office. "Why are we here and not over there?" He motioned to the rows upon rows of storage.

"You need the code to drive in," I said.

"Or we can walk."

He pointed to the left of the car entrance. There was a small door to allow the young and carless to get to their stuff, too. I was glad they were concerned with transportation equality. "It's probably locked," I said.

"Let's find out."

I watched him get out the car, casually walk across the driveway, open the door, and walk in. I waited for sirens to go off or Buster the world's hungriest pit bull to charge him. When neither happened, I took that as a sign I should join him.

I quickly glanced at the office. Aubrey would kill me if he knew what I was doing. Neither Aubrey nor the employee was paying me any attention. I took that as another sign and got out the car. I booked it across the driveway and scurried through the door. It took me five minutes to find 8A.

Omari was standing in front of it. We stood there a minute and stared. "You should open it," Omari said.

"So I can be the one who gets arrested?"

"Because I have a crappy memory and left my old cell in the car. Don't act like you don't remember the numbers, Rain Man."

He was right. I did. I took a breath, then grabbed the lock. I was so nervous it took a couple of tries to hit the exact numbers. I finally did and slid the lock off. Omari pulled the door open.

I don't know what I was expecting to find inside. Maybe a note saying "Hi, our names are X,Y, and Z and we stole everything in here." What we did find was stuff. Lots and lots of stuff. And there, on the ground in the front of the unit as if it had accidentally been dropped, was Emme's necklace.

SEVENTEEN

To be clear, it wasn't Emme's necklace. It belonged to her sister, Toni. There were only two of those necklaces in the world and they were unmistakable. "WTF?!" Emme said.

For the first time in the three years I'd known her, I had her full attention. She'd even taken off the headset I would've bet money was surgically attached to her head. She held Toni's necklace, staring at it, while playing with its twin around her neck.

On impulse, Omari and I had reclaimed the necklace, wiped my prints off the lock, and hauled butt straight to Emme's place. We'd spent a good ten minutes detailing how Toni's necklace had gotten into our possession. This was the first time Emme had spoken. "What was it doing there?"

I hadn't the slightest clue. It shouldn't have been there. It should have been around Toni's neck, in whatever exotic location she was shooting. "She would have mentioned if she'd been hit by the Rack Pack," Emme said.

"Maybe she doesn't know," I said. "She's been in Antarctica since the *SVU* finale."

Toni was a fellow *Law & Order* addict. I remembered talking with her about the finale back in May when she'd stopped by Emme's on her way to start filming her latest movie.

Emme grabbed her phone and dialed Toni. It rang four times before the automated voicemail greeting kicked in. Emme hung up and redialed as she spoke. "She has an alarm. Security cameras. Gates. A guard who drives around in a stupid golf cart. She couldn't have been robbed, Day."

Omari and I shared a look. I made sure to keep my voice as gentle as possible when I answered her. "The necklace says otherwise. Em, I'm sorry, but Toni was hit by the Rack Pack. We just need to figure out when."

"We could if she'd answer the freaking phone." I thought Emme was going to fling her cell across the room. Instead, she just hung up when she got voicemail once again and immediately hit redial.

I lost track of how many times she dialed, but it would have put a crazed fan voting for their favorite singing competition contestant to shame. After the kabillionth time, someone picked up. "She's sleeping!"

It was an assistant. Toni went through them like toilet paper. Half of Los Angeles probably had signed confidentiality agreements saying they'd never discuss their time working with Toni Abrams. From the tone of the voice, this one wouldn't last either.

"Wake her up," Emme said.

"She had a late call last night," the assistant said. "She needs her sleep."

"It's an emergency."

"Regarding?"

The silence was long enough to indicate a standoff. Emme had no plans to tell the assistant what was going on and the assistant had no plans to wake Toni up until she knew. Just when I thought we'd have to call in the United Nations, Emme spoke. "Does Toni know you answer her phone?"

"I'm just doing my job."

"No. That would be getting coffee and packing suitcases."

There was a pause then, and it was a full thirty seconds before anyone spoke again. "I'll tell her you called," the assistant finally said.

Yeah, right.

"Can you at least give me Ben's private line?" Emme asked.

But the assistant had already hung up. Ben

was Toni's take-no-prisoners manager. About the only thing he didn't do for her was brush her teeth, and based on my encounters with him, he would if she asked.

Emme threw her phone down and grabbed her wallet. "I'm going to Toni's."

Omari and I looked at each other again, then scrambled up. "I'll drive," he said.

The ride over felt like forever, especially since it was dark out by then. I rode shotgun, while Emme sat behind Omari and continued to call Toni. The assistant was smart enough not to pick up again.

Toni lived in the hills. Technically, the Hollywood Hills separates Los Angeles proper from the Valley. In reality, it separates the haves from the have-nots. Celebrities and the people with enough money and power to make them famous like to buy houses built on the side of a mountain. It affords them a grand view of Los Angeles, literally letting them look down on the little people.

The closer we got, the more butterflies entered my stomach. Toni lived in a gated community with the aforementioned golf-cart-driving security guard and his pal who manned the entry gate. Just like everything else in Hollywood, you only got in if you knew someone and were on the list. We weren't.

"How are we gonna get in?" I asked. "Even if we get past the guard, we still need a key."

"Getting in is obviously not a problem," Omari said as he pulled up to the gate.

I threw him a look. He caught it and lodged one back to me.

"Too. Soon," I whispered. Now was not the time to be making jokes about Toni's security or lack thereof.

"Maybe, but I do have a point." He did, but still.

Emme spoke from the seat behind him. "I have a key."

Great! Hopefully we'd be able to finagle our way past the guard so we could use it. From the looks of him, he wouldn't make it easy. He was too young and too fat to have once been a cop. And judging by how precisely his stretched-to-the-limits shirt was tucked into his pants, he took his job way too seriously. Toni probably hadn't been robbed on his watch.

Omari rolled down his tinted window as the guard approached. He seemed cautious, like he knew we didn't belong. And we didn't. Omari was now technically famous, but he was "first-season, semi-hit television show on broadcast TV" famous. Up here, he may as well have been begging on the side of the road.

"Hi, folks, this is restricted property." The guard didn't even bother to bend down. Omari stuck his head out the window to talk to him.

"We know," Omari said. "We're going to Toni Abrams' house."

"You on the list?"

"No, but we're good friends of hers." Honesty was not the approach I'd have gone for, but maybe it would work.

"Even good friends need to be on the list." Or maybe not.

From her perch in the backseat, Emme rolled down her window. I could only see the guard's big belly, but I could tell his whole demeanor changed when he saw her. It didn't quite shake like a bowl full of jelly, but it came close. "Ms. Abrams! I didn't know you were back there. I'm so sorry. Let me get the gate for you."

He rushed back to his itty-bitty guard house to open the gate for us. "You three have a great day," he called out as he waved goodbye.

We were already gunning it through the gates. The best part? Emme never said a word.

Toni's house was at the tippy-top of the

neighborhood. The road was so steep, it felt like heading up the world's scariest roller coaster. It made where Aubrey lived look like a mole hill. We survived the initial ascent and parked in her driveway.

The house looked small. But like everything else out here, what you see isn't always what you get. The place had to be at least 5,000 square feet, most of which clung for dear life to the hillside. From the front, however, the most impressive thing about it was the security lights spaced out every few feet. This was the only spotlight you didn't want to be in around here. Toni had so many lights because she didn't have room for a gate.

Emme was out the car before Omari could even put the thing in park. We scrambled to catch up, but she was already pushing the front door open when we got there. We were greeted by silence. There was none of that familiar beeping that signaled an alarm.

"WTF?" Emme stormed in and checked the alarm panel a few feet from the door. Sure enough, it said *unarmed.* "Idiot."

"You think it's been unarmed since she's been gone?" I asked.

Emme threw me a look that said I, too, was an idiot.

I looked around, expecting to see the

house in disarray. There were two rooms off the foyer: a library and what Toni called the media room. Both looked dusty but otherwise untouched. The thieves had even left the television.

Omari and I followed Emme like she was the Pied Piper. Instead of music, we were led by her thoughts regarding her sister, her sister's assistant, and mankind as a whole. Her words were few but they were choice. If this were a movie, we'd get an NC-17 rating based on her rant alone. We wouldn't even need a peek of boob.

We got to the back, where Toni had her main living area that served as both dining and living room. The space was huge, featuring floor-to-ceiling windows with sliding glass doors that opened onto a clear deck. When you stood on it, you could look down and see her pool below. It had always freaked me out, especially if I was drunk.

Emme went to turn on the chandelier, only to find the switch already in the On position. It must've burned out. She opted for a nearby table lamp. It clicked on, illuminating everything in its path.

Like the front of the house, this room also looked untouched. The press reports weren't lying. The Rack Pack was neater than most housekeepers. I finally ventured to speak.

"You said she has video cameras?"

"Really expensive ones, like you find on cruise ships. They're motion-activated so it only films if someone's there."

"Does it keep everything?" I asked.

"IDK."

"One way to find out," Omari said.

Just when I didn't think it was possible, I managed to get even more excited.

The main living area was in the back center of the house. To the left, nestled behind the three-car garage, was Toni's master suite and personal office. We went in that direction. The office was done in various shades of white. Toni had even managed to find a snow-white desktop computer. Emme booted it up.

As we waited, my phone rang. "That your boyfriend?" Omari asked.

If he meant Aubrey, he was right. We'd left the storage place without saying goodbye. I knew Aubrey wouldn't approve of my stealing, even if it was from thieves. I was too excited to listen to a lecture. I hit ignore and watched Emme open the surveillance program. This was the equivalent of Christmas morning and Santa was bringing me exactly what I'd asked for: a murderer.

Several files were listed, the last one dated August 16th. "That's not right," I said.

"That's only two days before Haley died. Way too soon. The Rack Pack waits at least a month between robberies. Look for something older."

Instead, Emme just opened the file. The video was black and white and as fuzzy as an old stuffed animal, but we could make out what was going on. I immediately recognized the deck. It was night, but thanks to the high-beam spotlights, it might as well have been high noon.

She strode into frame. Yes, she. The face was covered by a hoodie, but it was most definitely female. A rail-thin one at that.

I was surprised. I was expecting someone big, bad, and, well, male. Not this itty-bitty thing making her way toward the sliding doors off Toni's main room. The three of us stared at the computer screen, entranced. "We should call the police," Omari finally said.

I flashed back to the car chase and how the Range Rover had become off-limits as soon as those a-hole patrolmen arrived. No way, José. Luckily, Emme nixed that idea first. "Ben'll take care of it."

That settled, I refocused on the computer. Even without the hoodie, the camera distance made it impossible to make out any features. The intruder was about three feet from the door when she stopped. It looked like her mouth moved, but I couldn't hear anything. In fact, I didn't hear anything at all. "What's she saying?"

"IDK," Emme said. "No sound."

Blurg. I should've known I wasn't that lucky. The person continued to talk sound-less words when an object flew past the camera. "What. The. Heck. Was. That?" I asked as another object missed the camera by mere inches.

"One of her cohorts is trying to take out the spotlight," Omari said. He was right.

As if on cue, a second image popped up from the other camera in the area, this one aimed right at Toni's sliding glass door. We watched the two pieces of footage in tandem as the rock traveled from one camera's area to the other's. After the fourth try, the rock hit its target. Both cameras went black. "We lose the stream?" I asked.

"It's still on," Emme said. "She's there."

"You mean, they," Omari said.

He was right. Without the spotlight, we couldn't make out much more than figures, but there were definitely two of them. *Just* two of them. "What happened to the Pack?" I asked.

We couldn't even tell if the second person was a man or a woman. It was too dark. I found it hard to believe that these two shadowed stick figures had robbed over a half million dollars' worth of stuff. They walked up to the sliding glass door. "They're deciding the best way to get in," I said.

"They'll probably take out a glass cutter and cut a hole in the door," Omari said.

"Or better yet, use one of those long ruler-looking things and jimmy the lock," I said.

That was a thief staple. At least it was on television. I was more than ready to find out if it was true in real life as well. We watched as one of them reached for the handle. A second later, the door slid open. After all that, it turned out it was unlocked. "Well, that was anticlimactic," Omari said.

Who was he telling? "My sister has to be the dumbest person on the planet," Emme said.

A light turned on in the window to the left of the door. The aforementioned chandelier. I spoke up, all excited-like. "Shouldn't it switch to the inside cameras?" I was more than ready to put faces to the shadows. My heart increased in speed. I was close. So very close.

"No," Emme said. I must've looked dumbfounded, because she clarified the obvious. "No cameras inside."

"That's stupid!" It slipped out of my

mouth before I even thought about it.

"My sister's not stupid," Emme said, although she'd spent the last fifteen minutes stating otherwise. I'd forgotten Emme was the only person allowed to say a bad word about Toni. "She had that incident a couple of years ago when someone tried to sell that video of her getting undressed," she continued. "She had all the cameras removed after that."

"Well, that make sense," I said. It didn't, but I didn't dare admit how disappointed I was.

We sat in silence watching the black screen. When it was clear they weren't coming out anytime soon, Emme hit fast-forward. A sped-up forty-five minutes later, the back door once again slid open. A lone figure came out, dropped what looked like a bag, then turned around and stormed back inside. A few minutes later, the two of them returned to drop off another bag.

The bags had to belong to Toni since they hadn't had them when they came in. Geez. It really took balls to steal someone's stuff using their own carry-ons.

They stood there. Then there was shuffling. In the dark, it looked like two angry shadow puppets. It took me a second to realize what was going on. "They're fighting."

The argument escalated, the figures moving quickly. A shoving match. Someone got off a particularly good push and his or her cohort fell, landing smack-dab into the patch of light coming from the room. It was the one in the hoodie.

We could finally see her clearly, but since she was looking down, the hoodie covered most of her face. "Look up, just look up."

I doubted Omari even realized he was talking out loud. He was reading my mind, though. If I could just see her face, I could give a positive ID to the cops.

She moved, causing her hoodie to fall back slightly, teasing us with a quick glimpse of a nose. But that's all we saw. The hoodie stopped its descent before we could see any other identifiable features north of said nose. I held my breath.

"Just look up."

From below the hoodie, I could see the woman's lips moving. Judging by the speed, she was pissed. She struggled to get up, resulting in her hood inching another centimeter back.

"Lookuplookuplookup," Omari said.

She finally stood, slapping her hands together in an angry attempt to rid them of dust and gravel. She flung her hair out her face, taking the hoodie down in the process.

I had never been so happy to see hair before in my life.

"Looook up, look —" Omari stopped abruptly because he'd finally gotten his wish. She looked up.

Emme immediately hit pause so we could have a clear image of her face.

It was Haley.

EIGHTEEN

I was too shocked to speak, though a million thoughts were racing through my brain. "Who is that?" Omari asked. "Not Haley?"

Yes, Haley. Haley with the boyfriend problems. Haley who gave her friends good advice. Haley with the great life motto. You were supposed to control your peanut butter, not steal it. I felt like someone had kicked me in the gut, snatched out my hair, said my mama was easy, and then revealed there was no Santa Claus. "You okay?" someone asked. It might have been Omari. I was too busy drowning in a sea of surprise to tell.

"Yes." No. "Keep going." I motioned to the video.

Emme hit play and Haley looked directly at the camera, as if realizing it had caught her. She jumped up, her arms disappearing into the inky blackness where they must have latched onto her shadowed accomplice.

The person didn't join her in the spotlight despite Haley trying her utmost. When her arms came back into the light, all she was holding was a baseball cap. The shadow figure ran away. Haley threw the hat down and chased after her elusive partner.

Video from another camera popped up. The first figure ran by, bags bouncing at his or her side. A second later, Haley followed him or her. Emme fast-forwarded, but it was the last we saw of either of them.

"What did I just watch?" I asked, still in disbelief.

"Motive for a murder," Omari said. "Your girl and her partner were robbing rich people's houses and had a big falling-out. Literally."

He was right. I thought out loud. "The car used in Kandy Wrapper's robbery was the one that killed Haley. And it seems like there's only two robbers. One was Haley. So if Haley wasn't driving the car, her partner was." Then it hit me how I'd been right all along. "It wasn't an accident. She was murdered, just like I thought."

"By who, though?" It was the first time Emme had spoken, and it was a valid question.

I glanced back at the now blank screen. "The hat," I said. "Neither of them came

back, so the hat's probably still outside."

Omari was already heading to the door before I could finish speaking. Emme and I fell in line behind him. We ran to the living room and opened the door to the glass deck. It was still unlocked. We stepped outside, almost exactly where Haley had fallen. I looked a few feet to the left, saw the hat immediately, and went to pick it up.

"Don't touch it. There might be prints!" Omari said.

He had a point. I did as requested. Instead, we all stared at it, revolted, as if it were a decaying animal carcass. It was maroon with the letters *S* and *C* intertwined in gold letters, the logo for the University of Southern California.

"I need to call Ben," Emme said. "His number must be in there somewhere."

She made her way inside, glancing back at the hat every few seconds like it might get up and walk away. Omari and I must've felt similarly. We stood as if guarding the President of the United States. We were like that for minutes until Omari finally spoke. "Whose is it?"

I thought I knew. "Her BFF, Marina. She did everything with Haley and doesn't seem to own an item without the USC logo printed on it."

"Makes sense. I doubt your girl just walked up to someone on the street and said, 'Hey, let's go rob some rich people.' She would choose someone she trusted. A friend."

"Or what *was* a friend," I said, thinking back to the fight.

I liked Marina. I couldn't picture her coming to blows any more than I could picture her running down her best friend in cold blood. But then again, a few minutes earlier I couldn't picture Haley masterminding a string of celebrity home invasions. So what did I know?

"She have an alibi?" he asked.

"Don't know, but I'm gonna find out."

If this were some cheesy TV show, the screen would have cut to black so the network could spend the next five minutes trying to get you to buy toothpaste you already bought anyway. It wasn't. Instead, Emme came back. "Ben's calling the police. They won't use their sirens."

Two hours later, Emme and I were back at her place. Omari had dropped us off and regretfully gone home. He had an early call in the morning. True to his word, Ben had had the cops show up in an unmarked car. As impossible as it seemed with the Rack

Pack being the talk of the town and all, the robbery would not be making the papers. Only someone with Toni's standing could pull that off. It wouldn't be the first time.

It was after midnight, but I'd left a message with the tip line about Haley being one half of the Rack Pack and Marina being her accomplice/possible murderer, to cover my bases. Aubrey had called me two more times and was greeted by voicemail on both occasions. I wasn't avoiding him as much as not wanting to talk to him at that *exact* moment. Yes, I had new information, but it wasn't like I'd seen the killer. I figured I could wait at least a day to call him back.

While I was avoiding calls, Emme had finally spoken with Toni. Of course, her assistant hadn't given her the earlier message. Toni was more concerned about sentimental things being taken — like the necklace — than the free shoes and handbags she'd gotten from random designers. She wasn't concerned enough to come back home, but she did make Emme promise to personally go through the house and find out exactly what was missing.

I'd told Emme I suspected Marina was Haley's accomplice and wanted to investigate. For once, she didn't object. Instead, she offered to help. Now that it was personal, I was no longer dumb for putting my life in danger by confronting a killer. I should've been mad, but in actuality I was happy for the help. I needed as much background on Marina as possible. No one was better at that than Emme.

She wasted no time getting started. "Let's have some fun," she said.

Only Emme would define fun as cyber-stalking someone. Unfortunately, Marina didn't come up in a search of the LAPD's records. A background check also proved uneventful. Worse than that, she barely used her Facebook account.

So Emme delved deeper, even hacking into Marina's bank account. Yes, it was illegal, but at least Emme was using her powers for good. She found Marina's email address and tried to log into every bank website using the email and 1234 as the password. She finally got a hit on Wells Fargo's site. It recognized the email address, but of course the password was wrong.

Emme took care of that in mere seconds, and we were logged into Marina's account. "Her balance is $6,234?" I asked.

"And thirty-four cents."

"How does a nineteen-year-old paying private school tuition and making minimum wage have that much money in her account?"

"Especially since four months ago her balance was six dollars."

Any lingering doubts I had about Marina's possible guilt went vamoose. I'd found my murderer. I just needed to prove it.

The only thing that stopped me from going to Clothes Encounters first thing the next morning was I didn't know what to say to Marina. So I did what I normally did in these situations — talk to Sienna about it. Since I'd gotten home from Emme's place after Sienna left for the club, I had to wait until the morning to give her an update. She was as shocked as I'd been. "So what should I say?" I asked.

"I know what you shouldn't say. 'Did you steal from famous people and then run down your best friend with a stolen BMW?'"

"Figured that was a bit too on the nose, as the screenwriters say," I said.

Her eyes lit up. "Looking at it like a screenplay is actually a good idea. What do you want to get out of the scene?"

The last time I'd heard someone say that had been in acting class. This was way more fun. "To get Marina to go straight to the police station and say, 'I confess, now give Dayna Anderson her $15,000 reward.' "

"That doesn't even happen in the movies. You need to trick her into revealing something that'll prove she did it. Let's brainstorm." Sienna got a pen and paper. "The most obvious way is to find out where she was the night Haley died. Was she with Haley?"

"She wouldn't tell us if she was. I might be able to trick her into admitting something about one of the robberies."

"Like Toni's necklace!" Sienna said. "Far as she knows, the necklace is still safe and sound in storage, right?"

"Yep. Maybe I can ask her if anyone is selling something similar. Say I want it as a gift."

"Perfect! And what about her bank account?"

It was a full minute before inspiration hit. "I'll casually bring up all my student loan debt. Ask her how she's paying for hers."

"Sounds like a plan," she said.

That was easy. I went to grab my purse to go. About halfway to the door, I realized Sienna wasn't behind me. "Aren't you coming?" Her look said it all. "Oh. Montgomery."

"We're having a meeting, but we'll be

done by two at the latest if you want to wait that long."

I didn't. I was instantly annoyed. "Have fun. I'll just go to meet a possible murderer on my own."

"I could cancel."

She may have said it, but she didn't mean it. It was like when you're on a date with a dude and you pretend to reach for your purse to pay knowing darn well he'll stop you. Except I was going to make her pay. "Okay."

I looked her dead in the eye. For the first time ever, I won a staring contest. "Are you sure you can't wait until after my meeting?" she finally asked.

"I'll be fine." I headed to the door.

"Text me," she called out after me. "You need to be careful if she killed her friend."

I answered by slamming the door.

I seethed the entire trip to Clothes Encounters. That Montgomery guy was getting on my last nerve. I knew I was being a selfish baby, but like most selfish babies, I didn't give a crap. The good thing was that by the time I got to Marina, any possible fear I may have had was replaced by anger with a pinch of jealousy mixed in, and I did my best when I was 85 percent mad and 15 percent jealous.

I marched into Clothes Encounters with purpose. Nat and Marina were standing by the counter. Both glanced in my direction when I walked in. Marina seemed happy to see me. She was all braces-adorned smiles. "Hey, Dayna!"

Nat, however, looked like she was afraid I would try to peer pressure her again. "Betty's not back yet." She sounded like I'd tried to force her to jump off a bridge, not give me one little name. Geez.

"I know. I'm here to shop." I focused on Marina. "Where are your necklaces?"

Turned out they were in the other room. Way in the back. Marina accompanied me over. I would have preferred staying near the window, where any pedestrians strolling by would notice if Marina suddenly decided to become a serial killer. I had enough problems; I didn't need to add being dead to that growing pile.

Since I didn't have a choice in the matter, I took the risk. As we walked, I thought of the checklist Sienna and I had come up with: (1) Find out if she knows anything about the necklace. (2) See if she has any details about the other robberies. (3) Ask where she gets money for school. (4) Confirm she has no alibi for the night Haley died. "I'm looking for something simple," I said. "Silver, not gold. A solitaire diamond if possible."

"Sounds like something I've seen recently."

Check one off the list.

We looked at the display. Not surprisingly, no such necklace was there. "Okay, maybe we sold it," Marina said. "I'm sorry. I'll definitely keep my eye out for anything similar."

I followed her back to the main room, relieved to be with Nat and the other customers. Safety in numbers and all that. "Have a good weekend?" Marina asked, by way of small talk.

Sensing an opportunity, I threw myself at it like a groupie at a ball player. "I was at Toni's. Her place is amazing."

"I bet," Marina said. "The view alone." She knew where Toni lived. Check. "Just staring at the beach and the sunset every day."

Beach? Sunset? "Where do you think she lives?" I asked as I pretended to look at clothes. I didn't want to leave just yet so I needed a stalling tactic.

"I thought someone told me Toni Abrams lives in Malibu." Marina turned to Nat, celeb-whore extraordinaire, for confirmation.

Nat looked startled by the random question, then realized what we were talking about. "Don't they all? Either there or the Hills."

She might have elaborated, but a customer had a question. Nat walked off to help her while I mentally erased the check mark and moved on to the next item on my list. "What about you?" I asked. "What did you do this weekend?"

"Worked."

"It must be hard to juggle school and work. I have so many student loans, Navient is going to be sending statements to my grave. Hope you're not in the same boat."

"I was, but then I got some money from a relative. Not a lot, but it helped this semester."

Nice try but something didn't make sense. "So why are you still working here?"

"I actually quit," she said. "I only came back after Haley died. Betty needed help, and I already knew the store . . ."

"That was sweet of you. I'm impressed you're balancing it all. I wouldn't be able to if my best friend passed away. I wouldn't even leave the house."

"I don't. Well, besides school and work," she said. "Haven't really felt up to going out. I just dread the idea of going to the spots we always went to and Haley not being there."

I felt bad for her and had to remind myself that I was talking to a possible killer. I flashed on the checklist again. "You guys at least get a chance to hang out before she died?"

Marina shook her head. "I didn't see her. She was supposed to hang out with Victory that night, but they were fighting as usual, so I don't know if they did."

"So you stayed at home?" No alibi. My mental pen was poised over my mental checklist, just a waiting.

"I went to a friend's birthday party. A former coworker from here, actually. I kinda drank too much and sort of passed out on her couch." She looked embarrassed as she said it.

Fudge. Marina had an alibi. "What'd you get her?"

Marina looked at me, confused, so I elaborated. "For her birthday. What'd you get this coworker?"

"Allie. I just picked her up something from here."

I nodded. I didn't know what to do at that point, so I made some lame excuse and left. As soon as my heel hit the sidewalk, I had my phone out and was texting Emme. *Ma-*

rina not looking good. Money came from rela-
tive & at bday party when Haley died. Friend
named Allie. I was hitting send when I
walked straight into what I thought was a
short brick wall. "Ms. Anderson," it said.

I looked up to find Aubrey staring at me.
"Hey, Aubrey!!!" I was a bit too enthusiastic,
but I was going for the offensive.

"I have been telephoning you, Ms. Anderson." His voice was even more formal than
usual. If this was his bad cop voice, he probably got plenty of confessions.

"And I've been meaning to call you back.
Any leads from the storage unit?"

"Unfortunately, it was a dead end. If you
had called me back, I would have told you
that. I had some additional news for you as
well."

"Me too!"

He said nothing, then. I intended to wait
him out, but I was never one for silences. I
was speaking again in less than half a
minute. "So you want me to go first or
should we rock, paper, scissors it?"

"The police arrested Haley Joseph's boyfriend."

NINETEEN

Victory had been arrested for Haley's murder? Wave bye-bye to my reward. I had a vision of my mother getting dragged by police out of her house past a big fat foreclosure sign. They didn't even give her a chance to put on her wig.

"He was arrested for stealing a car on Thursday," Aubrey said. I was instantly relieved. "He was on Martin Street."

It took me a minute to register what he was saying. That was when and where we had our car chase. Victory was probably driving the Range Rover, which meant there actually was a good chance he killed Haley. The cops obviously hadn't connected these dots — that the driver of the Range Rover was also probably the same person using Clothes Encounters to sell stolen goods. I could still be the one to let them know. My brain removed the foreclosure sign from the front yard and placed the wig back on my mother's head.

"Mr. Malone has a history of alleged car theft, dating back to his days as a juvenile offender in Sherman Oaks," Aubrey said. "He also has a history of his parents making sure he was never convicted — until now. They refused to bail him out and bring him home. He has spent the last three days in the county jail."

I was way more comfortable with the idea of Victory killing Haley than Marina killing her. Not that I was comfortable with murder, but still. Even without the rap sheet, I could see Victory being Haley's Rack Pack partner. From what I could recall, he had the same physical characteristics of the person in Toni's surveillance video.

The more I thought about it, the dumber I felt for not thinking of him first. "It makes sense," I said, causing Aubrey to look at me strange.

I remembered that he, like everyone else, wasn't a mind reader. Given my frequent not-so-nice thoughts about him, this was probably a good thing. I launched into what I'd been up to since the storage locker, making it seem like Toni just so happened to realize she'd been robbed. "The killer left a USC cap. I'd thought it was Haley's best friend, Marina, but it seems like it belongs to Victory."

"We can ask Mr. Malone tomorrow when he finally is released."

I liked the sound of that. "What time do you want me to pick you up?"

Sienna met me at the door when I got home. We spoke at the same time. "Good news," she said.

"I got great news." I laughed. "Jinx. You first."

She was happy to oblige. "Montgomery's going to talk to some of his contacts at a few networks about me doing a reality show."

"That's great!"

And unrealistic to think it would actually make it on air. That wasn't a knock against Sienna as much as it was against Hollywood. Talking to a network executive did not a reality show make. I hoped she was the one in a kajillion who did make it. She deserved it. "I'll keep my fingers crossed!"

"Thanks! What about you?"

"Marina has an alibi. But Aubrey found out Victory was arrested stealing a car a few blocks from our car chase. I figure he took it after abandoning the stolen Range Rover. We're gonna talk to him tomorrow."

"Nice! I was telling Montgomery this

morning that I hoped this would be over soon so you'd stop running around investigating."

Running around investigating? I was tempted to point out that she'd been right along with me. But since I didn't want to fight, I changed the subject. "It's Blind Item Day!"

Blind Item Day was when Anani Miss shared a tidbit about a celebrity so juicy she couldn't use actual names. Luckily, she made sure to pepper enough clues into her wording to help readers guess who it could be. Sienna and I had made a game out of it. She'd read. I'd throw out names, and she'd supplement the blind item with info from her own sources. Needless to say, it was my favorite day of the week. And in all the hubbub of "running around investigating," I'd completely forgotten about it.

"Already got the site open," she said. "Ready?"

I was, so she began reading as I listened like a four-year-old during story hour. "Thanks to an oh-so-fine body . . ."

"Oscar Blue!"

"And actual acting skills . . ."

"Not Oscar Blue." Beautiful man, but couldn't act his way out of a paper bag. Even the biodegradable, reusable ones he

loved so much.

"This star of one of the fall's hottest new shows has already climbed from obscurity to near TV's A-list faster than a ride on a bullet train." That kind of sounded like Omari, but it couldn't be. "The only thing needed for him to cross that fine line to the next level of the Hollywood caste system is having the right lady on his arm."

That was the second mention of the word *fine*. Omari's character on *LAPD 90036* was Jamal Fine. I hoped it was a coincidence, not a clue. Sienna continued on. "And it looks like Mr. Bullet Train finally found her, the Liz to his Dick. The Beyoncé to his Jay-Z. The Miss Piggy to his Kermit. I'm not talking reality A, or even TV A. Not to put too fine a point on things, but I'm talking valedictorian-of-the-class A-list."

Another *fine*. No. No. No. Oblivious to my impending panic attack, Sienna kept going. "Things are getting pretty steamy pretty quickly. Our spies spotted our Bullet Train and his Lady Love arriving at said diva's house, where they weren't seen for *hours*. Maybe next time we'll see them in the 90036 . . ."

Sienna's voice trailed off as she realized what she was saying. I almost choked . . . on air. The 90036? That wasn't a clue as much as a blinking bright pink neon sign alerting us that Omari Grant was getting some.

Sienna looked at me like I might run to the window and jump. I was tempted. "There are, like, four guys on that show." She didn't sound like she even believed what she was saying. "It could be any of them, but definitely not Omari."

How I wanted to believe her. "Have you heard anything about him dating anyone?"

"Nope. And you know I would, since everyone knows we know him."

"Because you would have told me . . ." It was more question than statement.

Sensing my hesitation, she switched tactics. "And even if it was about him, it would be BS. The *spy* was his publicist. Didn't you say she was a bit overzealous?" I did indeed say that. "I'm just surprised Anani fell for it."

Maybe Sienna was right. I started to feel better, but still. "Can you ask around?"

"Will do when I go out tonight."

The doorbell rang. Sienna looked relieved. She started to hand me the laptop but thought better of it. Maybe she assumed I would use it to bash my head in. She carried it with her to the front door. A few moments later, she and the laptop returned with Montgomery in tow.

"Hey, you," he said, then he turned to Sienna. "Sorry for dropping by out of the blue, but I always like to share good news in person. I heard back from Oxygen already. They're interested."

That got my mind off Omari real quick. Sienna practically did a double back handspring. "So we're gonna have a meeting? When? What should I wear? I need to go shopping!"

"Calm down," he said, laughing as he did so. "You'll have a meeting. Eventually. They want a sizzle reel first. I'll film you, put together some footage, and send it to them. And if they like it . . ."

"I'll have my own show. On Oxygen! I already have the name: *Lady in Red!*"

She looked at me all excited-like. "Congrats!" I said.

I was happy for her. I admired people like Sienna who kept trying and trying year after year after year to break into Hollywood. I, on the other hand, was a bit too pragmatic to follow the long, winding, twisting boulevard of dreams that ultimately lead to a dead end. It was why I'd retired and why I wouldn't be in her reality show when she undoubtedly asked me to. I just hoped she wouldn't get too mad.

My phone buzzed, signaling I had a text. It had to be Emme. Bill collectors weren't allowed to text. I knew because I'd looked it up. I grabbed my cell and headed to my bloset. As I disappeared inside, I heard Montgomery talking about me. "What's up with her?"

Closing the door before I could hear her answer, I checked my texts. Emme had sent me a message saying to check my email. I pulled out my tablet and found a Facebook link waiting in my inbox. I clicked on it. A photo album called *Allie's Legal!!!!!!!!!!!!!!!!!!!!!!!!!!!!!!!!* came up. There were almost as many pages of photos as there were exclamation points. Emme had found Allie's birthday party, thereby proving Marina's alibi.

I scanned photo after photo of people smiling in clusters of twos and threes. Interspersed was the occasional shot of food and lots and lots of alcohol. I couldn't blame Allie. The girl was turning twenty-one, after all.

I was surprised to see quite a few pictures of Nat, but since Allie had worked at Clothes Encounters, it made sense Nat would be there. And be there she was. Nat sure loved the camera, and she dressed way better than she did at work. She posed in every photo, even kicking her leg up so we'd get the full effect of stilettos. Like every other woman in LA, she was rocking Pink Panthers.

I went through each picture, then checked them all again. Something was missing. Or should I say someone. I texted Emme. *Where are the photos of Marina?*

Emme hit me back almost instantly. *There are none.*

Doesn't mean she wasn't at the party. Camera shy?

Another lightning-quick response. *Camera shy people don't move to LA.*

The girl had a point. *Thanks.*

NP.

I dialed Aubrey to tell him the news. He didn't answer, so I left a message and went to bed.

The next morning, I saw red. Literally. I woke up ten minutes before my alarm to find Sienna hovering over me in yesterday's clothes. She held her tablet about two inches from my face. "I need a new paint color. What do you like better? Cherry Tomato." She pointed at a deep red paint, then swiped the tablet, revealing another swatch of deep red. "Or Carriage Door. I can't decide."

"Carriage Door." They looked exactly the

same but Carriage Door was a much cooler name.

"I was leaning toward that one! I really like the undertones of blue."

"Exactly. So you're painting?"

"And getting new furniture! My couch should be here this afternoon." She swiped her tablet again. A furry red couch popped up. It looked like someone had skinned Elmo. "I'm redoing the entire apartment."

I was almost too afraid to ask. "In red?"

"Of course," she said, already walking out the door. "I want to be prepared in case my show gets picked up. I've got to order this paint. You're on your own for breakfast."

"Not even red eggs and ham?"

But she was gone. I forced myself out of bed. I had a busy day. After Aubrey and I spoke with Victory, I planned to help Emme go through Toni's house to catalog what was missing.

I completed my daily cleansing ritual, then squeezed into my dress, threw on my Pink Panther heels, and headed into the living room to find Sienna staring at the hardwood floor. "You get a chance to ask about Omari last night?" I asked.

"Ended up not going out. I was up all night redesigning. Think I can get new carpet installed by noon if I call right now?"

She didn't wait for an answer, just reached for her phone as I said goodbye.

I made it downtown to the LA county jail in record time — meaning only five minutes late. Neither Victory nor Aubrey was around. I was obsessing about Omari and this girlfriend when Aubrey opened my car door and invited himself to take a seat. Again. He didn't bother with a good morning.

"Ms. Anderson, we cannot mention anything to Mr. Malone about how we suspect he killed Ms. Joseph. He will be more apt to slip up if he thinks we do not know. We need to get him to admit he was her partner. The only person besides us who would know the same car was used in the robbery and the hit-and-run is the killer. He has to bring that up first. Do you understand?"

"Do I get a lollipop if I don't tattle?"

"Lollipops are nothing but sugar cubes that will rot your teeth."

"Only if it's done right!"

This insightful exchange was interrupted by a Victory sighting.

This was my first real life, in-person viewing of someone using his "get out of jail" card. It was nothing like television. Victory didn't walk past a long row of fences. He wasn't holding all of his life possessions in a

273

box. He didn't even have a car waiting for him. I figured at least his mom or maid would be waiting to take him back to their house in the Valley.

He just walked out the front door and proceeded to cross the street *without* looking both ways. Criminals today. Such risk-takers. At least he had enough sense not to steal a car right outside of jail.

I looked him over. He barely topped five foot seven. His lack of height was complemented by his lack of weight. Haley's shadowy accomplice on the video was also lacking on both the vertical and horizontal fronts. It could easily have been Victory.

I heard a door open. It was mine. Aubrey was out the car and taking off after him. Never one to be left out, I joined the procession and caught up with them across the street. "Oh goodie," Victory said when he saw me. "You brought your friend."

Aubrey ignored this. Big surprise there. "So will you answer a few of my questions?"

Victory looked from Aubrey to the keys in my hand. "If you give me a ride."

"Sure," I said, the sarcasm as thick as good quality bacon. "Aubrey brought his bike. Just jump on the handle bars and we can get this conversation over and done with."

"He means your car, Ms. Anderson."

"Really? I didn't realize that," I said. Sometimes I wondered if he truly thought I was stupid, but I was too afraid to ask.

Victory just rolled his eyes. "We got a deal or naw?"

Unfortunately, we did. The only thing I wanted more than Victory not being in my car was to know his whereabouts the night Haley died. Maybe if I drove and talked fast, he would be out before he infected the seats with his ickiness. I motioned to my car. "Fine, but you ride in the back."

Victory followed me to the Infiniti, then laughed when he saw the paint job. "Nice. If I ever want to cure my nausea, heartburn, and indigestion, I'll just lick the hood."

"It is *not* the color of Pepto!" I said, but he was climbing into the car.

Aubrey started to get in next to him. "You ride back there and I'll be expecting a tip," I said.

Victory, to his credit, laughed. Aubrey did not. "You did not tell me you wanted me to bring cash," he said.

We both looked at Aubrey with the same expression, then shared a look. It's a bad day when you're bonding with a car thief who might have run over his girlfriend and then left her for dead, but Aubrey had that effect. "She wants you up front, man," Victory finally said.

Aubrey climbed into the front seat while I assessed the situation. This could work. I could be good cop to Aubrey's weird cop. Maybe we could get something. "Where are we going?" I asked.

"Just drive," Victory said. "I'll tell you where to go. Get on the 101 South."

Whatever. I took off in the proper direction and gave Victory my best good cop smile, just like I'd seen on *The First 48.* "All comfy back there?"

"Cut the crap and tell me what this is about."

So much for that. "We have reason to believe you were one of the last people to see Ms. Joseph before she died," Aubrey said. "We wanted to see if you had any information that might help us solve her murder."

"I didn't see her," he said.

"Our sources say you did."

"Marina?" He smiled, showing off dimples and perfect teeth that probably had cost his parents the gross national product of a small country. "Next time you see her, tell her it wasn't *me* Haley was with that night."

I rolled my eyes as I got on the freeway. "That because of the fight you had when you robbed Toni Abrams' house?"

The dimples abruptly disappeared. "Marina tell you that too?" Was he saying Marina knew about the robbery? "Haley and I liked things that didn't belong to us. It was one of several things we had in common. She chose houses. I chose cars. Only cars."

"You expect us to believe that you two never overlapped?" Aubrey asked.

"Houses don't go zero to sixty in six seconds. Get off at the next exit."

"What were you doing if you weren't robbing that house with Haley?" I asked as I got off the freeway. Might as well let him think I believed him.

"I was at home. Alone. Smoking some bomb weed."

"*That's* your alibi? You didn't rob a house because you were doing drugs? You'd admit that in court?"

"Sure, right after I showed them my medical marijuana card. I get really, really, really bad migraines."

I didn't know how to react to his admission. Drugs as an alibi never came up on *The First 48.* "Turn at the next light," he said. I did, barely registering we were now in a residential area.

"What about your arrest the other day?" Aubrey asked. "Why did you steal a car from Martin Street?"

"Wrong question. Turn left at the stop sign. You should be wondering why I got caught stealing a car from Martin Street. Next stupid question."

I hated to admit that he was right. All the questions running through my head were indeed stupid. There was a nine-months pregnant pause as I tried to wrestle back control. "You own a USC hat?"

"I'm a Bruins fan," he said, name-dropping the UCLA mascot. "Here's my stop."

I realized where we were — a couple of blocks from where Aubrey and I had our car chase. A couple of blocks from where Victory was caught jacking the car. "Where are we?" I asked him.

"My place."

"You don't live in the Valley?"

"I did until I started subletting from my friend a couple months ago. You need a place to stay? I do need a roommate. It's a great neighborhood." Victory climbed out the backseat, then bent down so he could show me his dimples one final time. "Except for all the car thefts."

TWENTY

Having two of something normally was a good thing. Socks. Dumbbells. Twinkies. Earrings. Shoes. Parents. Boyfriends. The list went on and on. Unfortunately, it didn't include murder suspects.

I thought about the latest revelation as I attempted an awkward K-turn while Victory stood on his lawn and watched. I could still see him in my rearview mirror as I turned back onto Vermont. Living there was a good reason for being in the area, and maybe that's why "Jamie Smith" led us here during our goose chase. He was going home.

Victory hadn't even bothered to come up with an alibi. Marina, on the other hand, did come up with one. It was just shaky as all get-out. Not to mention the influx of cash that had found its way into her bank account. When we got to the next light, I was ready to talk my thoughts out with Aubrey. "So we have two strong suspects."

He looked genuinely confused. "One."

"Victory, that's one. And Marina, that's two. You got my message, right?"

"I would not refer to Ms. Choi as a strong suspect."

"She lied about her alibi."

"You *think* she lied about her alibi. She could have not wanted to be photographed. Perhaps because she was drinking underage."

"What about the hat? She goes to USC."

"The Trojans are the top-ranked football team in the country. If we arrested everyone who wore their paraphernalia, there would only be two people left in all of Los Angeles."

"She came into money," I said, making sure not to get into the specifics of how I knew that. "Enough to help with her tuition."

"Very nice, Ms. Anderson, but also very circumstantial. We can place Mr. Malone at the scene of our car chase. He was probably heading home."

"But you can't prove that," I said, conveniently forgetting I'd just had the exact same thought.

"Mr. Malone also has no alibi."

"If he killed her, wouldn't he be smart enough to create an alibi?" I was well aware

I was whining.

"You are referring to someone who got caught stealing a car from his own neighborhood. Smart is not part of his equation. When you do not give an alibi, there is no chance of anyone saying your alibi is a lie. I have a few additional things I want to look into in regards to Mr. Malone."

He wasn't the only one who could investigate. "Fine. I'm going to go see this Allie. Prove Marina's alibi is fake."

I wish I could say he got out the car at that point, but we still had five more minutes driving together. It felt like five hours. He spent the entire time lecturing me on proper lane-changing technique and pointing out things like traffic lights and other cars.

As soon as I got rid of him, I pulled out my tablet to hunt down Allie. I started with her Facebook page. It was private, but I could still see the basics. She wore a cheerleader uniform in her profile pic. Her hometown was listed as Crater Falls, Iowa, and her place of employment was the Forever 21 at the Americana.

Bingo.

Next, I placed two calls — phone card be darned. The first letting Emme know I'd be late. The second to Forever 21. It took a simple "Is Allie working today?" to confirm she was.

Getting Allie to break Marina's alibi probably wouldn't be so easy. I got on the 110 North and tried to figure out my best approach. In a perfect world, I'd walk up and ask if Marina was at her party, then walk out with an answer and a cute pair of jeans that were on sale. Unfortunately, this was the real world. For some strange reason, people didn't react kindly to strangers asking them to implicate a friend in a murder.

I had no clue how to play it. I came up with nada on the drive over, so I had no choice but to wing it when I got there.

I parked in back of the garage to avoid the growing crowd of people stopping by during their lunch break and made my way to Forever 21. As soon as I stepped inside the over-air-conditioned store, Allie was easy to spot. She looked just like her Facebook party photos. Only sober. I plastered on my sweetest smile and sashayed over. Allie's saleswoman spidey senses must have been on full alert because she turned when I got within five feet of her orbit and smiled. "Can I help you?"

Good question. I opened my mouth and prayed for brilliance to come out. Instead, I said, "Uhhh . . ."

I was still dragging the word out when I

saw her face change. "I know you. You went to Hanover High, right?"

And there it was. I opened my mouth again, all ready to explain I didn't attend Hanover High. That she didn't know me from a hole in the wall. That I happened to be on TV once upon a time selling fried chicken and my soul. "Yep," I said then flashed back to her Facebook profile. "In Crater Falls."

I silently talked to the man above, praying for forgiveness and thanking him for the invention of Facebook, and then spoke out loud. "You look super familiar too. Kinda like this cheerleader I went to high school with . . . Allie."

"I am Allie! Oh my God, it's been forever. How are you?"

She leaned in for a hug. I had a good five years on her but she didn't seem to notice. Black don't crack and all that. "I know! You look great, Allie."

"You too . . ."

She stretched that last word out, as if hoping to remember my name. I decided to help her out. "Dayna."

". . . Dayna. Oh my God. You hung out with Sassy?"

"Yep. That was my bestie."

"Oh my God. How is she?"

"Great. She's thinking about law school."

"Really? She rang me up at Stop and Shop last time I was home."

Oops. I immediately changed the subject. "I actually heard you were out here. I ran into someone who knows you. I was at this spot in Silver Lake. Clothes Encounters. This girl, I forgot her name. She was Asian, had braces."

"Marina! Oh my God! I love Marina!"

"Yes, Marina! We started chatting. Found out we both knew you. Small world, right? She mentioned she hadn't seen you in a while and I was like, 'Oh my God. I got you beat. I haven't seen her since high school!' "

"Yeah, it's been months and months since I've seen Marina. Oh my God. I should call her."

Months!!!!!!!!!!!!!!!!!!!!!!!!!!!!!!! My thoughts had more exclamation points than the name of Allie's photo album. I was right. Marina had lied about her alibi. "Months?" I asked, albeit a lot more calmly.

"I invited her to my birthday party, but she didn't make it. Oh my God, I wish I'd known you were out here. I would have invited you."

I tried to keep the excitement out my voice. "I'll definitely come next year. Well, I should go."

It was abrupt, but if I stayed any longer, Allie was bound to see me break out in song and dance. And I might ruin the stereotype that all black people had rhythm. I turned to go, but Allie stopped me. "Have you heard about Sharon Cassidy?"

"No." It was the first truthful thing I'd said since meeting her.

"Oh my God! Pregnant again. Three kids. Three baby daddies."

"What?" Three kids by three different men before twenty-one was kind of a lot.

Allie spent the next ten minutes updating me on all the Hanover High gossip. Donald Whathisname lost his football scholarship to Wayne State. Maiya Whosit had gone lesbian her junior year but then ended up marrying a dude. Cara Thingamajig was now dating Principal Martin. Sassy's law school aspirations would be a Facebook thread before I left the store.

I finally was able to claw my way out the door. To say I was excited would be an understatement. If I had enough minutes on my phone, I'd call Aubrey and scream "nani nani poo poo" while sticking out my tongue and putting thumbs in each ear.

As I drove to Toni's house, I put on a full-length concert in my car, singing along to the radio as it played "old school" hits barely five years old. I was driving up the road to her house when I saw Emme standing on the side of it, next to the fence that separated Toni's street from the public road. I stopped and rolled down the window. "Hey, sexy! Need a ride? Where can Daddy take you?"

She smiled when she saw me. She opened her mouth to speak but the voice I heard was decidedly male. "You got enough room for two?" Omari emerged from a hole in the fence.

I smiled at the sight of him, then remembered he had a girlfriend. Maybe. "What are you doing here?" I asked him.

He assumed I wanted to know why they were outside. "Trying to figure out how Haley and her partner got past the security guard," he said. "We think they parked on the side of the road and cut a hole in the fence."

I was torn. Part of me was intrigued, the other part of me was still mad Omari was there. Emme could tell, too, because she spoke. "Any luck on your end?"

"Some. Marina's alibi is shot. Allie confirmed she wasn't at the party. Victory has no alibi the night Haley died."

I was about to say more when we were interrupted. "Everything okay here, Ms.

Abrams?" The security guard from the other day rolled up in his golf cart.

"Yes," Emme said. "Just out for a walk."

She and Omari jumped in my car. Omari took the front seat. He smiled when we made eye contact. Why was he in such a good mood? His girlfriend must have given him some that morning before she left to go be famous. I glared at the thought. "Seriously, what are you doing here?"

"Glad you're happy to see me," he said.

"No, like seriously."

"I was third runner-up. She called me in a panic an hour ago and said you'd bailed on helping her."

I fastened my glare on Emme, who didn't even look at me. "You did," she said.

"I told you I was coming. I just didn't know when." Emme rolled her eyes as I refocused on Omari. "You didn't have plans?"

"Oh, I did. Plans with the most fascinating person on Earth," he said.

Was that his A-list girlfriend? Was this the aforementioned mind-blowing sex? I was almost afraid to ask. "Who would be . . . ?"

"Me, myself, and I. I was gonna watch *The Wire.*"

Just like that, we were friends again. *The Wire* was great but not greater than mind-blowing sex. No way he'd choose a TV marathon over a sex marathon. It was looking more like Sienna was right. The blind item *was* BS. "Which season?"

"Four."

Good choice. We pulled into Toni's driveway and trooped inside. "We've spent all afternoon in the closet," Emme said. "We're done with the clothes and on to shoes."

She didn't sound like she looked forward to it. I couldn't blame her. Out of all the rooms, Toni's interior designer had spent the most time on where Toni hung her clothes. The hard work had paid off. It wasn't a closet as much as a showroom. I'd never been to Rhode Island, but rumor was Toni's closet was bigger.

The centerpiece was the shoes. It was clear where Sienna had gotten her inspiration for my bloset because Toni's collection was lined neatly on shelves on two walls. Her stylist had left them in boxes and carefully attached a photo of each pair to the box for easy pickings.

I took it all in as they ran me through what they'd been doing. We were to go through each box to see which shoes were missing. It'd have been easier if Haley and her partner had left the empty boxes in a pile on the floor. They hadn't. What did it say that Toni's burgled closet was neater than my non-burgled one?

"If they're missing, take the photo and put it in a pile over there." Emme motioned to a pile just as her phone rang. She checked it. "It's Ben. BRB."

Once she left, Omari and I got started without her. It would have been more effective to start on opposite sides and work our way to the middle, so, of course, he wanted to start on the same side. Since he was taller, he went for the top shelf. I started at the bottom. He pointed to a photo of silver stiletto sandals. "No way they took these."

"Au contraire," I said. "Those are the Prada. Definitely goners."

"Wanna bet?"

"Bring it on."

He reached for the box. I could tell it was empty by the way his face dropped. "Wanna go for round two?" he asked.

I pointed to the nearest photo, a pair of simple black platform heels. "Red soles," Omari said. "Those are Louwhoevers. Definitely gone."

"Definitely last season. They're here." I grabbed the box. Sure enough, it wasn't empty. "Three out of four?" I asked.

It was his turn, so he grabbed a photo. It was a stiletto with a Pink Panther print.

"Oh, these are definitely still here. Every other chick I see on the street has these on. Bet Haley already owned these. Or at least already had stolen them from someone else."

"Those are definitely gone."

Of course, I was right. He looked at me with admiration. "I forgot you were the Shoe Whisperer."

"More like every girl you've seen has a knockoff. That shoe was the original, made just for Toni by Mr. Louboutin himself. The only difference is Toni's has a five-inch heel." I glanced at the photo. "I will say Haley had taste. I would've stolen these myself if Toni's feet weren't so freaking small."

We laughed like we used to, then spent the next few minutes working in a comfortable silence. After a few boxes, he spoke up. "So I know your excuse for being late. What's Sienna's?"

"She's redecorating our place in anticipation of her reality show being picked up."

He didn't even blink. "Right," he said. "About —"

"Her quest to set a world record for wearing red every day."

"Let me guess, you'll be wearing blue."

"You know blue's not my color. I was

290

thinking lime green." Then I got serious. "She and her new manager are shooting a teaser but I'm not gonna be in it. I'm retired. You know that."

He ignored that. "Seems like this manager's legit, at least."

"I hope so. He's all she talks about. 'Montgomery said this. Montgomery did that.' She even told me the other day they both agreed I should stop investigating because it's getting too dangerous. You believe that?" He shrugged. "You're the only one who hasn't told me I was stupid, foolish, or crazy for doing this."

"Because I know you'll quit." He had the nerve to laugh after he said it.

"Why would you think I'd quit?"

He looked at me and saw I was not amused. He sighed out an answer. "Because that's your MO, Day. At the first sign of trouble, you quit."

"That's bull."

"Monopoly," he said.

"That game takes forever."

"Harold Miller."

"I was going away to college."

"Business school."

"To follow my dreams."

"Acting."

He had me there. "Retiring and quitting

are two different things," I said.

"You don't 'retire' if it's really your dream." He actually used air quotes. "I didn't. Took me almost ten years. Sienna hasn't."

"Emme also quit acting."

"She was five."

He had a point, but still. Emme and Toni had shared the role of the precocious youngster on a family sitcom back in the day. Emme hated every minute of it and retired as soon as the show was canceled. Toni, obviously, had not. "It doesn't matter," I said. "She still quit, as you call it."

"You'll quit this, too."

I hated how sure of himself he sounded. All the good will I felt for him possibly not having a girlfriend evaporated. In fact, I suddenly hoped he not only had one, but that she cheated on him every chance she got and gave him an STD. Pissed, I yanked a shoe box off the wall. The photo was for a horrid pair of black flats. I didn't even know why Toni kept them. I ripped the box open and looked inside.

That's when I screamed, dropping the box in the process. Photos rained down like dollar bills in a strip club.

TWENTY-ONE

"What is it?" Omari sounded understandably alarmed.

I couldn't speak, instead just pointed at the photos now littering the area around me. He reached down to grab one.

The shoe box held pictures, and they definitely weren't of shoes. I wished they were. I glanced down at the photo closest to me. Toni stared back at me. To say the photo was explicit would be an understatement. If she weren't famous already, those photos would've been enough to get her and her extended family a reality show on *E!*. I quickly started picking them up; each was worse than the one before it.

The ones that weren't of Toni were of Luke Cruz, Toni's on-again, off-again boyfriend, and, unlike every character he played in those romantic comedies he was in each year, he was a grade-A a-hole, the "A" standing for "A-list." Toni was naked in all her photos. Luke was clothed. Unfortunately, it was in Toni's underwear.

Omari stared at the photo he was still holding of Toni. "Quite the close-up," he finally said.

I snatched it from him. "We cannot tell Emme about this."

"Tell me what?"

Emme stood at the doorway, her eyes boring down on the shoe box in my hand. Fudge.

"Uhhh . . ." I was surprised I even managed to get that out.

I stood frozen as Emme walked toward me and looked into the shoe box. She grabbed a photo. She focused in on it, realized what she was seeing, and then dropped it on the ground like it was on fire. She took out another. And another.

Then she snatched the box from me. Tucking it under her arm, she pulled out her phone and placed a call on speaker. "Speak," the voice said. I recognized it immediately as belonging to Toni's manager.

"Ben, did Toni tell you about any photos of her and Luke?" Emme asked.

"No. Where were they?"

"A shoe box. I don't know how many there are or if any are gone. They're pretty bad."

"Hmmph." There was no surprise in Ben's voice. No anger. It was as if he'd been doing this so long, he'd surgically removed his ability to be shocked anymore. "Guess that one wasn't a nut job after all."

Omari and I exchanged glances. Neither of us had the slightest clue what he was talking about. I wasn't sure if I wanted to know. But Ben continued on as if we'd asked him to explain. "About a month or two ago, some chick calls, won't tell me her name. Just wants me to call her H. This H claims she has compromising photos of Toni. Threatened to go public if we didn't pay her off. Blah. Blah. Blah."

He paused. I waited for him to continue, but I guess Ben assumed we already knew the end of that story. "Did you?" I asked, then flicked a look at Emme. She still wore no expression.

"Of course not." Ben sounded as offended as if I'd called his baby ugly. "You know how many calls like that I get? I told her what I tell everyone else: I was taping the call, and I would have my investigator on her so heavy I'd know her menstrual cycle."

All righty then. "You tell Toni?" I immediately realized this question was even dumber than my last one.

"I did my job — handled it — so she

could do hers. The woman never called back. Then the next fire came up and I had to piss all over that one."

"What about the photos?" Emme asked. "One of the robbers is still out there. We think we know who —"

"My people will take care of it," he said and hung up.

I stared at Emme. She looked me dead in the eye and said, "I'm gonna put a GPS on Marina's phone."

"That legal?" Omari asked.

"That matter?" Emme asked. Touché.

"How, though?" I asked. Someone — who definitely was not me — once asked Emme to track her boyfriend's cell phone and was told she didn't have the technology to do that. That someone was very disappointed.

"Has to be a way," Emme said. "And if there isn't, I'll make one."

I woke up the next morning thinking about Haley. Just when I thought it could get no worse, she'd managed to shock me even more. A lot of aspiring actresses had secondary jobs. Haley was more ambitious than most. Actress/secondhand-clothing saleswoman/world-class thief/not-so-great blackmailer. The hits kept coming.

When Sienna knocked on my door, I was

happy for the interruption. Since it was her door, I told her to come in. Her arms were piled high with clothes. All red, of course. "I need help picking an outfit."

With all the excitement, I'd forgotten she was scheduled to start shooting her sizzle reel with Montgomery. I glanced at the alarm clock. He was coming in a few minutes. From what Sienna had told me, he hadn't had time to put together a crew, so he was doing it solo. I hadn't had a chance to tell her I wouldn't be in it. I doubted she needed me. She was more than ready.

Her bedroom and the living room were now redecorated. Much like its owner, Sienna's apartment was rocking red from head to toe, or should I say ceiling to floor. I'd read somewhere that putting people in an all-red room was a Chinese torture method. I was sure it was just a myth, but after just two hours in our redesigned apartment, I was more than ready to share state secrets. If this was what my eggs felt like every month, no wonder they escaped.

"Didn't you mention the dress with the sparkles?" I asked.

"I did, but then I was thinking pants. Let me try on a few things and you film me."

I threw a quick glance at my phone, wondering if Emme had figured out how to put a GPS on Marina's cell. I was hoping I was quick enough Sienna wouldn't notice. She did. "Look, if you're too busy, I can have Fab help me. He should be here in a few minutes."

Fab? Here? Few minutes? Of course, wherever there's a camera, Fab would be close behind. "He must have smelled fame in the air and called you," I said.

"I called him. I need a sidekick, after all."

WTF? *I* was her sidekick, not Fab. Why ask him and not me?

She read my mind. "Montgomery suggested I ask you, but I told him how you were done with the whole Hollywood thing."

She was right, but still. At least ask. I was upset. To make matters worse, I was upset that I was upset. I *was* done with Hollywood. Yet here I was angry about not being asked to be on camera. I needed out of the apartment, so I said the first excuse I could think of. "I'm gonna go exercise."

Sienna was too distracted to remember I hadn't worked out in six months, so my escape was easy. I did manage to exercise, walking for an hour straight. Proud of myself, I stopped at a frozen yogurt store on the way back and requested samples until they figured out I wasn't going to buy anything and suggested I leave.

street. Thank God Fab was there. I gathered myself and came out the bathroom to find Sienna and Fab crowded outside the door. "We need to call the police," she said. "Report that someone tried to hit you."

"Someone tried to hit me?"

I wasn't saying it to be an a-hole. I was truly confused. Someone tried to hit me? Wait, someone tried to hit me? Me? *Uh-uh,* I thought, then tried it out loud. "Uh-uh."

Sienna pressed the back of her hand on my forehead. "I think you have a concussion."

"It was an accident." I sounded downright insistent. "It wasn't like they ran me over on the sidewalk. They couldn't see me around the bend."

"We need to call the police."

I didn't respond. Since I was still having trouble grasping that someone had almost killed me accidentally, I found it nearly impossible to believe he or she might have done it on purpose. The doorbell rang, signaling Montgomery's arrival.

Fab went to let him in while Sienna followed me to the bloset. She grabbed her landline and called Emme. I sat there still in shock while Sienna filled Emme in. Luckily, Emme was Team Accident. "IDK," she said. "Killers don't honk."

Sienna rolled her eyes before speaking. "So they weren't trying to kill her. They were trying to scare her. That make you feel better? She needs to stop with this investigation."

"But she's making progress." That I was.

"Which is why she almost just got killed. If they killed their best friend or girlfriend, why wouldn't they kill her?"

Good point.

"So she quits," Emme said. "Who's to say they won't randomly decide to kill her one day? The only way for her to ever feel safe is to put them behind bars."

Another good point. They might as well have each climbed on a shoulder. The only problem was I wasn't sure who was my devil and who was my angel.

Before I could decide, Montgomery barged into the room, Fab right at his heels. "You okay?" Montgomery said.

"She's still in shock," Sienna answered. "Emme thinks she needs to keep on with this investigation."

"After someone just tried to kill her?" Montgomery sounded genuinely shocked.

"It was an accident," Emme said.

"You need to call the police," Montgomery said. "Now."

I was about to tell Sienna to go ahead

when my father popped into my head. I thought it over. It didn't feel like a threat to me. It felt like an accident. And Emme was right. I was close to figuring things out. What if it *was* an accident? I would have quit for no reason.

I was scared, but would quitting make me less scared? Especially if there was a killer out there who knew where I lived and knew that I knew something important. The best bet seemed to be to solve the murder. Haley's killer couldn't run me over if he or she was sitting in a jail cell.

Besides, my family still needed the money. Time was running out to pay the bank.

"I'm not calling the police," I said. "It was an accident."

Sienna actually dropped the phone. I picked it up, then practically shoved the three of them out of my bloset. I slammed the door, but I could hear them talking loudly about how crazy I was acting. I spoke to Emme. "Any luck tracking Marina's phone?"

"Yes, but we have to physically download the GPS tracking software onto it."

"By we, you mean me?" I said, knowing full well that Emme had filled her leaving-the-house quota dealing with this Toni situation.

"Yep."

"You really think it was an accident?"

She didn't even hesitate. "Yep."

I really hoped she was right.

My life would have been easier if Marina could afford a doorbell. Any other day, knocking on a door wouldn't have been a problem. Any other day, I wasn't about to meet a potential murderer to secretly load GPS software onto her phone. My hands were shaking so badly they barely made a sound as my knuckles rapped on her door.

It had been surprisingly easy to get Marina to agree to hang out. I harbored no delusions that downloading the software would be quite so simple. I was scared out my mind. I wasn't willing to risk one of my friends' lives by having them come with me, but it would have been nice to have backup. Instead, I settled for taking a girl's other best friend. Not diamonds. Pepper spray.

I told Marina I'd pick her up at 9:00 p.m. so I got to her apartment at 8:30, figuring her cell and I could have alone-time while she finished getting ready. When she answered the door, she was wearing a robe, and only one eye had shadow. "Sorry I'm early," I said. "I got done late and it didn't make sense to go home, so . . ."

I half expected her to whip out a knife and stab me right there. Instead, she flashed me her braces. "No prob."

She ushered me inside, sat me down on a futon, and disappeared down the hall. I took in my surroundings. Not that there was much to take in. Besides the aforementioned futon, the only other furniture was a card table with a couple of folding chairs. Forget cable — there wasn't even a TV. The Rack Pack obviously hadn't taken home any of the things they stole. I use the term "obviously" because it would have been easy to hide something in plain sight.

What Marina and Haley lacked in furniture, they made up for with stuff. That was the only way to describe it. Papers, magazines, and textbooks were piled high on the table, both folding chairs, and half of the futon. Judging from the stack of magazines teetering dangerously in a pile next to my feet, Marina's version of "cleaning" for company was moving the pile from the futon to the floor. I briefly wondered if any of it had belonged to Haley, then reminded myself that I didn't care.

I had a cell phone to find. It felt impossible under these circumstances. I spied Marina's purse in a pile by the door and tiptoed over.

"Did you see the first movie?" she called from down the hall.

We had plans to see a *Man in Danger 2: Man in More Danger,* starring wholesome family man/A-list action star Todd Arrington. "Yes, but I fell asleep halfway through."

I opened the purse. She had three lipsticks, a wad of crumpled tissue, a couple of stray pieces of gum, and some pepper spray of her own. But no phone. "He tends to bore me when he's fully clothed," I said.

She laughed. "Good thing they always manage to get him out of his shirt ten minutes in." I went to the card table. "He and his family just did a sit-down interview for *E!.* He gave a tour of his place. It was so nice. Serious house goals."

I threw a few three-year-old issues of *InStyle* on the floor. She wouldn't know the difference anyway. No cell phone. "Really?" I said, barely listening.

I was about to check under the futon when I spied a USC book bag in the corner. I walked over. The phone was in the front pocket. Bingo.

I slipped it into my jacket pocket and went to sit back down, all ready to resume the innocent act. That's when I saw the second cell phone peeking out from between two of the piles on the futon.

I didn't know how I'd missed it. Both were the latest Galaxy phone and both had sparkly cases, except this one was pink and the one in my pocket was purple. Fudge. I bent down to examine it.

"Blurg adak awk jad."

That wasn't what Marina said. Just what it sounded like. Her voice was close, like "stab me in my back with a knife for stealing her cell phone" close. I screamed.

"I scared you, I'm sorry," Marina said.

I'd been so caught up in my search that I hadn't noticed she'd walked into the room. Thank God my back was to her so she couldn't see what I was doing. I tried to catch my breath, then gave up. Palming the pink cell and hiding it in my sleeve, I turned around. "It's okay," I managed to squeak out between inhaling large gulps of air. "I was just admiring . . . your lovely collection of magazines. What'd you say?"

"Have you seen my cell phone?"

Yes. "No." I smiled my way through the lie and prayed she didn't notice my teeth chattering. "When'd you last have it?"

"I'm not sure."

I watched Marina check all the places I'd checked a few minutes before, the phone feeling like a hundred-pound weight in my hand. She wore that same look we all got when we couldn't find something we'd just had. "Maybe I should call it?" she said.

That was a horrible idea. "That's a great idea. Let me call it for you."

I grabbed my purse a few feet away. My back to her, I slipped the second phone into my jacket pocket with its twin. I made a show of taking out my cell phone. I found the number and hit to connect. "I'm calling."

I just wasn't calling her. Instead, I called Sienna, knowing she wouldn't pick up since she was filming. As it rang, I made a show of looking around, as if straining to hear her cell. Marina was doing the same thing, except for real. Right before it went to Sienna's voicemail, I hung up. "Maybe the battery died," I said, then scooped up my purse and changed the subject. "Where's your bathroom?"

Still focused on her phantom phone, Marina motioned toward the hallway. As soon as I was in the bathroom, I breathed for the first time since entering her apartment. That had been close. I, of course, had to use the facilities. I did it quickly and then took the cell with the purple cover out of my pocket. I hit the button to remove the screen saver and swiped the touch screen to unlock it.

God must've taken pity on me because there was no pass code.

The photos confirmed it was Marina's. Give it up one time for people loving to take selfies in dirty bathroom mirrors. I had more of my own than I cared to admit. I used her phone's browser to visit a website Emme had created for me and downloaded the GPS software. Luckily, part of the software's appeal was that it didn't show up in your icons. I then made sure to remove the site from Marina's browser history. The whole thing took less than thirty seconds.

I put Marina's cell back in my pocket then pulled out the second one. It had to have belonged to Haley, the one Victory was so eager to get back. It could be Marina's old phone, but it was too new. It was also off. I turned it on and waited impatiently during the thirty seconds it took to boot. Like Marina, Haley didn't have a passcode. Two in a row!

There were lots of pictures of Haley solo and with Marina and Victory — including a few nude shots of him. TMI. I moved to her texts. The last one was to Victory. Of course, the new messages were at the bottom and you had to scroll up. There were about three messages on the current screen.

The top was from Haley. *NP TOOK THE CASH.*

Sent at midnight the night she died.

I'd been friends with Emme long enough to know what *NP* stood for. I just wasn't sure what the "no problem" referred to. *Took the cash* could be about the Kandy Wrapper robbery. Haley really was a fan of the caps lock. Punctuation, not so much.

Victory was no better. His response: *GTFOOH acting like everything ok w/us*

Victory was mad, but then, when wasn't he? What were they arguing about?

Her: *GOI TOLD U IT WAS JUST BIZ*

Get over it. I told you it was just business. So they were arguing about business, but what business? And why hadn't she included Victory?

Him: *& I told u Id kill u. GOI that u hoe.*

Whoa. He was threatening to kill her. Thirty minutes before she died, at that.

I scrolled up, hoping to find out more, when a Kandy Wrapper song started blaring somewhere near my privates. What the heck? I had no clue what it was, but Marina sure did. She banged on the door. "Is that my phone?"

And that's when I dropped Haley's phone in the toilet.

TWENTY-TWO

"Victory and Haley weren't only partners in life. They were partners in crime. He an expert at stealing cars, she at breaking into houses. They combined their skills to form the Rack Pack. Everything was going well until they decided to rob Toni Abrams while she was out of town shooting a movie. They cut a hole in a fence to enter the gated community, then found a sliding glass door Toni's assistant forgot to lock.

"But something went wrong in that house. Partners became enemies. They fought inside, which led to fighting outside. It turned physical, Haley striking first. But it was Victory who gave the push that sent her over the edge, or should I say into the spotlight. Haley was caught on tape. She knew it, too. Her days numbered, she pressured Victory for one last hurrah, one final break-in. They chose Kandy Wrapper, who'd bragged on record about keeping ten

Gs in her house at all times. They decided to find out if it was true.

"They got the money, then went their separate ways; Victory took the car while Haley visited her job to quit it. Maybe they planned to meet up later to split the money. Maybe not. I don't know. What I do know? Haley taunted him via text. Telling him she took *all* the cash. This enraged Victory, who threatened to kill her. An hour later, she was dead, hit by the same BMW used in the robbery, the same BMW Victory stole. Haley took the cash. So Victory took her life."

I took a much-needed breath, then spoke again. "So? What do you think?"

The Voice finally spoke. "Don't get paid to think. I get paid to write down tips."

I'd wanted to call the tip line as soon as I made my "Ooh, how did your phone get in here? Girl, my Aunt Flo just arrived and these cramps are killing me" excuse to Marina and hauled butt out of there. I'd left Haley's phone floating in the toilet. I was tempted to take it, but let's just say that I'd neglected to flush. I figured the police could just get Haley's cell phone records anyway. I was sure Marina would eventually notice the present I'd left in her toilet but as long as I wasn't around when she did, I was fine with it. She'd called me a few times after I left, but I blocked her number and spent the entire night staring at the clock, praying for morning. It finally came. Just as I was about to call the tip line, my phone rang. Of course, the temp agency would call me at that moment to work a last-minute job.

And work me they did. I didn't have a spare moment all day except for lunch. When I called the tip line, I got voicemail. My theory was too good (and too long-winded) to leave after the beep, so I waited until I got off work at four, calling the Voice as soon as I got to the lobby. It took me all the way to Robertson to get my story out. "Did you at least write it down?" I asked the Voice.

"It's in your file, 1018. Right next to my notes about Montgomery Rose, BMW owner. Right next to you swearing up and down the killer was the boyfriend of a quote PrimaDonna6969. Right next to you letting us know a Marina Choi did her friend in. Your file is fatter than a contestant on *Biggest Loser* at the first weigh-in."

She'd summed up my investigation in four rude but succinct sentences. I suddenly felt *a lot* of sympathy for the boy who cried wolf. "Have you subpoenaed Haley Joseph's cell phone records?"

"This is the tip line, not the information line. We aren't 411."

"Victory's been desperate to get that phone back. He knows it can prove he killed her. Talk to Marina. She'll tell you."

"You mean Suspect Number Three?"

I chose to ignore that. "Those texts should be enough to bring him in."

"Bring him in? You've gone from too much *The Young and the Restless* to too much *Law & Order.*" I'd actually gotten that last bit from *The First 48,* but she didn't need to know that. "How do you know about their text conversation, anyway?" she continued.

Oops. "Gotta go," I said, then yelled one last thing before I hung up. "Get the subpoena!"

That was a waste of five phone card minutes. Yes, I'd been a bit too eager to share my theories, but the last thing I wanted was for Victory to get away because I'd called the tip line a few too many times. Aubrey was right. Victory was the strongest suspect. I'd be darned if he got away with it. Before I knew it, I'd driven past Sienna's apartment on my way to Victory's house.

It took me getting there, parking, ringing the doorbell, being mad he wasn't home, and stomping back to my car to wait to realize what an idiot I was being. A man had threatened to kill his girlfriend and said girlfriend ended up dead in one of the cruelest ways possible. And here I was about to confront him by myself.

I'd done it with Marina, but I'd been scared out my mind the entire time. Victory was a hundred times scarier. Sociopath scary. Confronting Victory wasn't the bad idea, though. Confronting him on my own was. I needed backup. Sienna was mad at me. I was mad at Omari. Emme wouldn't leave her house. That left one person: Aubrey.

He answered on the first ring. I cut off his customary "Ms. Anderson" and told him what I'd found, trying my best to make it seem I'd happened across the phone while it was in the open with the texts already on the screen. Then I casually mentioned that I happened to be outside Victory's house. I expected to be yelled at, but Aubrey surprised me. Instead of a lecture, he hung up with a promise to meet me in twenty minutes.

It took him eighteen. I spent every second praying Victory didn't beat him home. For once, luck was on my side. Aubrey got in, snapped on his seat belt even though we weren't going anywhere, and opened his mouth. *Here it comes,* I thought; *he was just waiting to yell at me in person.* "Good work, Ms. Anderson."

I beamed, then did what you're supposed to when you receive a compliment. I gave one right back. "You were the one who first thought it was Victory."

"Yes, but you found what might be the nail in the coffin."

"Thanks to you."

We kissed each other's butts for the next five minutes. It took half that long for my ego to take up the entire backseat. An hour later, I was ready to climb back there with it. If I'd been hoping for some buddy-comedy-style bonding, I would have been severely disappointed. Investigation aside, we had nothing to talk about. He thought *The First 48* was a movie by "that African-American comedian," and I didn't give a hoot about hockey. So we mostly sat in silence.

The last time I'd spent more than ten minutes alone in a car with a dude where no talking was involved was college. That was a lot more fun, even though I had an imprint of the gearshift on my back for the next week and a half.

It was dark by the time Victory pulled up and parked. He was in his own Toyota for once. Though he wasn't breaking that law, he was clearly breaking another. Drunk, he zigzagged his way toward his front door, leaning more than the Leaning Tower of Pisa.

We caught up with him halfway up his walkway. He reeked of alcohol and bad life choices. "Mr. Malone," Aubrey said. Victory turned in slow motion and regarded us as if he'd never seen us before. "We need to talk to you about Ms. Joseph's death."

Victory nodded, though I was pretty sure he hadn't understood a word Aubrey said. He was too drunk to even hold his head still.

"We would like to know if you want to change your earlier statement," Aubrey continued.

Victory opened his mouth and I fully expected vomit to come out. Instead, he managed to speak. "Think I'll keep it: 'I was alone.' " He moved his hands as if picturing it being written somewhere. "Has a special ring to it. Don't you think?"

"I've heard better," I said.

He managed to focus his eyes on me. "Why are you two so obsessed with pinning this robbery on me?"

"Because we know you were involved," I said. "You stole a BMW, probably to blend in with the neighborhood, then robbed Kandy. Problem was Haley took all the cash you guys stole. Didn't share it with you."

"Sharing is caring." He laughed like it was the funniest knock-knock joke ever. Just as suddenly, he stopped and spoke like we hadn't just gone through this two seconds before. "Why are you so obsessed with pinning this robbery on me, anyway?"

"She baited you about how she took the money," I said. "Right before you threatened to kill her."

He looked at me, then Aubrey, then back to me again before settling on a point somewhere between us. "Oh, I see. You just did some roundabout way of saying I killed her. Why not just start with that?"

"Actually, *you* said you killed her, Mr. Malone," Aubrey said. "There are text messages."

He acted like he hadn't heard him. "Number One: it was an accident. And even if it wasn't, which it was, Number Three, I was at home."

He missed Number Two, but whatever. "At home texting her that you planned to kill her?" I asked.

"Pretty much."

"Then why do you want her phone so bad?" I asked. "You were desperate because you knew it linked you to her death."

"Or because I shelled out three hundred bucks for the thing and she only had it for two weeks. Waste of my hard-earned money."

He really was an a-hole. "You denying you threatened her?"

"No, but words don't mean jack. I could say 'the sky is burnt magenta.' Don't mean it's true."

"Are you saying you were joking?" Aubrey asked. "You weren't mad at her that night?"

"I was pissed." He let the word drag out, like a snake, then smiled.

I wish I could say his honesty was refreshing. "Why?"

" 'Cause I found out she was cheating on me. Some old dude, too, which is just gross."

"So it was just a coincidence she died that same evening?" Aubrey asked.

I chimed in. "But you didn't do it, right? What happened? Too lazy to follow through? Something good on TV?"

Between his cockiness and drunkenness, I was expecting Victory to say, 'Yep.' Instead, he surprised the crap out of me. "I realized cheating or not, I couldn't live without her. Didn't mean I didn't hate her as much as I loved her. I did love her, though. Couldn't live without her. Wait, I say that already? That I couldn't live without her?"

I was about to say he was managing quite well, but then I thought about it. Was he? He was high half the time, drunk the other half. Stealing cars from right outside his house. Not signs of a man thinking clearly. Could it be his way of mourning? If Victory *wasn't* Haley's Rack Pack partner — and I still wasn't 100 percent sure he wasn't — then he had to know who was. He just needed to tell us already. "If you didn't kill her, who did?" I asked, not really expecting an answer. I didn't get one.

"Wasn't there. How'd I know?" Victory said.

"Because you know her partner in the Rack Pack," Aubrey said. "Her death was no accident, Mr. Malone. Her partner killed her."

Victory thought about it but quickly dismissed it by shaking his head. He smiled, that copyrighted cockiness peeking out oh-so-briefly before he spoke. "Don't know who you're talking about. Know what? I do want to change my statement. I didn't even know Haley was in the Rack Pack or had a partner. And I'm very, very, very surprised at this latest turn of events."

He knew something and he wasn't telling,

which pissed me all sorts of off. I went in. "I'm talking about the person who got into a fist fight with her at Toni Abrams's house, then waited for the prime opportunity to seek revenge. It came two days later when said partner mowed her down while she was crossing the street, leaving her to die a slow, painful death. The news said she choked to death on her own blood. It took her five long minutes."

I got him. At least for a split second, then he was gone again. "Fights don't mean guilt. I know that more than anyone. You need more than that to convince me she killed her."

She? Victory didn't realize he'd let it slip that Haley's partner was a woman because he continued on. "It was an accident."

I immediately flashed on Marina. Was I right after all? I peeked at Aubrey to see if he'd caught it, but he was too busy still trying to convince Victory to snitch. He did it with the bombshell. "The car used in their last robbery was the same car that ran her over."

That sobered Victory up real quick. He went from drunk to angry. Really, really angry. He still didn't snitch, though. "Like I said, I don't know who you're talking about."

"If you loved Haley as much as you say you did, you need to give us a name, Mr. Malone."

"I get you might be trying to protect them," I said. "But a person like that doesn't deserve protection."

I'd tried to appeal to his heart. It backfired. "Get off my property before I kill you."

He pushed past us and went inside.

Thanks to a police chase involving two helicopters and a conga line of cop cars, it took me almost three hours to drop Aubrey off and get home. I was cranky, starving, and wanted nothing more than to eat the leftover chili Sienna had made while vegging out to a new *The First 48*. I could only hope she hadn't thrown out the leftover chili to spite me. It had happened before.

I came home to find Sienna and Montgomery using her desktop computer to watch footage. So much for my plans. "Hi!" I said with way too much enthusiasm. Sienna and I had managed to avoid each other ever since our little disagreement over whether someone tried to kill me or not.

She matched my tone and raised me tenfold. "How are you?"

"Great. Your day?"

"Great. Yours?"

"Great."

"Great," she said.

"Great!" I said, then, "Okay, well, I'm gonna go to my room now!"

"Okay!"

Things were weird between us now that I'd made the decision to continue looking into Haley's death, but we were acting like they weren't. Which just made things even weirder. We were still smiling at each other when my phone rang. Sienna turned back to her computer to continue editing. I answered my cell. "Marina," Emme said when I picked up.

I literally squeaked. Sienna was doing a good job of ignoring me because she didn't even turn around. Montgomery glanced in my direction, then went right back to work. "We should cut to a talking head interview of you mad at what Fab did," he said.

"Where is she?" I asked Emme.

"The hills above Hollywood Boulevard."

"She lives by USC. She has no good reason to be up there. What's the address?"

"Don't have an exact address, but it's accurate within five hundred feet."

"Give me the five hundred feet."

I looked around the room for a pen. I found one. Unfortunately, it was mere inches from Sienna. I ran to her desk and wrote down Marina's approximate whereabouts. Sienna must have been reading over my shoulder because she said, "Todd Arrington lives on that street."

She reached into a drawer and pulled out a Celebrity Homes Star Map and pointed. Sure enough, there was a star on the street with the name Todd Arrington on it. He was the lead in *Man in Danger 1* and *2*, who I'd talked about with Marina the night before. She'd mentioned how nice his house was when he showed it on *E!*.

It looked like she was checking it out for herself.

TWENTY-THREE

I was so excited I was practically screeching. "Marina was telling me how much she loved Todd Arrington's house yesterday. And now she's in his neighborhood! I don't need Victory after all."

"What are you talking about?" Emme asked.

I was too anxious to explain, so I put the cell on speaker and gave everyone the Cliffs Notes version. "I spoke with Victory today. He let it slip Haley's partner was female, but he wouldn't say who. He knows something he's not telling us. And he wouldn't budge, even after we told him the same car was used in the robbery and the murder. But now I don't need him."

"You're sure she's there?" Sienna asked Emme.

"IDK exactly."

"Only one way to find out. Emme, I'll call you when I get there." I hung up and grabbed my keys. To my surprise, Sienna got up too.

Montgomery was as shocked as I was. "We still have an hour left of footage. You can't go now."

I wanted her to come, but I didn't want her to know I wanted her to come since we were beefing. I could've called Aubrey, but we'd had enough alone-time that day.

"You can finish up, right?" she asked him.

I could see Montgomery hesitate. He *could* finish up. That didn't mean he wanted to. "How about we let the police handle it and all review the footage together?" he said.

Sienna wasn't having it. "I'm not going to let her roll up on a potential robbery by herself, and we know Day's not gonna call the police."

I ignored the jab, mainly because I wasn't. Not until I'd confirmed Marina *was* at his house and called the tip line first.

"So you're not going to let the police handle it?" Montgomery watched Sienna throw on her red shoes. I just opened the front door. "Freaking crazy. The both of you."

We left him sitting at the computer.

I'd hoped Sienna coming meant things were getting better between us, but the car ride negated that notion. We barely spoke. I tried not to focus on it and instead concentrate on the task at hand. Marina was at (or at least within five hundred feet of) Todd Arrington's house. She was either robbing him or in the bushes — five minutes away from a restraining order.

Though Todd Arrington lived in the Hills, it was not a gated community. Thank God for small favors. We turned onto his street, almost running into a paddy wagon doubling as a craft service truck there to feed a hungry film crew. A movie was being shot down the street. It wouldn't be LA without someone shooting something somewhere at all times. Based on the small number of trucks, it was an independent production.

Though his neighbor's house was getting plenty of action, Todd Arrington's wasn't. The two-story monstrosity was pitch black, or at least looked that way from behind the fence surrounding it. The street was narrow, so there wasn't much in the way of parking options. I was going to comment on wanting to be inconspicuous but remembered I was driving a (non-Pepto) pink Infiniti. So much for that. I parked directly across the street, pulling into the neighbor's driveway to turn around and do so. If they called the cops, then win-win all around.

I cut the lights and we sat in the dark.

Neither of us spoke, and we were both painfully aware neither of us was talking. I finally decided to be brave. "Thanks."

"I'm only here to make sure you don't do anything stupid."

I wish I could say it was all she said, but it wasn't. She continued like that — taking full advantage that I was stuck in the car and couldn't leave. Not wanting to start an argument, I didn't speak until I had something worthwhile to say. When I did, it was, "Look." I pointed at the Arrington house.

"Don't try to change the subject."

"Seriously, look." I could make out what looked like a small circle of light bobbing about in an upstairs room. "You see it?"

"I do." She said it like she really hadn't expected anything to happen except for an opportunity to lecture me.

"There it is again!" It was bigger, as if the person was farther away. I was suddenly very nervous. "If we start seeing shadow puppets, I'm leaving."

Sienna ignored me and got out her phone. "I'm calling the police."

"Wait." I grabbed my own phone. "I need to call the tip line first. Otherwise, it doesn't count."

"The tip line? This is exactly what I'm talking about, Day."

"You don't want me to have, quote, almost gotten myself killed, unquote for nothing, right?"

She didn't even bother to look at me, just started dialing. I did the same. She only had three digits to my ten. She was going to beat me to it.

My break came because she was calling in LA, where 911 gets a lot of traffic. The tip line? Not so much. It picked up on the second ring. Unfortunately, *it* was the voicemail. I listened as the Voice told me I'd reached the tip line and watched Sienna smile at me. She must've gotten a human. "Hi, I'd like —" She abruptly shut up as her eyes narrowed. "Fine, I'll hold."

Yes! I made it to the beep. "Yes, hi, this is 1018 leaving a message at precisely" — I glanced at my watch — "11:38 p.m. Pacific time. I'd like to report a break-in at the home of Todd Arrington. It's related to Haley Joseph's murder. And I was right before." I realized that due to our many conversations, I'd have to clarify. "Before as in the other day, not before as in today, because today I thought it was the boyfriend, but now I *know* it's the best friend."

I hung up as Sienna's 911 operator came back on the line. "I need to report a break-in at Todd Arrington's house. Yes, the robbery is in progress . . . no, I'm not in any immediate danger . . . what do you mean you'll send a car as soon as one is available? Did you not hear me? I said Todd Arrington. As in *the* Todd Arrington. A-list celebrity."

The operator must not have been a fan because Sienna rolled her eyes before speaking. "Can't you just transfer me to the VIP department?" She listened for a second and then hung up. "They're on their way. Can you believe they don't have VIP? This is LA! Everywhere has VIP."

I had to admit I felt better I'd left the message *and* the police were coming. I just wanted them to come soon. Who knew how long Marina would be in there.

Five minutes later, there were no police. We knew Marina was still inside because we occasionally saw a spurt of light bouncing off a window. I was about to call the police again (or rather ask Sienna to use *her* minutes to call) when we saw headlights. The police. Thank God.

I was all ready to go talk to them when the car pulled into Todd's driveway. It wasn't a cop car. It wasn't really a car at all, but a huge, bright red Hummer with pitch-black tinted windows. I halfway expected it to just mow down the gate and keep going, but it managed to stop long enough to let

the gate open.

Todd was home.

"Maybe I should honk . . . ?" I suggested. "Alert Todd someone's in the house."

"And alert Marina that Todd's home?"

Good point, but still. "I couldn't live with myself if Todd surprised Marina and something happened to him."

"He's Todd Arrington," Sienna said. "He took out the entire ISIS with nothing but a shoelace, a can of expired hair spray, and his bare hands."

I nodded. The climax of that first *Man in Danger* was pretty impressive. Then I realized something. "It was probably his stunt double."

"The cops are gonna show up." Sienna sounded pretty confident. "They always do in his movies."

"Yeah, right after the climax is over and someone's died."

"Usually it's not Todd, though," she said.

Touché.

Neither of us knew what to do, so we did nothing at all. Just watched Todd's garage door close and the flashlight in the upper window immediately go off. I sucked in a breath. "Maybe she'll jump out a window," I said. A girl could hope.

The window remained closed. A glow

emanated from behind the fence. Todd was inside turning on lights. They were both officially in the house. I couldn't take it anymore. I jumped out the car and ran to his gate, all ready to ring the buzzer. There wasn't one. "This house is worth like fourteen million and it didn't come with a buzzer?" I asked Sienna when she showed up a few seconds later.

"He probably had a billion people with star maps buzzing him all night and day." Including us, but this was for a good cause.

We had to get inside. The fence was made of wide mahogany panels so close together you couldn't even peek in to see what was going on. "We could climb it," I said, tentatively looking up.

"Not in these heels."

"Not in this butt," I agreed.

If we couldn't go high, maybe we could go low. I kicked the fence. Nothing happened. So I took out my cell phone and used it as a light to examine the fence. Since there were no streetlights, it was the only way I could see anything. The panels looked pretty sturdy in the glow of my wallpaper. I walked until I found a small panel that looked loose. I kicked it and it jiggled. I glanced at Sienna.

"Don't look at me," she said. "I just got a mani."

There were very few things worth ruining your manicure for. This wasn't one of them. It was up to me. I bent down, grabbed the board, and yanked it out. I stood up to examine my handiwork. Nice. "After you," I said.

Sienna ducked down and went through. She had a bit of a holdup when she got to her boobs but still managed to squeeze past.

I was not as lucky. I chose to go feet first. I stuck the first leg in and got up to my thigh before I quickly realized it wasn't going to work. If my leg couldn't make it, my stomach didn't stand a chance. Sienna must've come to the same conclusion. She spoke through the fence. "I can meet you at the gate."

Great idea. I de-wedged my leg with only the smallest of cuts, then hobbled back to the gate and waited, thanking the heavens it was too dark for the neighbors to see what we were doing.

I stood there for a full minute before I got worried. Where was Sienna? My thoughts flashed to Marina doing something to her. Sienna was my best friend, whether we were talking or not. If Marina even put a scratch on her . . .

I was about ready to scale the wall when Sienna finally opened the door. It took everything I had not to pull her into a hug. "I heard noises," she whispered.

"Think he caught her?" I whispered back as we looked at the house. There wasn't much to see. The lights were on, but the curtains were drawn.

"I think *she* caught him."

No! Sienna and I grabbed each other's hands as we tiptoed toward the front door. We had a good thirty feet of lawn to cover. It felt like forever. Once we got there, the front door was locked. Big surprise there. "Maybe we can get in through the back," Sienna said.

I nodded. We made our way to the back of the house. Much like me, the place was wider on the side than the front. It took us a good five minutes to get to the back.

Any normal day, I'd say the view of the city was worth the wait. That night, I didn't even notice it. I was too busy staring at the house. Like Toni's place, the first floor was made up entirely of floor-to-ceiling windows, which gave me a front-row seat to Todd Arrington tied to a chair, his mouth bound shut with black tape.

Marina was nowhere to be found. Sienna gripped my hand tighter.

"Let's untie him while we have the chance," I said. "If Marina shows up, I'll try to distract her."

She did know me, after all. I'd been to her house (where I'd put a GPS tracker in her phone, but still). Maybe I could reason with her long enough for Sienna to get Todd out of there.

"Good plan," Sienna said. "Only thing is we need to get in to do it."

I looked around and picked up the biggest rock I could find. People in glass houses and all that. I was all ready to throw it when Sienna walked to the sliding glass door and pulled. It opened. If she wanted to do it that way, I wasn't going to put up a fight. I put the rock down and followed her in.

Todd jerked when he heard the door, his eyes getting wide as he watched us come in. His saviors. The irony of two black chicks saving the white action star was not lost on me at all. He started speaking but, of course, we couldn't understand him through the tape. I put my finger to my mouth in the universal "shut the heck up before you let Marina know we're here and we all die" gesture.

He got the point because he stopped trying to talk. We rushed over and worked on his hands first. Marina must have had a Girl

Scout badge in knot-tying stowed some-where because it was impossible to undo. It didn't help that we stopped every few seconds to look toward the door. We were finally making progress when my phone rang. Loudly.

Not good. "Turn it off!" Sienna hissed. I got it out and hit ignore without even look-ing at who was calling, but it was too late. We heard steps. And they sounded angry.

Needing to hide and hide quickly, Sienna and I bolted behind the couch just as the footsteps made it into the room. "I thought I told you to be a good boy," Marina said.

I heard ripping. Marina was removing the tape from Todd's mouth. She wasn't gentle, either. I hoped he wouldn't rat us out. I was more than content to spend the rest of my life behind that couch. I would have, too, except my phone rang.

Again.

Fudge. Forget Marina, Sienna looked ready to cause me bodily harm. I mouthed an apology as I got the thing out my pocket. As I did, I heard the footsteps stop right above me and freaked. "No, Marina," I screamed, throwing my cell phone in her general direction.

"What the . . . you almost hit me." She sounded appalled. And now that she was closer, she also sounded nothing like Marina.

I looked up, right into the eyes of someone who definitely was not Marina. Her blonde weave was cheap, her Double G implants even cheaper. She'd chosen to put all her money into lip injections. Her top lip alone was big enough to double as a flotation device. She was wearing a burglar's outfit she must've found during an after-Halloween sale next to Naughty Nurse and Sexy Maid. Something told me she was getting paid by the hour.

I glanced at Todd, who looked as blissfully happy as when he'd killed a baker's dozen of bad guys with just a machete in the *Man in Danger 2: Man in More Danger* trailer. He spoke. "Are your friends gonna cost me extra?"

I was broke, but not that broke. Sienna and I both popped up and scurried back to the sliding door. I picked up my dropped cell as we did. "Wrong house," I said.

"What can I do to make it the right house?" Todd asked.

By that time we were out the door, booking it around the corner and through the front gate. I hadn't run that fast since a particularly competitive game of hide-and-seek when I was seven. We were halfway

337

down the street before I realized my car was still across from his house. Forget it. I could buy another one. It *was* the color of Pepto, anyway.

Sienna finally slowed down when we got to the house where they were filming. A lone crew member was taking a smoke break outside. As soon as we both caught our breath, we looked at each other and laughed. Only in Hollywood.

I called Emme. She must have been anxious because she picked up on the first ring. "You okay?"

"Physically, yes," I said. Mentally was a different story, but it didn't seem like the right time to get into what had just happened. We all didn't need to be scarred for life. "She wasn't there."

"Her phone's there," Emme said. "She could be hitting another house."

No way was I going to check. "We're gonna head home. I'll call you when we get there," I said and hung up.

I was about to ask Sienna if she wanted to call a cab when I found her chatting up the crew member. Nothing like being within yelling distance of a camera to get Sienna's mind off having just interrupted how Todd Arrington liked to spend his free time. "How's the shoot going?" she asked.

"Great," he said, giving her a once-over and then a twice-over. "You act?"

Sienna smiled. "Sometimes. I'm concentrating on reality TV right now. I have my own show."

"That's too bad 'cause you'd be perfect. Not for this film, but something else."

"What are you shooting?" she asked him.

"Brace Face 24."

It sounded like the title for some cheesy direct-to-video horror movie. Pass. "Never heard of it," she said.

"Really? *23* has over two million hits on YouPorn."

YouPorn? They were shooting a porno called *Brace Face.* Who would do a porno called *Brace Face*? I realized I might know someone. I finally spoke up. "It stars chicks with braces?"

"The bigger the better," he said, then, "Braces, I mean."

I bet. "You mind letting us take a look?"

It was my turn to get a once-over. He was nowhere near as impressed as he was with Sienna. He gave up halfway through, which was a shame because next to my eyes, my legs were my best feature. "Closed set," he said.

"Come on." I turned my Georgia Peach accent on full blast. "I have always wanted to see a movie being filmed. We did this star home map thing, but it's been a bust. Not a single celeb sighting. I would love to tell my friends back in Augusta I saw a real live movie being shot. We'd love it," I said. Sienna nodded and so did her breasts.

That was all it took. You'd think a set of breasts jiggling more than an inflatable Bounce House wouldn't sway him, considering his line of work, but then again, he was a man. "Sure, I can do that."

He stubbed out his cigarette and we followed him through the house until we reached the deck. LA was once again glistening in front of us. It wasn't the only thing.

Marina was there. The only thing she was wearing was her braces.

Twenty-Four

The good news, if you could call it that, was that Marina's only costars were a banana, a pineapple (trimmed, thank goodness), and every variety of melon you could think of. Suffice it to say, I wouldn't be eating fruit salad for a long, long time. I probably wouldn't be eating period.

Marina was so involved in her work that there was a delay noticing me. Her expression blank, her eyes lazily flicked toward us, then immediately came back to me while she started choking. "Cut," the director yelled.

No one came to help her. They just stared as she managed to talk between spitting out bits of fruit. "What are you doing here?"

The entire crew turned, their welcome nowhere near as warm as Todd Arrington's. Sienna gave a tiny wave while I spoke. "I came to see you."

The crew turned back to Marina. "You

followed me?" she asked.

All eyes were back on me. I wondered if Venus and Serena felt like this on the tennis court. "No!" I said, which was true. I'd followed her GPS tracker. "How long has this second career been going on?"

The director finally got tired of the back-and-forth. "Do I need to call security?"

I knew it was just a threat. All of his budget had gone to edible props. Marina stood and threw herself into a robe while she spoke. "They're friends of mine. I need a minute."

"We need to get this scene finished," he said, but he was talking to her back.

Her front was dragging me inside to the living room. Sienna followed. She was quick but not quick enough. Marina slid the door closed in her face, then shut the blinds. I felt bad about leaving Sienna out there, but she could hold her own.

Marina and I stared at each other for a minute, neither sure what to say. She spoke first. "You're not gonna tell, right?" She didn't give me a chance to answer. "You're the only person who knows about this. You can't tell. Anyone."

"Why are you doing this? Are you that hard up for money?"

Not that I could judge. I knew better than

anyone the crazy things one would do for cash. I'd been turned down to be a Bikini Barista, after all, but still. There had to be a better way for Marina to make some money.

"It's harmless," she said. "They cut my scholarship and I needed money for school and this pays pretty well, considering all I'm doing is eating."

I wasn't clear if she was trying to convince me or herself. "How long's it been?" I asked again.

"Since *Brace Face 18.*"

I quickly did the math. Seven movies. That was a lot of fruit. I suspected the filming date coincided with the first big deposit in Marina's checking account a few months ago. "So this was where you were the night Haley died? Why you lied about going to Allie's party?"

"Brace Face 21." She realized what I was saying. "Where'd you think I was?"

"Honestly? Kandy Wrapper's house."

"Why would I be there? It's not like I know her or anything."

" 'Cause that's where Haley was before she died."

"Haley was hanging out with Kandy?" Marina thought it over. "Wasn't that the night she got robbed? Kandy wasn't even at her house, why would Haley be . . ."

I could practically see the gears working in her brain. Thoughts processed at a rapid pace, putting two and two together until she got to: "You're saying Haley robbed Kandy Wrapper's house?"

I don't know which one of us was more surprised. I would've sworn she knew. Victory sure did. I'd assumed Haley hadn't kept it a secret. But Marina seemed genuinely shocked. And I'd just seen her filming a scene, so I knew she wasn't that good an actress. "There's no way," she said, sounding like she believed it. "Haley wouldn't do that."

"Just like you wouldn't do porn? Did she know about *your* little side hustle?"

Her expression told me she hadn't. As I said, everyone in LA had a side job. These two had just taken it to the extreme.

"Seems like you both had secrets. Haley's was being part of the Rack Pack. She got into a huge fight with her partner at an earlier robbery. Two days later, the same stolen car they took to Kandy's house ran her down."

"You thought it was me?!" Marina darn near choked again. "You think I killed my best friend?"

I had, but in my defense, her actions didn't really leave me much choice. She

344

could have saved me a lot of time and herself a lot of suspicion if she'd just been honest up front.

Marina was panicked. "I can prove where I was the night she died."

I knew she could. I just didn't want to log on to YouPorn to confirm it. Before we could continue the conversation, someone banged on the sliding glass door. "We need you back on set."

Marina wasn't quite ready. "I didn't rob anyone and I didn't kill her. You believe me, right?"

The thing was, I did. I did have one more question though. "If Haley was to partner with someone, who would it be?"

She didn't even hesitate. "Victory."

"Besides him? Any other girls you were cool with? Someone Haley hung out with when you were . . . at work."

She thought about it, then shook her head. It coincided with more banging. "I have to go," she said.

She slid the door open to find both Sienna and the director standing there. Neither looked pleased. "We only have the place for another hour," he said. I wondered if that included cleanup.

He seized her by the elbow and took her back to set, as if marching a convicted criminal to his death. I grabbed Sienna to leave. I peeked back one last time before we left. Marina was back in position and ready for her close-up. Her heart wasn't in it though. At least I hoped it wasn't.

She'd get over the shock of both her secret getting out and being accused of killing someone. Then she'd have to deal with learning her best friend was a thief who was murdered. That would take a lot longer. I didn't envy her. At all.

I spoke as soon as we hit the sidewalk. "It wasn't Marina. So I'm back to square one, not knowing who it could be."

"Well, at least it's not every day you get mistaken for a role-playing hooker and then walk in on a fetish video." Sienna was trying to cheer me up.

It didn't work. "Yeah, but I don't think it'll be one of those stories I'll tell people," I said. "No matter how many drinks I get in me."

We walked silently back to the car, both throwing a quick glance at Todd Arrington's place to make sure no one was lying in wait with a pair of fuzzy handcuffs. We got in the car and made it down the block handcuff-free. When we got to the corner, we passed the police heading in the opposite direction. I felt bad about them walking in on Todd, but calling the police wasn't like ordering on Amazon. You couldn't change your mind and cancel their arrival. Plus, he paid a lot of people a lot of money to keep this sort of thing out of the papers. He'd be okay, better than me even.

We were halfway home before I remembered that someone had called me. Twice. I figured it was Emme, but a glance at my cell told me the number had come up private both times. I had to do something I only did under extreme circumstances: I checked my voicemail.

Victory's voice filled the void after the beep. "It's me." He sounded like we were BFFs. He also sounded drunk. Big surprise there. "Need to talk about earlier. Got something you'll want to hear."

His second message was just a hang-up. When I called back, he didn't answer. Blurg. It'd been a very long, very crazy twenty-four hours. I'd illegally downloaded a GPS tracker, worked eight hours, broken into an A-list actor's house, been propositioned by said A-list actor, and crashed a porn shoot. I was tired, and now I was annoyed. If Victory had something to tell me, why not tell me? Why tell me you want to tell me? That's just as annoying as when someone says, "Can I ask a question?" Just ask the freaking question.

I tried Victory again with the same result. He was probably passed out in a drunken stupor. Knowing him, that could last for days. I'd have to go over there. At least I could find out exactly what he was talking about *and* give him a piece of my mind. But since I was angry and not stupid, I called Aubrey first. After a quick update, he promised he'd meet me at Victory's house in thirty minutes. I offered to drop Sienna off at home first, but she refused.

We beat Aubrey there. With all the lights on, Victory's house was as lit up as the blunt he'd no doubt smoked pre-pass out. His television was loud enough that we could hear it from our car — with the windows up. Between the loud music and the grand theft auto, his neighbors must have loved him to pieces.

We stayed in the car like good girls until Aubrey pedaled up, but I jumped out at the first glimpse of his shiny orange jumpsuit in my rearview mirror. "Is Mr. Malone inside, Ms. Anderson?" Aubrey asked.

"I'm about to find out," I said.

The three of us walked to the door and rang the bell. Victory didn't answer. I hoped he hadn't been playing with me with that phone call. "He can't hear us above all that racket," I said, sounding a bit too much like my mother for my liking.

I started banging. As soon as my palm slammed against the door, it swung open. He'd forgotten to lock it. Lucky for him, he was the only criminal in the neighborhood. I stomped into the house, Sienna and Aubrey close behind me. "Victory!" I yelled.

I didn't stop until I reached the living room just off the foyer. The place was even more of a mess than he was, his decor of choice being "Clothes On Every Surface." The furniture under his junk looked nice. I wondered if he'd stolen it or gotten it from his parents. Probably a combo. I found him on the couch passed out, his head propped so far back it looked like it might pop off. A belt hung off the back of the couch. I stomped over. "Wake up, you idiot."

I shook him. It was a bit too hard, because his body slumped off the couch and slid. His head hit the floor hard enough that it should've woken him up. It didn't.

I bent down and shook him again, but still no response. Something wasn't right. Aubrey appeared next to me. "Please step back, Ms. Anderson."

I was more than happy to do so, instinctively grabbing Sienna's hand as I did. She gripped me tight as Aubrey checked Victory's pulse. After a minute, he stood up and stated what had become obvious. "Mr. Malone is dead."

The only reason I didn't faint then and there was because I couldn't afford the emergency room bill.

TWENTY-FIVE

The rest of the night felt like a movie montage. Mainly because I was so in shock I only remember dribs and drabs. Aubrey ushering us out of the house while calling 911. The police responding way more quickly than they did for Todd. Answering the same questions over and over — just for different people. The cops letting us go. And, finally, me announcing to Sienna and Aubrey I was done playing investigator. I would just have to find a different way to help my parents out.

Omari could call me a quitter all he wanted. I'd get the word tattooed on my forehead if it meant staying alive. Let the police and Aubrey figure that crap out. I was finished, even if it meant someone got away with a murder — or in this case, two. It was better than three.

I went back to what I did best: looking for a job and not finding one. Yes, I was dead broke but it sure beat being just plain dead. The next few days involved a lot of phone calls to temp agencies I'd signed up with. I even signed up with a few new ones. Montgomery let me lie on my résumé and say I'd been his assistant. It made me find him a tad less annoying, especially when one of the new agencies immediately found me a few one-day assignments. It wasn't much, but I happily took it.

Victory's death made big news. The TV anchors reported that he'd been strangled with his own belt. If the police thought it was connected to Haley's death and the Rack Pack, no one had informed the media. Their official theory was drug deal gone wrong. I knew better but wasn't saying a word.

Sienna wanted to go to Victory's funeral, but luckily I had to temp that day. Though I wouldn't have gone even if I didn't. It felt wrong to go when I was the one responsible for his death. The idea that I'd told him something that led to him dying was too much. My guilt could fill the Hollywood Bowl. Victory was an a-hole, but even a-holes don't deserve to die.

A couple days after the funeral, my phone rang at precisely 11:08 a.m. I was expecting a temp agency. Instead, I got my mother.

"Boop, they're taking the house!"

I sucked in a breath. The jig was up. I wondered if my father knew. "What do you mean?" I asked, stalling for time.

"This here paper says we got one month till we have to leave the house. *My* house."

"It's a misunderstanding, Mama. There's nothing wrong with the house." I paced around the room. If God planned to strike me with lightning, I wanted to be a moving target. "Did Daddy see it?"

"He's at work."

Eek. The last thing I wanted was for my unsuspecting father to walk in on my mother mid-hysterics. I'd done it more times than I could count and each time was worse than the time before it. I needed to placate her. Stat. "I'll call the bank and get it straightened out."

I hoped that would pacify her, but it didn't. "You gonna tell the neighbors that too?"

"They stick a big 'Foreclosure' sign on the lawn that everyone can read?" I'd seen that in a movie once. It was quite embarrassing.

"They stuck a piece of paper on the door."

"Then, Mama, you're fine. The neighbors probably thought it was a flier."

"I don't think so. Miss Jenkins looked at me funny this morning when I waved."

Miss Jenkins looked at her funny every morning. "She probably was just mad because she thought the flier people skipped her house." Miss Jenkins was like that.

My mother hemmed and hawed for a bit, then decided I had a point. "You're gonna let me know soon as it's straightened out . . ."

"Of course. Let me get off the phone so I can call them now."

"Okay," she said and kept talking like she hadn't heard me. "I was coming back from Bed, Bath & Beyond when I saw that foreclosure paper. They had the prettiest curtains. Figure I could save up, maybe have enough to get them in a few months. 'Course they're on sale now. Don't know if they'll be then. Hate to pay full price."

I let her ramble. She was waiting for me to interrupt and offer to send money. I was tempted to tell her no, but then I thought about my father. The better mood that I could get her in, the better for Daddy's sanity — and safety. "I can always send you the money."

"No. I couldn't let you do that." I must've gotten my acting skills from her because she sounded like she meant it.

Knowing my part of this script well, my

next line came quick. "It's the least I can do."

"Well, if you insist."

We said our goodbyes and hung up. I immediately called Daddy's job but he was already gone for the day. He didn't have a cell phone so there was no way to warn him about Mama. I could only hope that she was too busy daydreaming about curtains to notice that he'd come home.

Of course, now I had to make a hundred dollars more appear out of thin air. My miniscule temp money was already assigned to my own bills. I knew what I finally needed to do. It was something I'd been avoiding, but couldn't any longer.

I went to the basement where Sienna's storage unit waited, chockfull of two walk-in closets' worth of my old size fours. At one point I'd been tempted to burn them in effigy for my failed career. But I'd kept them for a reason. I just assumed that reason would be I'd be able to fit in them again one day.

Grabbing two of Sienna's largest, most overpriced designer suitcases, I threw in every single article of clothing without even looking. You'd think they wouldn't all fit, but you have to take into account the length, or lack thereof, of my former wardrobe. The entire process took two minutes tops.

Factor in another five minutes to roll the suitcases to the car and an additional twenty-five sitting in traffic, and I was standing in front of Betty at a practically deserted Clothes Encounters within the hour. She was back from her vacation and judging by the new rock on her left ring finger, it had been a very, very, very good trip.

Her eyes flicked to the suitcase I had dramatically dropped on its side and flung open. Clothes spilled out, desperate to make their escape. It was as if they knew their fate. "We do a sixty/forty cut," she said. "And I don't take anything from H&M."

"It's all designer," I said. "Just a couple of seasons old."

"Perfect," she said. "Let's get started."

I threw the clothes inside and followed her to the back of the store. As many times as I'd dropped by, I'd never been back there. It was exactly what I'd expected. Clothes hung everywhere, all neatly labeled too. She opened the first door on the left.

Her office was as eccentric and fifties as she was. Lots of pink, of course. The walls were filled with old school glamour shots of Old Hollywood stars in their heyday. Even her computer was a "classic" — a late-nineties hot pink iMac. It sat on a pink chrome Formica table she used as a desk. The two chairs were also vintage. They sat next to a few empty clothes racks. The only unglamorous thing in there — myself excluded — was a large whiteboard hanging on the wall. It had one of those blank calendars, which she had dutifully filled in.

"Have a seat." She took a suitcase from me and opened it, using a much gentler hand than moi. She examined the clothes while she spoke. "We'll go through each piece so you can tell me anything I need to know. We'll look up items online and on eBay to come up with a price. The cut includes all hanging costs. You just need to pick up your check when an item is sold."

Sounded good to me. We got to work. I heard the bell above the door ring a couple of times, but Betty never stopped. There must've been someone I hadn't seen working the front desk. I hoped it wasn't Marina. I still wasn't ready to see her. Luckily, I didn't have to.

Betty was good at what she did so it only took an hour before she was hanging the final piece on the rack. "You have a nice collection," she said. "There shouldn't be any problem getting rid of it."

That's when it hit me. I was getting rid of my clothes, as in they wouldn't belong to me anymore. Someone else would own them. Someone else would wear them. Someone else would wash them and not just pay someone to do it like I did.

I felt like I was giving up a child. Someone else would be wearing my children. Not the best analogy, but it was as gross as I felt. Unaware of my internal crisis, Betty rolled the first rack out the door without giving me a chance to say a proper goodbye. "Let me just get these out of here and we can sign the contract."

A dress fell off the rack. She stopped. It probably wasn't a coincidence it was my favorite. I'd worn it during my appearance on the *Today* show. Of course it would want to stay with me as much I suddenly wanted to stay with it. I grabbed it off the ground, clutching it to my implants.

"Oh, thanks." Betty sounded like she expected me to hang it back on the rack. That didn't happen. She sighed, as if this was an everyday occurrence. She walked toward me, slowly holding her hand out. "It's okay." She reached for my precious dress, but I leaned back. "I'll find them all a good home."

She gently pulled the *Today* dress from

my hands. Surprisingly, I let her. She smiled like everything was okay as she hung the dress back up, but she was quicker when she resumed rolling the rack out. I turned my attention to the second rack and looked at my babies. I loved them all. I gently ran my fingers over each piece. It became too much. I forced myself to look away.

I made myself examine the photos on the wall. She had some beauties decorating them. Ava Gardner. Elizabeth Taylor. Lana Turner. Movie stars really were so much more glamorous before the invention of *TMZ*. I turned to the calendar. It looked like Betty used the whiteboard to track everyone's work schedules, writing in workers' initials to mark their shifts. There was a BX, which had to be her, MC for what had to be Marina, and finally an NP.

My internal light bulb went off. It wasn't one of those rinky-dink forty-watt energy efficient ones, either. What if the NP in Haley's text to Victory didn't stand for "no problem"? What if it stood for Betty's other employee, Nat Whatever-her-last-name-was? Was Haley telling Victory that Nat took all the cash from the Kandy Wrapper robbery?

Betty came back in. I called over my shoulder, "What's Nat's last name?"

"My last name is Peters. Why?"

I turned with quickness, coming face to face with someone who might just be Haley's killer. By that point, I had plenty of experience confronting Haley's would-be killers, so I knew the rules. Rule Number One: Don't let them know you think they did it. I forced myself to smile as I spoke. "Just wondering."

I followed it with Rule Number Two: Get out of there as soon as possible unless you have backup. I slipped past her and grabbed my purse. "Tell Betty I had to run. I'll sign the contract later."

I hauled butt and soon found myself sitting in my car contemplating this latest development. Could Nat be Haley's partner-turned-murderer? Even without the initials, she fit the profile. Victory had let it slip that Haley's partner was a she. Nat had the necessary lady parts. She was also small enough to be the shadowed partner. And she was obsessed with all things Hollywood. I'd never really thought about her because she and Haley didn't seem close.

I still wasn't sure. I looked at my Pink Panther pumps and got an idea. It was one of my better ones. Luckily, I'd brought my tablet. I hunted down some free Wi-Fi, logged into Facebook, and loaded the pics from Allie's twenty-first birthday party. It was Nat's alibi, but she could have always left the party early. Scrolling through until I found a full-body shot of her, I zoomed in on her shoes.

When I first saw the photo, I'd assumed Nat was like everyone else in Hollywood, rocking knockoffs of Toni's shoes. Now I realized she was *wearing* Toni's shoes. I peered close. The heels were definitely five inches. The knockoffs had gone for a more sell-friendly three-and-a-half. I called the tip line immediately.

"Tip li—"

I cut the Voice off. "It's me. Got something good this time."

"Oh goodie. They preempted my soaps for the stupid president."

I chose to ignore that, instead launching into what had happened the last week of my life. I went into Victory's slip-up, the NP on Haley's phone matching Nat's initials, and finally, the photos of Nat wearing Toni's shoes. "That's photographic evidence. Has to be enough for an arrest, don't you think?"

"I think you're getting us confused with the fashion police," the Voice said.

A vision invaded my head of some soap opera–handsome prosecutor thrusting a photo at the jury and exclaiming, "Look, they're not knockoffs." She had a point.

"I'll have something more for you in a day or two." I hung up before I could hear her smart-aleck reply.

I needed more, but I couldn't just confront Nat. She needed to confess, and I had to be there to catch it. Or at least catch enough to get the police to haul her in. But how? I started my car and pulled away.

I always did my best thinking when I was either in the car or in the shower. It was as if my brain went on stand-by, letting the important things break through the crowd of unimportant crap like what Angelina Jolie wore to the Oscars three years ago (Valentino). Within five minutes, I was busting a U-turn, knowing exactly how I'd get Nat to confess.

I waited until I got to a stoplight to call Emme and beg.

TWENTY-SIX

"You bring it?"

Aubrey presented the baseball hat without the least bit of fanfare. It was new. Too new. The maroon-colored brim was as stiff as a shirt that had OD'd on starch and the intertwined yellow S and C so bright they looked like they were glowing with toxic waste. He hadn't even bothered to take off the price tag stuck to the underside of the brim.

This wouldn't do at all. He watched, saying nothing, as I cracked the USC cap's brim, then bent down in the moonlight — in my Pink Panthers and a dress, no less — to smear some grass on it. Nothing wrong with being a bit dirty. At least that's what my first boyfriend out here claimed. If only he'd been talking about sex and not his bathing habits.

I shook off the excess dirt and examined my handiwork. "Much better."

Aubrey finally spoke. "I still think this is foolish, Ms. Anderson. We should call the police."

"We made a deal. Try it my way first and then do it your way if it doesn't work."

We were at Toni's house re-enacting the crime scene like I'd seen them do on *Snapped* and all those melodramatic news magazine shows.

It had hit me in the car that the best way to trap Nat was to use her love of all things famous against her. Toni was as famous as one could get. Everyone in an English-speaking country knew she'd been on location the past five months in Antarctica. Factor in Nat assuming Toni was interested in doing a movie on Haley's life and it all came together.

I'd driven back to Clothes Encounters, swallowed my fear like a stale peanut butter cookie, and walked back in under the guise of signing my contract. I'd also "finally" admitted we were not only developing a movie about Haley but had a studio interested. Nat ate it up as I told her Toni was flying back into town for just twenty-four hours to meet with the studio, and that she'd asked me to invite a few of Haley's closest friends to dinner the night before the meeting to get insight into Haley's life.

Betty, unfortunately, couldn't make it. It just so "happened" I picked a day she was working. Nat, of course, jumped at the chance. Who would turn down a free dinner, period, much less one with an A-plus-list movie star?

The only problem came when Nat insisted on knowing the restaurant. Already nervous, I hadn't thought that far ahead, so I said the first thing that came to mind: Chow House.

She was elated. Me? Not so much. It was only after I spoke that I remembered I could barely afford McDonald's, much less Chow House. But it was too late. I'd have to resort to the emergency credit card to pay for it. On the plus side, Nat might be less likely to become a triple murderer in a room full of half of *People's* World's Most Beautiful People list.

I told Nat that Toni was coming straight from the airport and we'd meet her at the restaurant. We'd wine and dine her and then, if we got lucky, take her back to Toni's for a nightcap. If all went well, she'd slip into something less comfortable — hand-cuffs. I was hoping that being there when we all visited the house for the "first time" since Toni had been on location and "dis-covering" the robbery would get Nat off her game, and she'd mention enough of her involvement to warrant an arrest. If she still didn't slip up, we'd pretend she'd been caught on tape. She hadn't been, but there was a good chance she didn't know that.

The crime scene was pretty easy to recreate. The Rack Pack had been neat and just taken clothes and jewelry. The only clues they had even been there were the unlocked door, a few left-on light switches, and the hat. All we had to do was unscrew a few light bulbs, unlock a door, and buy a baseball cap.

The only thing missing was Toni herself. Of course, I had the next best thing. Unfortunately, the next best thing took some convincing, but after I reminded said thing about her grandmother's stolen necklace and the whole double-homicide issue, she reluctantly agreed to pretend to be her sister.

Aubrey would be performing the role of bodyguard and Sienna would also be tagging along. I'd enlisted their help because any celebrity worth their weight in box office receipts was incomplete without an entourage.

I left Aubrey on the patio and went to check on Sienna and Emme. I found them in the dress section of Toni's closet — yes,

Toni's closet was big enough to have sections — standing a few feet back. I'd placed Sienna in charge of hair, makeup, and clothes. She was taking her job very seriously, her eyes roaming back and forth over Toni's dress collection like a hungry lion. She zeroed in on her prey and quickly pounced, coming back from the mass of clothes with a black dress made from silk that flowed like water. She held it against Emme and spoke. "This should hide the extra ten pounds."

Even though Emme was a size two, she had ten pounds on her sister. Toni was so itty-bitty that size zeroes had to be taken in to fit her. "On to makeup," Sienna continued. "Day, pick out some shoes."

Emme looked at me, wondering exactly what I'd gotten her into. "Sigh," she said, then followed Sienna out the door.

Extra weight aside, we had a few additional problems to overcome. Though they were identically beautiful, there were subtle differences. Emme had all her original parts. Toni? Not so much. But like with any good plastic surgery, the tweaks were not apparent at first glance. Or even second, third, or fourth glance. Slightly larger cup size. Slightly more refined nose. Slightly poutier lips. The result wasn't so much that Toni looked different. She just looked better. Thankfully, Emme didn't give a crap.

The only people who could tell the difference were family and stalkers. Nat definitely didn't fall into the former category. I wasn't so sure about the latter. I was worried she'd take one glance and know she was not in the presence of Hollywood royalty.

I spent the next few minutes shoe shopping in Toni's closet before deciding on a pair of peep toe stilettos. By the time I emerged, Emme was dressed and Sienna was finishing her eye makeup. I gasped. Emme looked like the Toni who'd been bought and paid for in full. I moved in close to see exactly what Sienna had done, but even close up, it was hard to tell. "What did you do?" I finally asked.

Sienna beamed. "Contoured the nose to make it look a bit smaller. The cleavage is a combo of Toni's best pushup bra and a bit of shadow between the boobs to make them look bigger. The lips come courtesy of white pencil to the middle of her top lip and a lighter lipstick."

"She's a work of art." I glanced at my cell phone. "One that needs to be in the car in five minutes."

We were in Toni's Mercedes in ten. Close enough. Sienna drove since she was the only one who could drive stick. Aubrey was beside her, while Emme and I sat in the back. The Emme-to-Toni transformation made me feel a kajillion times better, but I was still nervous as all get-out. If all went well, we were going to make a double murderer very, very angry. I didn't want to see what Nat did when she was angry. It was probably akin to doubling in size and turning green.

Five minutes from the restaurant, Emme realized she'd forgotten her cell phone. She acted like her left arm was cut off, even though I assured her it was intact. It was too late to go back. Her games of Candy Crush Soda Saga would still be there later. We had a reservation, and you weren't late for reservations at Chow House. Even if you were Toni Abrams, or at least pretending to be.

We got there with thirty seconds to spare. Pulling up to Chow House felt more like going to a premiere than dinner. The line for the valet was around the corner and the line of paparazzi and tourists lingering outside even longer. They all looked bored out their mind. Nat was supposed to meet us at the restaurant, but she wasn't outside. Where was she?

The paps recognized Toni's car as soon as

we got to the front of the valet line. They went bat crazy, which caused the tourists to go even crazier despite not knowing who was inside. Then Emme stepped out and mass hysteria set in. Flashbulbs popped like a microwaved bag of Orville Redenbacher's.

Emme froze, then glanced back like she wanted to jump into the car. She'd dealt with paps before, but never of this magnitude. She was like a deer in paparazzi lights.

Then Aubrey touched her elbow and she suddenly remembered she wasn't Emme at that moment. She held her head up high as they walked to the door, ignoring the paps as they called Toni's name.

The maître d' greeted us at the door. "Ms. Abrams. Welcome back to Chow House. We have your table waiting."

Sienna and I followed as we wound our way through the restaurant, past several well-known stars eating and, more importantly, being seen. A few tried to stop us to say hello to "Toni." They were ignored.

I bounced between checking out the celebs and checking out the decor. They'd redesigned since I'd last been there. Chow House's new designer was a big fan of three things: candles, mirrors, and orchids. All three littered the main dining room in random combinations, capped off by mirrored walls and ceiling. All the easier for diners to stare at themselves.

The room's centerpiece was a small pond sprinkled with orchid petals and floating votive candles. The bottom of the pond was, of course, mirrored, occasionally reflecting light from the three-foot-wide chandelier that hung above it.

It had a bridge we used to get to the VIP room. Even among the rich and famous, there were the more rich and more famous. The decorator had at least shown restraint with that room. Only two of the walls were mirrored, the ceiling having mercifully been left alone. A bottle of Evian joined the orchids and candles on each table. Only three of the ten tables were occupied, but the occupants accounted for half of last year's box office.

I expected to see Nat waiting at our table. She wasn't, which made me even more worried.

The maître d' pulled out our chairs, dispensed menus like Halloween candy, and hovered just long enough to make sure we didn't need anything. Once we confirmed that we didn't, he disappeared. I took a deep breath and opened the menu — scared of the big bad monster known as the price list.

My fears were well-founded. A glass of

wine was twenty-two dollars, and that bottle of Evian? Thirty bucks if we opened it. I felt myself starting to hyperventilate. My emergency credit card only had four hundred available. If we spent a penny more, I'd be singing for my supper — which wouldn't turn out well since my seventh-grade choir teacher once informed me I was tone deaf.

I looked up to find Sienna staring at me. She smiled when our eyes met. "This is fun, Day!" She sounded as if I'd invited her to Disneyland and not to catch a killer. "I'd really like to pay to thank you for inviting me."

"Actually, I'm gonna pay," Emme said. "Part of the reason we're doing this is to help my sister."

I smiled. They loved me enough to not only know I couldn't afford it, but also not embarrass me by saying it out loud. "Thanks," I said. "But my thing. My problem. My bill."

"What if we compromise and all pay for ourselves?" Sienna asked.

I smiled at her. "This doesn't seem like a place that does separate checks," I said, then changed the subject. "Nat's late."

"She's probably in that valet line," Sienna said. "She'll be here any minute."

Any minute turned into five, then ten. We

kept having to wave off the waiter who appeared every sixty seconds on the dot. I didn't know what to think. What if Nat stood us up? And even scarier, what if she didn't? Could we actually go through with it? I wasn't the only one feeling that way. Emme was sweating like a waterfall. "Your cleavage is running," I said.

The three of them — Aubrey included — looked at her breasts. A brown-colored line of sweat ran down the right one and disappeared into the crevice. "We need to take care of that," Sienna said and the two of them went off to the ladies room.

That left me, Aubrey, and no Nat. I checked my texts. There were none. "What if she doesn't show up?" I addressed my question to the door.

"Then she does not show up," he said.

Thank you, Confucius. I stood up and spoke. "I'm gonna check the front. Maybe the hostess is giving her grief."

I made my way over the bridge and to the lobby. Nat was nowhere to be seen. Deciding to check outside, I went out there just in time to see a Bentley pull up. The crowd moved toward the car, anticipating someone big. Like president-big. And I mean United States. Not just the Academy.

The driver got out and walked over to the

passenger side. He opened the door and a teeny, tiny blonde got out looking like she'd just bought the entire block. She wore sunglasses even though the sun was long gone. That was about all I could see before she was enveloped in a sea of flashbulbs, pens, and paper. Who was that? Aniston? Theron?

The herd made its way toward me. I braced myself. If I fell, I'd be trampled. Death by knockoff Louboutins was not any way to go. Someone opened the door and she walked by without so much as a glance, losing both me and the crowd like a sock in the dryer. It was only when she was already inside I realized it was Nat. Wow.

I managed to slip in right before the door closed on Nat's newly adoring public, then watched as the hostess greeted her. "Hi! Welcome to Chow —"

Nat cut her off. "I have a dinner reservation with Toni Abrams."

"Of course, Miss . . ." The anxious-to-please hostess trailed off, sure Nat was famous but coming up short on the name.

"Peters."

"Yes, Ms. Peters. I love your work in . . ." Once again, she came up short. So she wisely changed the subject. "Right this way."

They were about to head off when I

stopped them. "I'll take her. Hi, Nat. You look amazing." And she did. Not to get all cliché, but she was dressed to kill in a sleeveless dress made of a shimmering silver lace. I wondered whose closet she'd stolen it from. "We're in a private room in back," I said as we started off.

"Of course." Nat sounded as if she expected nothing less. "Toni already here?"

"Yep, she can't wait to meet you."

When we made it to the VIP room, I saw that Sienna and Emme were just sitting back down. As soon as Nat saw Emme, she bounded over and launched herself at Emme with the force of a rocket grenade.

Aubrey finally reacted, but it was too late. Nat was already on her. She looked like she was trying to squeeze the life out of Emme.

So much for safety in numbers.

TWENTY-SEVEN

Nat's embrace would impress even a polar bear. The only reason Emme didn't tip over like a bowling pin was that Nat had her arms around her. Sienna and I looked on, shocked, as Aubrey tried to pry Nat's hand off Emme. "Ma'am, please remove your hands from Ms. Abrams's midsection," he said.

"No, it's okay," Nat said. "I know her."

Though Emme may have lost her balance, she kept her wits. "Yes, of course, you're Nat."

She put her own arms around Nat — completing what had to be the most awkward hug in the history of time. As she did, she glanced at me over Nat's back and I knew I'd be paying for this by spending serious time helping her out on FarmVille.

"Thank you for meeting about the project." Emme sounded just like Toni. Besides being acronym-free, Toni's voice had no traces of a Valley accent thanks to a voice coach.

Nat took the chair closest to Emme, which had been my seat. Since I didn't feel now was a good time to bring that up, I sat between Sienna and Aubrey. I texted Sienna as the waiter came over to take our order: *She's not acting very killer-like.*

I heard a buzz and Sienna pulled out her phone as the waiter went over house specials as if he'd been practicing for this moment since he was a toddler. He spoke as if telling us about his life, not about chicken sauce. Unemployed actor no doubt. By the time he'd gotten to the climax — the final special of the night — I'd gotten Sienna's return text. *The good ones never do! That's what lets them kill people!!!!*

Touché. The waiter moved to the wine list. "May I suggest the Giaconda Chardonnay?" I snuck a peek at the menu. It was $150 a bottle. "It's an Australian wine aged underground. Intense, but also very light."

Intense or not, no way I could afford that. Aubrey, Sienna, and Emme knew that. Nat, however, didn't. "That sounds great."

Dangit. I forced myself to look on the bright side. At least that meant she'd be liquored up. The waiter waltzed off after swearing he'd come back for our food orders. At this rate, the only thing I could afford was ice, though they probably also charged for that.

My best bet was to get Nat out of there as quick as possible. I dove in, figuring I'd warm her up by starting off slow, then hitting her with the harder questions once the alcohol set in.

"You know we're pitching a story about Haley to Paramount tomorrow. We see this as a story not just about her death, but also about her life. Sort of a metaphor for every beautiful blonde who has come to Hollywood with nothing but a dollar and a dream."

Nat nodded, as impressed with my BS as I was. I was about to continue when she raised her hand like this was the third grade.

"You have a question?" I asked.

"Yeah." She turned to Emme. "How long did it take Marc Jacobs to design your Oscar gown?"

I would have preferred if she'd asked to go to the nurse's office. I doubted Emme even knew the answer. I jumped in. "So what would you like for us to know about Haley?"

I was straight-up ignored. "Did you have to go to his studio for fittings?"

Nat was relentless. I was about to inter-

378

rupt again when Emme spoke up. "He flew out here. It took him about two months to finalize the design. Fittings were at my house, though his studio is beautiful."

She sounded sure of herself. But was she accurate? Apparently so, because Nat smiled. "Marc Jacobs came to your house? I would have died!"

Emme smiled at Nat. "How long did you and Haley know each other?"

"Not that long. So did you tell him exactly what you wanted or did he show you his ideas?"

No way could Emme answer that. I prepared for the worst. "It's actually based on my grandmother's wedding dress," Emme said.

Even I didn't know that. The waiter arrived with the Chardonnay, which was a good thing because I suddenly needed a drink. He made a big production of pouring everyone's glasses, making it once again look like he was performing on Broadway. I lifted my glass. My very, very, very expensive glass. "A toast," I said, as the rest of the table joined in. "To Haley."

Sienna and I made sure to make eye contact when we clinked glasses. Neither of us wanted seven years of bad sex. Everyone else obviously wasn't as concerned, judging by the lack of eye contact from Nat, Emme, and Aubrey. After we finished toasting, I took a sip.

It was good, but then for 150 bucks, it darn well should've been. On my second sip, I realized Nat had put her drink down without even tasting it and cracked open the bottle of Evian. Add thirty dollars to my tab. Great. "Saving your wine for dinner?" I asked.

"I don't drink." She couldn't have told me that before she ordered the wine? I was not a happy camper.

"Come on, all the cool kids are doing it. We're gonna jump off a cliff next." I laughed at my own corny joke. "Just have a sip. You might like it. It's really good."

She spoke again. "I would, but my sponsor would kill me." *Cómo se* what? Nat was in AA? Eek. There went that plan. She turned to Emme. "I was at Betty Ford the exact same time as Amanda Bynes!"

Only in Hollywood is rehab something to brag about. The moment was ridiculously awkward. Sienna tried to lighten it. "Well, at least we have a designated driver."

"Definitely!" Nat said. "As long as it's not stick."

We were saved by the waiter. "Ready for your food orders?"

I wish I could say the rest of the dinner flew by, but it was the longest sixty minutes of my life. Nat ordered a fifty-five dollar salad, took a photo of it for Instagram, and then just picked at it.

Emme, Aubrey, Sienna, and I all brought up Haley several times, but Nat was more interested in Toni. I split my time trying to conjure up a question she'd actually answer and adding up the bill. I met trouble on both counts. The lone bright spot was when Nat accepted our invite to hang at Toni's afterward. It was a good thing, too, because the "discovery" of the robbery was now more important than ever.

When the bill came — hidden in a leatherbound holder — Aubrey reached for it. Perhaps he took pity on how bad things were going for me. I scooped it up before he had the chance but I couldn't open it, as scared as if I might find Freddy Krueger hiding behind the leather flap.

I was so busy willing the unseen check to shrink like a man's privates in nine-degree weather that I didn't notice the commotion at the door. Sienna practically kicked my leg off under the table. I looked up to see Toni's ex, Luke Cruz, coming in with his arm casually around some wisp of a model I'd seen on a magazine cover during my last late-night candy run.

He knew Toni better than anyone who hadn't shared a womb with her for nine months. He did a double take when he saw Emme and headed over, aware that every eye was on him. It felt like slow motion. The only things missing were a soundtrack and the sound of a guy two seats down loudly chomping on popcorn.

I was tempted to throw the wine bottle at him and scream, "Run!" The only thing that stopped me was it cost too much. He stopped a few feet away and gave Emme a once-over. "Not a lot of gyms in Antarctica, huh?"

He bent down for a quick peck, going for Emme's mouth. She recoiled and he settled for her cheek. "You didn't tell me you were coming back to town, Toni."

"That's because we broke up."

He smiled as if this were some game only he was playing. "I have about twenty sexts from last night that say differently."

Emme's eyes narrowed. Toni must not have told her sister she was seeing Luke again. Emme didn't look too pleased about it.

"Don't tell me you're mad I'm here with Anastasia," he said. "We have the same publicist. I'm just getting her some press."

"Cut the BS

"BS?" he rep   said.
shocked. "You've   anaging to sound
time with that we   ending too much
sister. That's somethin   mit you call a

Ruh-roh. Five more se say."
would be blown.   and our cover

"I sure have," Emme said
should dump you once and e thinks I
am."   ll, and I

Luke reached for her arm. Aub   inter-
cepted. "Please do not touch Ms. A rams."

"Come on, baby, tell this dude you only
joking," Luke said, but he kept his han to
himself. "This is how we communicate."

Emme stood. "Contact me again and I'm
leaking the photos of you in my thong."

She stormed off, Aubrey close on her
heels. Sienna threw Luke a glare and took
off herself. Nat hesitated, then snapped a
quick photo of him with her iPhone and
shuffled off — leaving just little old me and
the check. Luke looked at me and smiled.
"You know I dig black chicks, right?"

"Shove it."

"Especially sassy ones."

"I've seen the photos. Please tell me you
tucked."

I glared at him until he slunk back to
Anastasia. I had more important things to

worry about tha inability to fill out
women's und like how much the
check would b I had enough to cover
it. I reached thing tentatively, then
inhaled and. it.

It wasn't note from Mr. Chow himself
Inside Yow much he'd enjoyed her last
telling T how he hoped she'd come back
movie a nk. You. Mr. Chow. I just wished
soon. T d've told us this earlier. I would've
he wo he lobster.
ordered

By he time I left a tip and got outside,
the valet had pulled the car up. We got in,
accompanied by a symphony of flashbulbs.

The ride was more of the same as at dinner. Nat playing twenty questions about Toni's fashion choices. Though by that point we'd all given up on her answering a single question about Haley.

We were pulling up to the security gate at Toni's development when I finally figured out how to get Nat to talk about Haley — appeal to her ego. I leaned forward to look at Emme and asked, "Toni, have you changed your mind about playing Haley's best friend?"

I turned to Nat. "We're going for an unknown for Haley. But I've been trying to convince Toni to play the best friend. We're

384

toying with making the story more about that friendship. That loss of losing the person closest to you."

Nat perked up. "That's so smart. It's what I felt when I found out she died. We hung out all the time. I almost quit Clothes Encounters because it was too hard working there without her."

I just nodded. She was really laying the whole "we were BFFs" thing on thick.

"I even introduced her to her boyfriend," she added.

Nat knew Victory? Did not see that one coming.

"He and I went to high school together," she went on. "He just died too, you know. Strangled during a robbery. So I lost them both in like three months."

"I can't even imagine," I said. "What was the last thing you said to Haley?"

Nat hesitated, then pulled an answer out of thin air. "I told her I loved her, of course."

"Can you imagine if you hadn't? That regret. You'd probably carry the guilt for the rest of your life. Have you ever seen Toni play regret? She's a master."

"Toni also does a mean guilt," Sienna said as we pulled into the driveway. "It's too bad you guys weren't fighting before she died.

Toni would finally get that Oscar she deserves."

We got out as I spoke again. "The Academy lives for stuff like that."

Nat was suddenly eager to please. "That actually was what happened with me and Victory."

Interesting. We got to the porch. "Really? About what?"

She was about to answer when the front door swung open and Toni stepped out.

TWENTY-EIGHT

"You left the sliding door in the living room unlocked," Toni said, coming onto the porch as Aubrey slipped past her inside the house. "And who was that?"

I glanced at Nat. Her head was bobbing back and forth between the two of them as if wondering which was real and which was Memorex. I didn't blame her. I wasn't sure myself.

I turned around in time to see Toni give her sister a once-over, no doubt realizing Emme was wearing her dress, her makeup, and her best pushup bra. She opened her mouth to speak but I didn't give her the chance. "Emme!" I pulled Toni into a hug, pressing her face against my chest and hoping silicone muted any attempts to talk. "Didn't know you'd be here! That guy was Toni's new bodyguard, Aubrey! You haven't met him because he's been with her in Antarctica!"

I sounded way too hyper, but I couldn't stop speaking in exclamation points. I could practically see them at the end of each sentence. "Toni just got into town! We would've invited you to dinner, but you would've been bored! It was a business dinner about the girl who died in the hit-and-run! Haley Joseph! We're pitching her story to Paramount tomorrow!"

Out the corner of my eye, I looked at Nat, who still wore her confusion like an ill-fitting Oscar dress. Finally letting Toni breathe, I held her at arm's length. *"Toni"* — I gestured to Emme with a nod of my head — "wanted to take Haley's good friend Nat to dinner at Chow House! Since Toni" — another exaggerated gesture on my end — "is only in town for a day, we went straight to the restaurant from the airport! You know *Toni* hasn't been home in months! And no one's stepped foot in *Toni's* house, not even you."

A screenwriter would groan and settle into some diatribe about my dialogue being too "on the nose" and over-explanatory, but they weren't trying to catch a killer by tricking her into thinking one of the world's most recognizable actresses was actually her sister. I had to make sure Toni, the real one, knew exactly what was going on.

I finally managed to shut myself up and we all stared at Toni. I willed her to get the point and play along. After what felt like an eternity, she turned to Nat. She opened her mouth and my breath caught. "Hi," she finally said. "I'm Emme. Toni's sister."

Then she walked over and stuck out her hand. Thank. The. Lord.

Nat gave Toni a quick dismissive handshake before turning all her attention back to Emme. "I knew you had a sister, but I didn't realize how much you two looked alike."

Yes! "How was your flight?" Toni asked, getting into it now. Her voice had even taken on the remnants of the Valley accent Emme still carried.

"Flight was great," Emme said. "It was dinner that sucked. I ran into Luke."

My high plummeted at 10,000 miles per hour and crash-landed next to me. It was not the time or place to chastise your sister about her poor choice in men. Used to it, Toni took it in stride. "You two talk?"

"Yep. About how we've been sexting twenty times a day." Emme's eye narrowed with accusation.

Toni didn't even blink. "TMI."

We needed to get back on track. Pronto. I turned to Toni. "You said a door was unlocked?"

Toni nodded, still looking at Emme. "Yep. No alarm, either. I tried calling you. Went straight to voicemail, and you didn't answer any of my texts. WTF?"

"Sorry," Emme said. "I do that all the time even though I know how much it annoys you."

"NAA," Toni said. Not at all. "You can't always answer your phone just because I want to talk to you. Sometimes you have two hundred people waiting to film a scene."

"Or I just say that to get you off my back for having crappy manners."

It was Toni's turn to glare. "How about you KMPPA. Kiss my pale pink a—"

"We need to call the police, Ms. Abrams. There may have been a break-in."

Talk about saved by the Aubrey. He arrived just in time to remind us we had parts to play. Our faces all morphed into horrified expressions, except for Nat. Her face was blank, then she saw me looking at her and tried her best to look as shocked as the rest of us. "Are they gone?" she asked Aubrey.

Yeah, for two months now. "I think they have left, but I would like to check a few more rooms."

We all followed him inside. Emme turned

to Toni. "You didn't notice anything strange when you were traipsing around?"

"Besides mentioning the door was unlocked and the alarm was off?"

Emme stopped and looked around the foyer as if searching for telltale signs of a robbery. At least she was following that part of the plan. "Everything looks fine," she said. "They didn't take my Banksy."

She was right. Banksy was a well-known graffiti artist whose original works went for thousands. Toni's had been a gift from a particularly aggressive producer who'd wanted her for his film. She'd turned down the part yet kept the painting.

I turned to the family room right off the foyer. "TV's also still here."

We continued like this, going from room to room doing a quick visual inventory for Nat's sake. The cars and bike were still in the garage. The computer was still in the office. The People's Choice award was still in the den.

Nat didn't say much, probably because she didn't need a spoiler alert to know none of the big stuff would be gone. Then we got to Toni's closet, where she'd actually had done some damage. When we first walked in, she had no reaction. That alone was suspicious. I'd yet to meet a woman who didn't gasp in awe upon entering Toni's closet. Sienna had even cried. Nat, however, didn't even glance at the shoe department.

"Crap. I *was* robbed," Emme said right on cue. "I definitely am missing some clothes."

"We need to call the police," Aubrey said.

At the word *police,* Nat suddenly perked up. "How do you even know there's been a robbery?" she asked. "There's so much stuff. How can you tell if anything's missing?" She had a point. It really was impossible to tell at first glance. The closet was packed tighter than a Beverly Hills housewife's face fresh from her plastic surgeon's office. "Maybe she just left the door unlocked before her trip," Nat continued.

She had, but still. "What about the Rack Pack?" I paused long enough to gauge her reaction. Nada. "Everyone knows Toni's been out the country for months. It's not like it would be so out there for someone to break into the house while she was gone."

"In a gated community?" Nat asked. "People can't just walk in here."

Unless they're you. "There is one way to find out for sure," Aubrey said. "The video. We can check from the time Ms. Abrams left town."

I was banking on Nat not knowing

whether or not she was on tape and figuring the last thing she'd want was to find out. The plan was for Aubrey to pretend to watch the tape, then come back and tell Nat she'd been caught on camera. Then we would get to the part of the program where she'd freak the heck out.

I glanced at her. I don't know what I was expecting, but a smile was not it. "Great," she said. "Let's watch it."

Fudge. She either knew she wasn't on tape or was curious enough to find out. That tape was the last bit of leverage I had. No way could she see it, but I hadn't the slightest clue how to stop her. I couldn't ask if she wanted to play a quick game of Yahtzee. Panicked, I looked at Sienna. Her face only mirrored my own. We were screwed.

We trooped back to the office, each step taking me farther from my goal: Nat's confession. Emme sat at the desk as we crowded around her. She hesitated before hitting the power button and finally spoke. "You guys can at least put your stuff down."

Everyone was still holding their purses. "You sure we don't have to worry about anyone stealing it?" I said in a lame attempt at a joke. I was more nervous than I thought.

We set our things down in quick succession. My purse went next to where Sienna left her cell and the keys to Toni's car.

It took less than a minute for the computer to boot up and Emme to load up the video program. Ten screens appeared with the word "Standby" written in the upper left corner of each. We were looking at the live feed from the cameras outside. Since it was motion-controlled and no one was out there, the screens were black. "I should cue up the video," Emme said, sounding like that was the last thing she wanted to do.

I needed to stall her, but how? I was considering pretending like my left implant had suddenly burst when we were saved — by Nat of all people. "Can I use your bathroom?"

"Down the hall to your right," Toni said.

Behind me, I heard Nat grab her purse. As soon as she was gone, we spoke in rushed tones. "Ms. Peters knows she is not on tape," Aubrey said.

"Maybe one of us can go stall her while the rest of us pretend like we watched it?" I suggested.

Toni, Emme, and Sienna all looked at one another, no one eager to be alone with a murderer. "It won't take us long to pretend to watch it," I continued, not wanting to volunteer myself, either.

I was about to suggest Aubrey go stand

outside the bathroom door like some perv when Sienna spoke up. "It doesn't matter. She can still demand to see it."

"Then we tell Ms. Peters that will not be possible until she explains what she was doing at Ms. Abrams' house," Aubrey said.

"And if she doesn't?" Sienna asked.

"We're in trouble," I said. "We have nothing to connect her to the robbery."

Emme pointed to the computer. "Except one thing."

A camera had come to life. Nat hadn't gone to the bathroom after all. She'd snuck outside.

"She's looking for the hat! We catch her and we could force a confession!" I sounded overly excited but then again, I had a right to be.

"Once she finds it, she will leave," Aubrey said. "We need to guard the exits. How many are there?"

"Three sliding glass doors," Toni said. It was her house, after all. "She can't get to the front from the left side, but she can from the right. The doors are all locked except the one she went out of in the living room."

That was the middle of the house. Of course, we were on the left side. "Ms. Peters has only two possible exit strategies," Aubrey said. "We need to force her to come back inside."

He pointed at me and Emme. "Ms. Anderson and Ms. Abrams, head to the nearest door. I want you to scare her into going back into the house, where I will be waiting."

"What if she goes around the other side?" I asked.

"Ms. Hayes and the other Ms. Abrams can handle it. Do not try to stop her. I just want you to scare her into running back inside. Do you understand?"

We nodded and took off to our respective destinations. Emme and I ran to the nearest exit, which was Toni's bedroom. Emme slid the glass door open and we ran out. Nat was about twenty-five yards to our right. The hat was in her hand. "Nat, stop! You won't get away with it!"

I sounded pretty sure of myself because I was. We were to her left. Aubrey was waiting inside. Sienna and Toni were at the side exit to her right, or would be soon. Nat was stuck. I expected her to head back inside as we'd planned. Once again, Nat didn't do what was expected. It was getting kind of annoying. She headed for the right-side exit.

Unfortunately, I knew Toni and Sienna weren't there yet. Without even as much of a glance at each other, Emme and I took off after her. Though I could run in heels, I couldn't run fast and I didn't have the time to kick my shoes off. Emme, practically a heel virgin, wasn't doing any better. We didn't make up any ground.

Nat was about ten feet from rounding the corner to freedom, but she still had to run past the final set of sliding glass doors. I could hear the door being yanked open. Toni tumbled out.

I figured Nat would turn around when she saw Toni and the four of us could play a nice game of tag until Aubrey got there. Instead, she kept going. Toni planted her feet, figuring it was easier to let Nat come to her. And Nat sure was coming. She was almost at the sliding door when Sienna appeared out of nowhere from inside, flying through the air like a bird, a plane, or Superman himself.

Her intention was to take Nat down in a move worthy of WWE. Or it would've been if she hadn't missed. She was about five seconds too early. Nat saw her coming and slowed down. Sienna sailed right on past her like a ship in the night before belly-flopping smack-dab onto the cold concrete.

TWENTY-NINE

That left Toni.

Toni was ready for her, bracing herself and planting her feet like a defensive lineman for the 49ers. Nat came at her like a two-hundred-pound running back. She charged Toni full-out, having speed if not weight behind her. Toni went down like a sack of Russet potatoes. Nat jumped over her and disappeared around the side of the house.

Emme and I got to them seconds later. I instinctively went to Sienna while Emme did the same with Toni. I rolled Sienna over so she was staring up at the sky. "My face okay?" she asked.

I checked. "Beautiful as ever."

"Good. Now go get her."

"My pleasure."

I jumped up, rushing past Emme and Toni as determined as ever. By the time I got to the driveway, I was out of breath and Nat was in the driver's seat of the Mercedes.

Tired as heck, I was happy for the opportunity to ease up. Nat didn't have a key. We were going to be okay.

Then she turned the sucker on.

She must've taken the keys when she'd pretended to go to the bathroom. Great. I sped back up, getting to the front of the car just as she put the thing in reverse.

Slamming my fist on the hood, I considered jumping on it. I flashed to a vision of me holding on for dear life as Nat sped down the hill. Then I remembered this was real life. I didn't have a stunt double, but I did still have my sanity. No hood jumping was in my immediate future. I rushed to the passenger-side door with every intention of yanking it open and jumping in. Just as I touched the door handle, it locked.

Nat smiled at me as I glanced up. We both stayed like that for a bit, staring at each other. Then she hit the gas and backed out the driveway, staring me dead in the eye the entire time. She barely made it to the street before she threw it into first gear and took off.

I gave chase, running down the middle of the road. I made a vow right then and there to spend less time with Ben & Jerry and more time with Jenny Craig. I watched as

Nat got about thirty feet. Then the car stalled.

As I ran toward her, I could hear the gears grinding away as she tried to get the car moving again.

She'd said she couldn't drive stick. Good to see she wasn't lying about one thing.

I tried the driver-side door handle. It was still locked. "Open the door before I kick the glass in!" I yelled. I'd seen Todd Arrington do it once in a movie.

"Please do," Nat yelled back. "The only thing you'd break is a heel."

That made me even more pissed. I was tempted to go ahead and try it, hoping that maybe my anger would lead to the same super strength mothers got when they lifted whole cars off their injured children. I raised my foot up, poised to kick, and that's when I heard the beep.

Emme ran up from behind me, the spare set of keys in her hand. She practically knocked me out the way as she yanked open the door and grabbed Nat, who'd chosen not to wear her seat belt. Big mistake. "Don't you ever touch my sister again!" Emme yelled as she punched Nat square in her nose.

Dazed, Nat crumpled to the ground. Emme pounced on her, cocking her arm back, ready to once again make hand-to-face contact. She went for it, but Nat jerked to the right and Emme's hand glanced off her ear. Nat kicked, catching Emme right in the boob, propelling her backward.

Nat used the opportunity to scramble up and advance toward Emme. She got about two feet away when I saw the blur. Toni jumped on Nat's back and put her in a headlock. "Don't touch her!"

Emme got up quickly and served Nat with a backhand that would have made both pimps and tennis pros everywhere stand up and applaud. She was on her fourth go-round when Sienna appeared next to me. "What the . . ."

It was not every day you witnessed two rail-thin blonde carbon copies jump someone and do such an amazing job of it. Emme had told me once that she and Toni used to beat up their classmates in elementary school. I'd thought she was joking.

In the intervening twenty years, neither Abrams had lost a step. I'm sure Nat would have given them her lunch money if she wasn't losing oxygen by the second. Just when it was really about to get good, Aubrey appeared. "That is enough."

The sound of his voice made them both stop. He picked Emme up, carrying her over to us and depositing her in a heap by our feet. Toni just got a very stern look and an order: "Off."

She dropped off Nat's back and walked over to check on her sister. "Okay?" she asked.

Emme nodded. "You?"

Toni took a seat next to her, the two of them using their clothes to dab at wounds while glaring at Nat as if they were three-hundred-pound former bodyguards instead of former child stars. I walked over to Aubrey, who had handcuffed Nat to the steering wheel. She sat in the driver's seat huffing and puffing like she might blow the house down.

"Ms. Peters, anything you want to say before we call the police?" Aubrey asked.

She just looked at him and said nothing, which was fine by me. I wasn't up for much of a discussion anyway. "Anyone have a phone?" I asked.

Everyone shook his or her head. The only one of us who'd thought to bring her purse was Nat. I grabbed it. She glared at me while I rummaged through her bag and found her iPhone.

I called the tip line. Not surprisingly, the Voice didn't answer: it was late. As much as I'd wanted to gloat in her face, I happily settled for imagining her listening to my message. "This is 1018 calling about the Haley Joseph case. We just caught Nat Peters getting rid of evidence at Toni Abrams' house. We have strong reason to believe she's responsible for the murders of Haley Joseph and Victory Malone —"

I was interrupted by Nat's very sudden, very loud screaming. "What are you talking about? I didn't kill anyone, you idiot!"

I rolled my eyes. "Yeah, okay, I'll take your word for it."

I sounded cocky. It helped she was hand-cuffed to a steering wheel and I had the twin terrors standing guard a few feet away.

"You're a bigger idiot than I thought," Nat said.

"And you're going to jail. So who's really the idiot?" I was about to say more, then I realized I was still on the phone. "Anyway, let me know about the reward."

Then I hung up and called 911.

The next day, we were the talk of the town — at least Toni was. Everyone and their mama reported how she'd single-handedly taken down one-half of the Rack Pack while walking in on her mid-robbery. Accurate? Not at all.

But Emme, Toni, Sienna, and I didn't

discuss the discrepancy. In fact, we didn't discuss the previous night at all. Maybe because it was too fresh or maybe just because we were too drunk. We'd started drinking the moment the police carted Nat away and we hadn't stopped. I'd never been stone-cold drunk at nine in the morning before. It felt better than being hung over. Much, much better.

Toni's trip home had been a spur-of-the-moment attempt to cure a bout of homesickness. She had to fly back to Antarctica that afternoon, so we all squeezed into the car the studio sent to take her to the private jet the studio had paid for and drank the champagne the studio had left for her. We dropped her off and had the car take us to the condo — where we camped out and, you guessed it, drank.

Emme stood before us with two bottles. "White or red?"

"Red, dahling," Sienna said, grabbing the bottle. "The wine must match the outfit."

She giggled and started pouring, managing to get half of it on the floor. She looked down at the spill. "Oopsies," she said. "At least if we run out, we can just lick it up later."

"You are so drunk." I tended to state the

obvious when I'd had too much to drink myself.

"I'll drink to that," she said.

We clinked glasses. I tried to look into Emme's eyes but she avoided me. "Emme!" I yelled. "Eye contact."

"She wants you to have seven years bad sex!" Sienna said.

"I know!" I said. "Though I'd settle for any sex at this point, even if it was bad."

"I'll drink to that!" Sienna said and we clinked glasses once again. "Why don't you want to be in my reality show?"

Talk about an abrupt subject change. "Why didn't you ask me?" I asked.

"Because I knew you didn't want to." She changed her voice so it sounded like mine. "You're *retired.*"

"Of course I wanted to." My intent was to make her feel better, but as I said it, I realized it was the truth. "*You* didn't want me. You wanted Fab." I said his name like it was some disease.

"I wanted you. I just knew Fab would say yes."

"Oh." That made me feel better. "I'll drink to that!"

As had become custom, Sienna and I clinked, made eye contact, and sipped.

Emme finished her drink and spoke up.

"It's settled. You're on the show."

"I have an audition tomorrow," Sienna said.

"Ugh," I said. "Saturday auditions are the worst. It's always some bootleg production or last-minute casting."

"I know!" Sienna said. Clink. Stare. Sip. "At least the casting director said we could film it for my sizzle reel. You can come and give me advice. Amazing, wonderful advice."

"I'd love to!" We tapped glasses with each word, then each took a long sip.

I had reward money coming to help my parents, a reality show to be a sidekick on, and a full glass of wine. I was happy. Very, very happy. The moment needed to be captured for the ages. "Let's take a selfie!"

I grabbed my tablet. The three of us sat on the couch and crowded into the frame. There was barely enough room for us and our wine glasses, but we made it work. "To solving Haley's murder," I said.

"To finishing my sizzle reel," Sienna chimed in.

"To not leaving my house anytime soon," Emme said.

We clinked glasses once again and said "Cheese." The resulting photo was about as good as one would expect from someone holding a ten-inch tablet arm's length from her face in one hand while cradling a wine glass in the other. But at the moment, it was perfect.

I immediately uploaded it to Instagram and decided to also upload it to Twitter. But I got a bit sidetracked when I loaded the app. The first thing I saw was a tweet from Anani Miss: *It ain't the first time I've revealed a Blind, but it's the first time with visuals. Meet Mr. Bullet Train & his lady love.*

She had oh-so-thoughtfully included a link. Mr. Bullet Train? Why did that sound familiar? A thought started in the back of the brain. It took a moment to swim through the alcohol, but it finally made it to the front. Mr. Bullet Train was Omari!! Butterflies descended on my stomach faster than Sienna at a sample sale going for the last pair of size seven Louboutins.

"What's up?" Sienna asked. She looked alarmed.

Suddenly remembering Sienna and Emme were in the room, I attempted a smile. "Nothing. Anani's got pictures of Omari and his new girlfriend."

Emme and Sienna exchanged a look and a fleeting moment of sobriety. "You okay?" Emme asked.

"Of course." That was my story and I was sticking to it.

I clicked the link and waited. Why did I feel like I was about to look at photos of my boyfriend cheating on me? But Omari wasn't my boyfriend. He'd made it clear he had no feelings for me. He was allowed to date whomever he wanted. I was not allowed to be upset about it.

An error message came up on screen. I wasn't the only person interested in seeing who Omari was dating. "It's not gonna be him," Sienna said, though I noticed she was looking at the tablet as anxiously as I was.

I shrugged, hit the reload button, and got the same error. "Like I said, I don't really care."

I immediately tapped reload again. "Honestly, I just want to see who tied him down. That's it."

Another error message. I hit it again. "His love life is none of my concern."

And again. "We're barely talking."

And again. Still an error. "I mean, I want him happy, but with who isn't my concern."

I was about to hit it with my finger another time when Sienna placed her hand over mine. "We get it. You don't care."

"If you cared any less, my tablet would be broken," Emme said.

I rolled my eyes, but I was much gentler when I tapped the reload button the next time. The page finally began to load.

We all leaned in. The page loaded slow as molasses, doing that annoying thing where it loaded from the top, revealing more and more like a rolled-up poster. The first thing we saw was sky. Not very helpful. A few seconds later, we saw the top of a familiar brown head. I'd been right. Mr. Bullet Train was indeed Omari. I threw Sienna a look. "Oopsies," she said.

We got another spurt, Omari's face and the beginning of his love. Just from the scrap of head, she was a blonde and much shorter than him. "She's hideous," Sienna said, her voice so automatic she might as well have been a robot.

"Her hair color is horrid," Emme said, just as automatically.

Another few centimeters loaded and there she was.

Emme.

She was Omari's girlfriend? That didn't make sense at all. Sienna and I whipped around to look at her. She was as shocked as we were. No one spoke until the photo finished loading. Sienna finally turned to Emme. "You really might want to think about getting your hair dyed, though."

"STFU," Emme said.

"Don't get mad," Sienna said. "You said

it. Not me."

Her buzz back in full effect, Sienna giggled while I was just confused. "Where was this taken?" I asked.

"Toni's house," Emme said. "Probably by that idiot guard."

I looked closer. It *was* outside Toni's house. The guard had been there the first time we went and had mistaken Emme for Toni. He must've sold the story to Anani — omitting that I'd also been in the car — and then jumped at the chance to take some pics of Omari and Emme together while they were outside investigating how Nat and Haley had broken into Toni's place.

I started laughing like someone had just said the funniest thing in the world. Omari wasn't dating Emme. "He's single," I said. "Omari's single. And I care. I really care."

Emme and Sienna both rolled their eyes. "Duh," Emme said.

Sienna chimed in. "No question about that. The only question is why you're telling us and not telling him."

The girl had a point. I knew I should tell him. I'd been feeling that way for years. He had the right to know. I looked around for my phone, then realized it was in the bloset. I jumped up and the Earth shook.

Was this the Big One? My mother had

been right. California was about to fall into the Pacific Ocean. Then I realized I was the only one moving. I took another step and the ground shook again. No way I going anywhere.

I still needed to tell him. I sat and thought about it. Brilliance soon followed. If I couldn't call him, I could tweet him. It made sense. The world had a right to know. I went back to my Twitter app and @ed him. My mind went blank. "What should I say?"

Emme and Sienna wasted no time offering suggestions. "Ask him if he wants to shoot your club up."

"Take a lap in your pool."

"Smash your box."

"Hit your lotto."

"Tell him the amusement park is open for business."

"You're offering free admission."

"But he has to be this big to ride."

I won't mention how far apart Sienna's hands were. Amusing? Yes. Helpful? No. "No, seriously."

But they just kept on with the metaphors. Realizing I was on my own, I thought about what I really wanted to say to him. How could I express ten years of feelings in 140 characters or less? How could I tell him that

I wanted to be with him? That I'd been in love with him since that first rehearsal of *Guys and Dolls*?

I thought long and hard, then ultimately decided to keep it simple. I typed the message out.

I miss your hand.

I hit send, then replaced the tablet with my drink.

THIRTY

The morning came way too soon. My first coherent thought was that my head was killing me. The second was that I might have drunk-tweeted Omari. Fudge. I jumped out of bed — not the smartest thing to do coming off a twenty-four-hour drinking binge. I felt like I'd walked straight into an anvil, but somehow I managed to push through the pain. I had a Twitter feed to check.

I went to my Twitter page. There it was. I had in fact drunk-tweeted Omari. I deleted it and immediately felt better. Then the third thought came: *What if he already saw it?*

I clicked his Twitter handle. He hadn't tweeted for two days and even that was a generic tweet about his new show. It probably came from his publicist. I just might be safe.

Of course, not tweeting anything didn't mean he hadn't read any tweets *to* him. I typed his handle in the search bar and held my breath. The last tweet that @ed him had been sent seventeen seconds ago: *It's my birthday and all I want is a retweet from @OmariG90036!!!!!!!!!*

I scrolled down and down and down. And down. Based on my thirty seconds of research, he was averaging about one @ a minute. That was how many tweets since I'd sent mine? I was trying to multiply when I remembered two things: I was hung over and I sucked at math. Let's just say it was a lot.

I still felt a bit paranoid until I remembered the final safety measure: my Twitter handle. Boop618. Even if he had seen my one tweet, no way he could know it was me. For all he knew, I was some psycho fan with a hand fetish.

I was in the clear, which made me feel good enough to run up Runyon Canyon, well at least walk it very fast while taking frequent breaks. My revelry was interrupted by Sienna's voice in the next room. "Get in here. Now."

I dang near busted my ankle trying to find out what was up. When I got to her, she was staring at the TV slack-jawed. I turned to the flat screen. Nat stared back at me, rocking prison orange and shackles on her hands and feet. She shuffled into a room while a somber male provided the voice-over. "Just two short days ago, Natalie Peters was enjoying the high life. Dining at Hollywood hot spot Chow House. Getting her picture taken by paparazzi. Rubbing shoulders with the likes of Toni Abrams and Luke Cruz. Now? She dines in the prison mess hall, gets her photo taken for mug shots, rubs shoulders with the likes of thieves and murderers."

Nat spoke solemnly to someone off-camera. "I always knew I'd be famous. I just didn't expect it to be like this."

I guffawed. Like literally. Before I'd done it myself, I didn't even know what guffawed meant. "It's been two freaking days. She's already giving jailhouse interviews?"

The voice-over continued, over red-carpet footage of Rack Pack victims. "Peters is accused of being one-half of the Rack Pack. Police say she robbed the world's most rich, famous, and beautiful of millions in jewelry and clothing, then ran her partner over in cold blood. Peters, however, claims she was as much a victim as the celebrities she's accused of robbing."

They cut back to Nat speaking. "Haley and I were working late one night watching Joseline's show. I said I liked her shoes and wanted a pair just like them. The next day Haley asked me to hang out after work. I thought we were going to her friend's house."

More voice-over. "Haley Joseph rang the doorbell, then took a key from underneath the welcome mat and opened the door. It was only once they were inside that Peters realized it was the home of reality star Joseline."

"I panicked. I wanted to leave, but I couldn't since I didn't drive there."

"Police say the Rack Pack got Joseline's address from a friend and used the star's Instagram and Snapchat to learn she was in Las Vegas. Peters claims she didn't realize Joseph had taken anything until they were back in the car."

"She handed me the shoes," Nat said. "I wanted to tell the police, but Haley told me she'd tell them it was all my idea if I did."

Yeah, right, Nat.

The news cut to an image of Joseline at her most recent wedding. The reporter continued. "Police claim the two hit Joseline's house an additional five to seven times. It would take the reality star a month to realize she'd been robbed. By that time, the thieves had moved on to their next victim. The Rack Pack became the talk of the town, with their own catchy nickname. ABC News spoke with Alison O'Keefe, a close personal friend of Peters, who says the accused murderer bragged about the robberies."

They cut to Allie standing in front of Forever 21. She was doing her best to look solemn as she spoke. "Oh my God! Nat was always bragging about how she'd gotten this from Joseline's house or that from Oscar Blue's house. She was so proud of herself."

The voice-over returned. "Everything was going well until, according to police, the pair decided to rob Toni Abrams. Though Peters insists she was not there the night of the robbery, her friend O'Keefe claims Peters told her Joseph wanted to go against their usual routine."

"Nat said there was a painting Haley liked in the hallway, but Nat didn't want her to take it. She thought it would be missed. Oh my God. This is so crazy."

Voice-over again. "Joseph insisted, and things turned physical. ABC News has obtained exclusive footage of the fight caught on Abrams' security cameras."

They flashed to footage from Toni's video camera. Someone at the police force now had enough money to take his or her family to Disney World. I watched as Haley fell into the spotlight. She immediately scrambled up. The first time I saw the footage, it had felt like forever, but watching it again made me realize the whole thing only took a few seconds. Just as Haley took off after a retreating Nat, the report cut to images from Kandy Wrapper's last video. She licked a lollipop suggestively as the voiceover continued. "Two days later, the Rack Pack hit again."

They cut back to Nat's interview. "There was no way I could've been there. I was at a friend's party."

The voice-over returned as they flashed to Allie. "Oh my God. She was there, but she left early. She got a call from Haley and was bragging to everyone about how Haley was all apologetic and begging her to help her with one last robbery. Haley picked her up in a BMW."

The voice-over returned a final time. "It would be the same BMW that would later run Joseph down in cold blood."

They cut to a perky black news anchor with an even perkier voice. "Tomorrow, we'll have part two of our exclusive interview. You'll hear details about the hours before Haley Joseph's death."

They cut quickly to a close-up of Allie speaking. "Oh my God. The last time I saw

Haley was when she dropped Nat back at my place. I invited her in, but she said she had to return the car. I figured she was going to see her boyfriend."

It was the news anchor's turn to try and look solemn. She did a much better job than Allie. "Stay tuned for more of that interview, as well as details of the fateful night two days ago when Peters says she was viciously attacked by Toni Abrams."

Nat was on camera again, this time with tears streaming down her face. "She ripped out my hair! I'm going to need extensions. Extensions!"

She made it sound like it was a liver transplant. The news anchor came back on screen to send us to commercial and Sienna turned the TV off. "What a load of BS," I said.

"Can't blame a girl for trying to get her fifteen minutes of fame," Sienna said.

I was about to say something when the doorbell rang. Within thirty seconds, Montgomery was standing in front of us looking all excited. "Let it slip to my contacts at Oxygen you were involved in bringing down the Rack Pack. They're more interested than ever."

Sienna beamed. "Then let's give them what they want."

We followed him down to his BMW. I took the backseat, snapping on my seat belt as Montgomery shifted into first gear and pulled out. "They won't let us actually shoot the audition, so we'll have to do before and after, which is fine . . ."

He continued talking but I tuned him out. Something was bugging me. I just couldn't place my finger on exactly what. Maybe it was because it was my first time actually riding in the car Nat had used to kill Haley. It felt weird that it was still on the road. I had to remind myself it wasn't the car that was the problem. It was the driver. And she was behind bars.

It took us thirty minutes to get over the hill to the Warner Bros. studio. Of course, we needed to be on a list to get on the lot. We handed our IDs to the guard. After a few minutes, he handed back our respective identification, then checked the trunk for explosives and wrote down Montgomery's license plate. "Auditions are in Building 18," the guard said when he came back. "Today's slow 'cause it's Saturday. Only thing going on are the tours and your audition."

Montgomery nodded and drove in. "Let's find a quiet area in the back to shoot you prepping for your audition and then we'll

420

drive over to the casting office," he said.

Studios are where the magic happens. Unfortunately, that magic tends to happen inside huge beige buildings the size of airport hangars. From the outside, they all look identical. You can only tell them apart by their numbers. But step inside and you'll find anything from a complete first floor of a family's house to an underground cave that doubles as some villain's secret lair.

We continued straight down past about a dozen buildings, then Montgomery took a left at Studio 18 and suddenly we were in Oz. That's not a metaphor. I literally was staring at a yellow brick road. Dorothy, Toto, the Tin Man, the Cowardly Lion, and Scarecrow were standing in front of Dorothy's tornado ravaged upside-down house being confronted by a green-hued witch. "I'll get you, my pretty," the witch said.

Nonplussed, Dorothy responded by belting out the opening lines of "Over the Rainbow," accompanied by a recorded track drifting in from unseen loudspeakers. Dorothy was singing live, however, and singing well. It wasn't exactly canon, but the group of tourists watching didn't seem to care.

There were ten of them seated in an open-air tram pimped out in hot pink. If that wasn't weird enough, all the seats had been rearranged so they faced the left side of the tram. The effect was that of someone having ripped out the two partial rows of movie theater stadium seats and placing them in a moving vehicle.

As Dorothy sang her heart out, a tour guide in the front of the tram spoke into an intercom. "Ladies and gentleman, there is truly no place like home, just like there is no place like Warner Bros. Now for our next stop . . ."

The tram driver pulled off. Warner Bros. really was going all-out with its new studio tour.

As soon as the group was out of earshot, the music cut off and Dorothy abruptly shut up. The Cowardly Lion ripped off his lion tresses — it was a piece, who knew? — while Scarecrow lit up a cigarette. "I gotta pee," the Wicked Witch said and ambled off in what I could only assume was the direction of the nearest bathroom.

Dorothy called out after her. "Don't be all day. We only have twenty minutes till the next show."

The Wicked Witch just waved her off. The street finally clear, Montgomery continued on and found a remote spot in the back lot, where the studio housed its outdoor sets. We were in the middle of a Western town circa the 1800s. The guard hadn't lied. It was a ghost town. Leaving his keys in the ignition, Montgomery got his camera equipment from the back. "So the scene is Day dropping Sienna off to the audition and sharing some words of wisdom," he said. "Day, you'll need to be in the driver's seat."

I did as told. Montgomery took my place in the back and set up his shot. "When I say 'action,' Day, turn off the car and act like you normally do when Sienna's heading to an audition. Action."

I turned off the car but didn't know what to say. I was used to working with a script. I finally spoke. "So . . . good luck."

"Turn your heads more so I can get your profile," Montgomery said. "More. More. There you go."

Due to the angle, I wasn't really looking at Sienna as much as her ear. "Now talk," he said.

"Um, you're gonna do a great job!"

"No, ask her if she's nervous," Montgomery said.

All righty then. "You nervous?"

"Again, but like you actually mean it."

I thought I'd meant it, but suddenly I wasn't so sure. Forget Sienna, I was the one who was suddenly nervous. "You nervous?"

"I am," Sienna answered. "This could be

the break I need."

"Day, tell her you guys have practiced this scene and she'll nail it."

"But we haven't," I said. I didn't even have a clue what the part was.

"We'll film you practicing it later and make it look like you did in post. Now tell her!"

God, he was bossy. "We've gone over this," I said. "You know this scene like the back of your hand. You got this."

"Sienna, ask her for a final bit of advice."

"Do you have any advice for me?"

I waited for Montgomery to tell me what to say. After a few moments, I realized he wasn't. So I spoke. "When I was auditioning, I always would try to think of a time when I'd experienced something similar to the character. I know you can relate to this woman."

Sienna looked at me, or should I say, somewhere by my ear. "She's a crackhead hooker."

Huh? "Perfect!" Montgomery said. "Sienna, get out of the car, then walk to the driver's side."

The last thing I wanted was to be on video comparing my best friend to a drug-addicted professional streetwalker. "Let me do it again."

"No, it's great. Sienna, go."

Geez, reality TV was stressful. I promised myself if I survived this, I was getting a cupcake or two or a kajillion.

Sienna walked to my side of the car. I was afraid to look at her in case I messed up Montgomery's camera angle. "Sienna will say goodbye," he said. "I'll film you backing out like you're about to leave."

Um, okay. I went to put the car in reverse, then hesitated. "What's wrong?" Montgomery barked.

That's when I realized what was bugging me. "I don't drive stick," I said.

Neither did Nat. She wasn't lying. She didn't kill Haley.

THIRTY-ONE

If Nat didn't kill Haley, who did? My first thought was Victory. Except Victory was dead and sure as heck didn't kill himself. So who was left? Not Marina and not Betty. Yet someone else had to have driven that car.

I pulled bits and pieces from my investigation, trying to put them together like a puzzle. Haley's final word being "rose." Allie mentioning Haley had to return the car. Victory's claim that Haley cheated on him with some old dude.

It began to fit together quite neatly, and the completed puzzle looked just like Montgomery Rose.

I'd thought Haley was identifying the window decal, but she could've been identifying her killer, especially if he was "some old dude" she'd been messing around with. Of course, you don't normally call someone you're smashing by their last name, but I

could only imagine that one wouldn't want to use their final breaths trying to repeat a four-syllable first name. Identifying him just as Rose would be easier. Montgomery's alibi was that his car was stolen. But what if it wasn't? Stolen cars weren't returned. Borrowed cars were.

"You okay?"

Montgomery's voice sliced through my thoughts. He and Sienna had been staring at me while I'd been in La La Land. "We can fake like you're driving," he said. "Just put your foot on the clutch and turn it on." He smiled as he spoke. It took everything I had to smile back. "Everything will be fine, Day."

Yes, it would be, as soon as I managed to get Sienna and myself out of there. I was tempted to scream bloody murder but knew it wouldn't do much good. I hadn't seen a security guard since we'd come in. The last thing I wanted was to let Montgomery know that I was on to him. And screaming that he was a murderer at the top of my lungs would do just that.

I didn't want to alert him. Sienna, however, was a different story. "I have to pee," I said. "What about you, Sienna?"

I figured we could pretend to hit the bathroom and keep walking until we found a guard or two or three. Like me, Sienna *always* had to pee. "I'm actually good," she said.

Say what? "You sure?" She nodded. "Come with me anyway. You know us girls can't go to the ladies' room on our own." I smiled for Montgomery's benefit.

"Sure," she said. "Let's just finish this scene first. You can hold it until then, right?"

Just great. Luckily, I thought of another way to get us out of there. "Sure," I said, then looked at Montgomery. "So are you just doing close-ups?"

"You have a better idea?"

"It might be nice to get a few wide shots. Show we're actually on the Warner Bros. lot. Sienna and I can sit in the car and pretend like we're talking while you shoot from like ten feet back."

Then I could tell her you're a double murderer, and we could haul serious butt.

"Great idea," he said. I thought so too. A lifesaving one. "Let's shoot that after the audition. For now, I'm going to shoot over your shoulder." He got the camera ready. "Action."

Sienna leaned into the car, making sure to angle her face so it was still in frame. "Thanks for helping me."

"Of course," I said. "You know I love helping you run lines. I was actually thinking about the last time I helped you."

"This is a bad angle," Montgomery said.

He got out from behind me. I was tempted to whisper, "He killed Haley," but figured he might hear. He situated himself so he was standing next to the hood right in front of Sienna. "And action," he said.

"You do remember the last time we ran lines, right?"

She thought for a moment. We'd been staking out Montgomery's house because we were sure he was the driver who'd killed Haley. "Yeah, of course. We were —"

I cut her off. I wanted her to know where we were, not Montgomery. "We were right that day. We thought we weren't, but I realize now we were."

I stared her dead in the eye. She had to know what I was talking about. *She had to.* After an eternity, she finally spoke. "Okay."

She remembered. Thank. You. Now we just needed to leave without alerting Montgomery. "Great. Can we pee now?" I asked.

"Of course," she said. "When we finish filming."

Fudge. So much for her remembering.

I glanced at Montgomery. He'd brought the camera down and was just staring at me. We made eye contact. He didn't even blink.

He knew.

We smiled at each other then, both waiting for whatever came next. My eyes were still on him when I spoke. "Sienna."

"Yes?"

"Run!!!" I screamed like my life depended on it. And it did. I shoved her out the way and flung the door open. It nailed Montgomery and he went down. Sienna had stumbled back but quickly regained her footing.

I jumped over him and grabbed Sienna, who was staring at Montgomery writhing on the ground. "What did you just do, Dayna?"

"We need to go!" I pulled her, but she was dead weight.

Montgomery moaned from the ground. "Day, what are you doing?"

Sienna bent down. "Are you okay?"

"He killed Haley!" I yelled. "We don't care if he's okay."

I started off, expecting her to follow me. She stayed put. "Did you not hear me, Sienna?"

Montgomery pulled himself into a sitting position. Then he spoke, managing to sound surprised and hurt. "Why would I kill Haley?"

Sienna looked at him. "You didn't. Nat did."

I didn't want to explain myself but didn't have much choice. "His car's a stick. She couldn't have done it."

"Okay, so someone else did it," Sienna said. "Not Montgomery. His car was stolen. They didn't even *know* each other."

"Victory said she was cheating on him with some old dude." I pointed to Montgomery. "Some old dude!"

He sputtered out a laugh and struggled to his knees so he was kneeling. "Now I know you've gone crazy. You've accused everyone and their mother of killing Haley. Guess it's my turn." Sienna placed her hand on his shoulder.

"I was wrong about them but I'm not wrong now," I said. "He killed her and he killed Victory because Victory knew he killed her. Now he's going to kill us."

Sienna looked back and forth between us while I willed her to believe me. "How would he know Victory knew?"

"He probably heard us talking about it. I don't know. Ask him!"

Montgomery began to laugh. It was the scariest thing I'd ever heard. When he spoke, his voice reeked of sarcasm. "Good lord, you've truly lost your mind, Dayna. What do you think happened? Me and this Haley chick were screwing? What, did I somehow convince her to rob famous people?"

It sounded good to me.

He rolled his eyes then but didn't get up. "Let me guess: I acted as her silent partner. Told her where people lived, explained the best ways to get past gates, what to get. She probably just wanted silly things like shoes and clothes, but I probably showed her how to get big money. Things like Rolexes, cash, and wait, better yet, information."

I flashed back to Toni's manager telling us about the failed blackmail attempt. Joseline and Oscar Blue's places probably housed bigger secrets than naughty pictures of a boyfriend wearing women's panties. Montgomery was telling the truth, even though he was saying it in a way that made the whole thing seem ridiculous.

"But then, why would I kill her if she was giving me money *and* sex?"

He looked like he thought I would actually answer. I didn't say a word, refusing to do him any favors. So he glanced at Sienna, who spoke. "He has a point, Day."

Realizing she was a lost cause, I turned to

him. "If I'm crazy, then prove I am. Let Sienna and me walk out of here. You can even call the police and have me arrested for assault. I'll happily do my time and apologize. Just let us leave."

He stared at me for a beat, then smiled that smile of his. "No problem," he said. "Go."

I wasn't expecting that, but I was happy to take it. Afraid not to have him in my sights, I started to move away backward. "Come on, Sienna."

She hesitated, then turned to follow me. She'd barely taken half a step when he reached out and pulled her legs out from under her. She hit the ground, her forehead making contact with the pavement.

"Oops," Montgomery said.

Before I could move, he was on her back and had her long black hair wrapped around his right hand. He used her hair to lift her head a few inches from the ground. "One step closer and I'm banging her head against the concrete. Repeatedly."

I immediately stopped. Sienna was out cold, and the only thing moving was the blood streaming from her forehead. "Don't kill her! Please!"

"I didn't want to hurt her. You got her into this."

And I had. He was the fourth person I'd accused of killing Haley. The first three had all stated how wrong I was. I missed that now. Desperately. "Take me instead. Kill me. Just don't touch her."

"What makes you think I won't kill you both?"

I screamed. Montgomery didn't even react. He just watched me, hands still using Sienna's hair as a weapon against her. No one showed up, so I kept on screaming. It lasted until I ran out of breath. When I gulped in air, he smiled. "If a soon-to-be dead girl screams on an empty studio lot, does anyone hear her?"

I hoped so, though I figured he was right. The only people we'd seen were the tour group. Dorothy had mentioned there were twenty minutes until the next group. We'd wasted fifteen of those twenty minutes. I wasn't sure if we could make it through the last five.

Sienna moaned and I saw her eyes flick open. I tried not to react, but I must have. Still staring at me, Montgomery casually lifted her head and banged it against the pavement again.

I knew then that I couldn't wait for the tour group. If I couldn't get Sienna away from him, maybe I could get him away from

Sienna. He was about fifteen feet away from me. I screamed again and took off running toward the nearest building. As I turned the corner, I heard footsteps. They sounded like he was moving in fast-forward. I knew he'd be on me within minutes.

I went right then cut left, managing to lose him. I cut left again and found myself in front of a small two-story building with about four doors. I tried them one by one. The third one was unlocked. I stepped inside, hoping for both safety and a phone.

A seven-foot grizzly bear greeted me.

I was in the prop house, where the studio kept all past, present, and future props for their projects. Not a good place to be when you were already scared out your mind. I needed a phone. A real one. Not a prop. I went searching. Luckily, there was just enough light from a window to see where I was going. I stumbled about and found the office. It was next to an impressive collection of knives. I tried to open the door but it was locked. Great.

I moved on to Plan B: find a weapon. I grabbed the biggest, scariest knife I could find. It was straight Rambo, the blades as long as the claws jutting out of Wolverine's hands and twice as thick.

I touched the tip. Plastic. I pressed it into

my arm. The blade disappeared into the handle, making it look like I'd stabbed myself. Much too scary to be real. He'd know it was fake. I put it back.

I heard a muffled scream. Sienna was awake. I knew I needed to get to her before Montgomery did. I grabbed a prop steak knife and ran out the door. I looked left and found him waiting for me.

He was about twenty feet away. Not much of a head start but better than nothing.

I had two options: the yellow brick road or the woods. I chose the latter, kicking off my heels and running for all it was worth. I immediately heard him behind me.

Warner Bros. had gone all-out with its outdoor woods set. Pine trees. Palm trees. Oak trees. It was all there and all real. I made noise every time I stepped on a stray stick or branch. I cursed myself for not going the other way, but I kept going and so did he. I could hear his labored breathing getting closer and closer with each step.

I finally reached a clearing. Safety was within my sight. That's when he caught up with me. I glanced back in time to see him lunge. I jutted to the left and he hit the ground. He quickly scrambled up, but I was ready for him. "I should have run you over when I had the chance. You were just standing there in the middle of the street. Yapping away to Fab."

"But you didn't kill me then. Just like you won't now." I hoped I sounded way more confident than I actually was. Facing him, I raised the prop knife. "One step closer and I stab the crap out of you."

He looked at it and smiled, way too happy to call my bluff. "What set did you get that fake crap from?" he asked.

So much for that plan. He advanced toward me. I was too scared to move. As soon as he got within arm's distance, he punched me in the stomach. It was the worst pain I'd ever felt. And it pissed me off. I screamed and lunged at him with the knife, forgetting for a moment it was fake.

It hit him right in the chest, a few inches from where his heart would have been if he had one. I figured the plastic would disappear into the handle.

But it didn't.

We both watched as blood — real blood — began to seep out. I don't know who was more shocked. Him or me.

I quickly stepped away as his hands went to the knife — the real knife — sticking out his chest. We stared at each other, both wondering what now?

Someone yelled behind me. "That's right,

girl. Show him who's boss."

I turned to see a tram filled with tourists watching, more than one taking photos with cell phones. They thought we were part of the show.

"I just knew she was gonna fall like the white chick always does in the horror movies," another said.

"*He* fell, though. Nice twist."

I glanced at the two uniformed employees in the front of the tram. They both stared, shocked, knowing I wasn't part of the tour show but not knowing what to do. I stumbled toward the tram and grabbed at a tourist filming me. I reached for his phone. He didn't know what to do so he just handed it to me.

I touched the phone icon and dialed 911. They picked up immediately. "I'm at Warner Bros. There's been an incident. Two people are injured, one of them a double murderer."

I hung up and immediately fainted.

My last thought was that I had indeed survived. I was definitely getting that cupcake.

EPILOGUE

It took me weeks to get my cupcake. In my defense, it had been crazy. Sienna and I went to the hospital, where our injuries were deemed non-life-threatening. Once home, we both spent the next few days in bed. Emme came over to play caretaker.

Nat was also confined to a room. Of course, hers was a cell. Though the murder charges were dropped, the robbery charges stuck. ABC dragged its "exclusive" interview out for an entire week, especially once it found out she didn't kill anyone. On day four, Nat talked about how Victory was innocently dropping her off at work one day when they were accosted by Toni's goons (read: me and Aubrey), forcing them to drive for their lives while we tried to run them off the road.

Marina stopped by and told me Nat was close to a plea bargain that included two years in prison, giving all the celebs their stuff back, and making reparations, whatever that meant.

Even with the prison time, Nat was in better shape than Montgomery. Physically, he was okay. He'd survived our encounter since I missed all major arteries. And he dodged the death penalty after bypassing a lawyer and — in true manager form — negotiating a deal of his own. As part of the deal, he confessed to killing Haley and Victory and got life in prison. No parole.

All the local news channels carried his sentencing live. He spent over an hour speaking. It was quite the show. He had in fact been telling us the truth about how Haley started robbing houses. It was all his idea, though Haley and Nat were the ones who decided to siphon the goods through Clothes Encounters. It had been going great, until Toni's house.

He said Haley freaked because she got caught on camera. She knew they'd ID her as soon as Toni got back from location. Haley wanted to skip town, but she needed money, since she apparently spent it just as quick as she stole it. She called Montgomery right after she left Toni's house and demanded he give her enough cash to leave.

He didn't have it, which pissed her off. She told him about some photos she had of him, which in turn pissed him off. The blackmailer didn't take too kindly to being blackmailed himself.

Montgomery said he told her that he'd get her the cash, and also let her know about the money Kandy kept at her house. He sent an anonymous message to Victory, telling him that Haley was cheating, and let Haley borrow his car for her last robbery.

He told cops the car was stolen and waited. When they met up so Haley could give him the car back, she was mad because Nat had taken the cash from Kandy's house. Montgomery claimed his money was still at his house, so she went to say goodbye to Betty and he was supposed to pick her up there. He did. To directly quote him, he "just didn't stop first."

The press ate it all up. Sienna took her manager being a two-time murderer in stride. She said she still planned to wear red every day. Her face was not only okay, but thanks to her plastic surgeon and a few extra nips and tucks, it was better than ever.

Emme went back to a world of poker, editing, and Candy Crush Soda Saga.

Toni got both her Pink Panther shoes and her photos back. She also fired her assistant. Emme immediately hated the replacement's guts.

Due to calling 911 that last time and not the tip line, I was deemed ineligible to receive the reward for (finally) discovering Haley's killer. It worked out for the best, though, because Toni gave me her own reward for returning her Grandma's necklace. It was way more than $15,000.

I wasn't going to accept it, but then remembered she spent that much in two hours at Saks. The money was enough to get my parents' house out of foreclosure with a bit left over to live on until my next check. I was hoping that would be coming soon. The LAPD was offering $25,000 for information on an assault outside Dodgers Stadium. When I told Aubrey about it, we agreed to partner up. I hoped that I'd finally had found my calling, and I didn't plan to quit it anytime soon.

Omari stopped by my hospital room, but I was asleep so we didn't get to see each other. He then worked five straight twelve-hour days, followed by some time in New York filming a special two-part episode. Though I didn't see him, we texted, mainly small talk with him checking in every day to see how I was doing. I told him how I'd been desperate for a sweet potato cupcake and we made plans to meet up to get one as soon as he got back from the East Coast.

When the day came, I actually beat him to the cupcake place. I sat down and the waitress hustled toward me. I spoke before she'd even entered a five-foot radius of the table. "Sweet potato cupcake and a hot chocolate, please."

She didn't bother to write it down. I didn't know if she was that good or my order was that easy. I was about to ask when she glanced past me and did a double take. Someone had come in. "You need a menu?" she asked, cheesing up a storm.

She sure wasn't talking to me. I followed her gaze, turning just in time to see Omari slide into the seat across from me. Now I understood why the waitress was so happy. I couldn't blame her. I was pleased myself.

"What's she having?" he asked.

"Sweet potato cupcake and hot chocolate."

"I'll take the same," he said.

"Will do," the waitress said, though she didn't walk away.

After a few moments I spoke, just to mosey things along. "Thank you."

It took her another thirty seconds, but she did eventually leave.

Omari turned to me and smiled. I couldn't help but smile myself. It felt nice to finally have my friend back. Texting him every day had reminded me how much I missed him. I looked forward to getting back to normal, even if it was in the Friend Zone.

We stayed like that for a few seconds, just smiling it up, until he finally spoke.

"So what's this about missing my hand?"

Shit.

ACKNOWLEDGMENTS

I would probably be disowned if I didn't start by thanking my parents, Valerie Scott and E. Wyman Garrett. I was five when I first told them that I wanted to write books. Though they were the first to support my silly dream, they certainly weren't the last.

This dream wouldn't have been possible without the awesome Brenda Drake creating Pitch Wars, which lead to the incredible Sarah Henning picking me to mentor, which lead to the amazing Michelle Richter offering to be my agent, which lead to the wonderful Terri Bischoff and Midnight Ink buying my book.

Michelle, you believed in Dayna even when I didn't and you continue to hold my hand even though your job is technically done (and done well at that). And Sarah, you were the first stranger to tell me that they liked my book, and I'm so glad that our relationship has evolved from mentor/

mentee to friends.

Terri, Katie Mickschl, Sandy Sullivan, and the entire Midnight Ink staff, thank you for realizing that there aren't enough mysteries written by people of color and deciding to do something about that. I am so thrilled to be a Midnight Ink author.

My siblings Donielle, Ernie, and Nikki. No one knows me — and accepts me as is — like you guys do.

My aunties Shelly, Monica, Renee, Donna, Marlene, Barbara, and the grande dame of them all — my Great Aunt Bernie. You have been amazing role models and I still aim to be just like you when I grow up.

The menfolk — Grandpa and Thad. I can't convey how much I appreciate you both — even if I don't always show it.

My grandparents Anna Will Stewart, Phyllis Scott, and Robert Scott. Even though you are no longer physically here, I know you've been with me every step of this journey.

Lateefa, Bianka, Iman, and Jasmine. You guys are proof that you don't have to share blood to be family.

Mocumba Dimsey, Felicia Harvey, Carucha Meuse, Raven Britt, and Maiya Hayes for taking on the sometimes impossible task of keeping me sane for the last two decades and being the best friends a girl could ask for. Rue, thank you again for taking my author photos!

My ultra-supportive, ultra-talented writing group. Mocumba, Linda Halder, and Stephanie Dodson, you have both been there since day one and have happily read every word — even when the words sucked.

Brandon Walston, Joanna Lovinger, and Shireen Razack, for saying yes when I asked you to read this out the blue. Your notes were so helpful.

My fellow Chicks on the Case: Marla Cooper, Lisa Q. Mathews, and Ellen Byron. I'm in awe of all three of you and I still can't believe you let me hang out with you.

Roselle Kaes, Sonia Hartl, and Claribel Ortega. Who knew that you could find your writing soulmates on Twitter and Facebook?

My fellow '17 Scribers Kristen Lepionka (who helped me find my talented illustrator, Richard Méril), Laura Heffernan, and of course Mary Ann Marlowe. I'm so glad we're going through this debut author journey together.

The Pitch Wars crew, especially Vanessa Lillie, Elly Blake, Kelly Siskind, the Mentee Class of 2014, and the CD. I'm going to go broke buying all of your books!

My iHeartMedia family. You guys have

made me feel like part of the team since my first day and I'm so lucky to work with such a supportive, talented, and fun group of people.

And finally, the youngins Mallory, Julian, Ian, and Jace. You bring me so much joy and I look forward to one — or all — of you taking care of me when I get older!

ABOUT THE AUTHOR

Kellye Garrett spent eight years working in Hollywood, including a stint writing for *Cold Case*. People were always surprised to learn what she did for a living — probably because she seemed way too happy to be brainstorming ways to murder people. A former magazine editor, she holds a BS in magazine writing from Florida A&M and an MFA in screenwriting from USC's famed film school. Having moved back to her native New Jersey, she spends her mornings commuting to Manhattan for her job at a leading media company — while still happily brainstorming ways to commit murder.